Flying Blind

Alaska Adventure and International Intrigue

* * * * *

Ron Walden
Alaskan True to Life Crime Writer

ISBN Number: 978-1-95-726333-5
eBook ISBN Number: 978-1-95-726334-2

Library of Congress Number: 2020940622

Copyright by Ron Walden
2020 - First Edition
2022 - Second Edition

Manufactured in the United States of America

Contents

Chapter 1

It was mid-morning when Robert "Bobby" Halstead returned home from his mail run and morning coffee with the guys. He practiced this ritual each morning he was home, since he was gone much of the time as a professional big game hunter and guide. This had been his chosen work for all his adult life. He was licensed to guide in several assigned guiding areas in the state of Alaska, including the North Slope, Alaska Peninsula, and the Wrangell Mountains along the Canadian border. Bobby had taken a job as an assistant guide with an old timer and master guide during the summer following graduation from high school.

The old timer liked Bobby and taught him the business while working him hard. The boy learned quickly and loved it. The aging master guide admired the young man's skills and work ethic enough to pay for his flying lessons at the end of his first season.

The youngster never returned to the classroom for a college education but became one of the top guides in Alaska with the instruction from his mentor and boss. The old man loved Bobby and schooled him in the ways of the wild. He taught him to trap for fur, taught him survival skills and the tricks of woodcraft. Seven years later the old man retired from the business for health reasons, leaving his client list and hunting areas to young Robert Halstead.

Bobby made his home on the Kenai River near the small town of Soldotna. His morning trip to the post office and the coffee table to talk politics with the local boys was about all the social life he wanted. His work day was filled with repairing gear and flying his small Cessna 185 to one of his cabins around the state to maintain the properties, stock up on firewood, and gather the bedding and linen to be properly cleaned after the season. Some of the cabins needed to be "bear proofed" for the winter as Alaska brown bears are known to break into cabins and use them as dens for the winter or just hunt for a food source before denning up and sleeping. Few people enjoy their lives as much as this young hunting guide.

He was planning a short, day trip to one of his cabins on the McArthur River on the west shore of Cook Inlet. His huge Dodge Ram truck was parked behind the log hangar at the end of the small airstrip behind his home. Bobby had been working for nearly an hour inspecting the aircraft and re-fueling the Cessna from his 500-gallon tank beside the hangar. He was busy checking the fuel for water in the plane's wings when his cell phone rang.

"Halstead Guide Service," he answered.

It was Don Halstead, Bobby's younger brother. He could hardly make out the words from the other end of the phone. Don spoke barely above a whisper, "Bobby, don't ask questions now, but you have to go to my place and get Jenny. She's in danger. Some men are after me and have threatened my daughter. Hurry; get her out of there and away. I'll call you when I can."

"What's this ab...." The line went dead.

The message had been secretive and urgent. Don was not one to be spooked by anyone, but, in the past, he had spoken of the safety of his family. Don's wife, Doris, had passed away two years ago from a long battle with cancer. He was raising his thirteen-year-old daughter alone with occasional help from Bobby. On the phone Don had sounded frightened.

Bobby thought about his options as he preflight checked his airplane. 'Don didn't panic easily and cared deeply for his daughter,' he thought as he walked around the plane. 'He was scared,' thought Bobby. It was time to act. He walked quickly to his big Dodge pickup truck and climbed behind the wheel. Being late summer, Jenny would be at home alone. He started the engine and pressed hard on the throttle of the big HEMI engine, tossing gravel skyward from under the huge lug tread tires as he took off.

Traffic along the route was heavy making profess slow to just under speed limit pace and making

Bobby irritable. He stopped at the first two traffic lights which, of course, were red. The third light however was green allowing a quick left turn toward the upscale subdivision where Don's home was located. Bobby could not stop thinking about the tension he heard in his brother's voice as he hurried up the front walk. Don was not one to be easily panicked, but something or someone had spooked him.

He pressed the doorbell button and waited, looking around the neighborhood as he waited. Moments later Jenny answered the door wearing blue jeans and sweatshirt.

"Hi, Uncle Bobby, what are you doing here?"

"Hi there, Jenny," he replied, not knowing exactly how to tell the girl this was not a social call. "Come on in," said the teenager. "Would you like some iced tea?"

"No thanks, honey, I have to hurry. I had a call from your dad and he asked me to get you out of here immediately. I don't know why, and he hung up before I could ask. So, pack a bag with a couple of changes of clothing and come with me."

Jenny looked shocked, "Why, Uncle Bobby? Why?"

"I don't know, but we'll figure it out later. Right now get a move on. We have to go."

Jenny started to say something but stopped. She turned and walked quickly to her bedroom to do as she had been instructed. There was a small carry-on size bag in the hall closet which she took to her room and tossed several items inside. She then went to her bathroom for a toothbrush and toiletries and tossed them into the small bag before zipping it up.

"I guess I'm ready," she said as she handed the bag to Bobby. "I'll have to lock the house when we leave." The two made a quick walk-through of the house, turning off lights and appliances. Once the front door was secured, they climbed into the tall truck.

"Where are we going, Uncle Bobby?" she asked.

"My airplane is fueled up and ready to go. I was heading to one of my cabins on the west side of the inlet. I think we should go there and try to figure out what's going on. I have cell phone coverage there in case your father calls." Bobby was now speeding through town and onto the Sterling Highway. He monitored the rear view mirror the entire distance to his home where he stopped beside the spruce log hangar.

Jenny helped push the Cessna 185 out of the hangar and climbed into the right seat for the trip. Bobby tossed the bag into the rear seat as he climbed into the pilot seat. He pushed and pulled on the yoke, flipped several switches and turned to the girl.

"Are you ready?" he asked.

"Yeah, I'm ready," she replied.

The engine caught on the second blade and roared to life. The pilot turned on the radios and looked around the sky for any traffic in the area. It was a warm summer day and the airplane seemed ready to fly. He taxied into position at the end of the runway and watched the gauges as he made his run-up. He checked the seatbelt on his passenger a final time.

"Here we go," he said as he pressed the throttle to the stop. He then pointed at the headset hanging from the overhead panel, his own already in place. Now with the airplane in the air and the flaps retracted he established a steady rate of climb to reach a safe altitude at which to cross the waters of Cook Inlet before speaking into the microphone connecting the headsets.

"Do you still like flying?" he asked his niece.

She adjusted her mike and spoke. "Are you going to let me drive?" she asked.

"Sure, take the wheel and level at 5,500 feet on this compass heading." She took the yoke and control of the airplane as he crossed his arms over his chest and leaned back into the seat.

Twenty minutes later he said, "I'll take her now. Good job, Jenny."

Bobby dropped the nose and descended to 1,500 feet once they were over dry land. At the cabin he circled to check the area and the runway before landing. On the north end of the runway stood a huge bull moose. He pointed it out to Jenny and circled around to buzz the moose and drive him off the landing strip. He circled once more to make a final check before landing and taxied to a tie-down spot near the cabin. Once the plane was secured he pulled her suitcase from the rear seat and handed it to her. He reached into the rear of the airplane again and retrieved a bolt action rifle which he carried to the cabin.

The cabin was small, a single room with two bunks on the west wall, a small kitchen on the south wall and a dining room/living room in the front. The cook stove was propane, but the heat was a wood burning contraption made from a barrel located in the center of the open area. It was cozy and efficient.

"You can have the bottom bunk. I can go outside when you need privacy, just ask." He hung the rifle by the sling from a peg near the front door. With that he exited the cabin returning in a few minutes with a large plastic cooler he had retrieved from the Cessna.

"We have no electricity here except for the generator out back, so try to be sparing on perishable supplies. Now come and sit down and we'll try to figure out what's going on."

Jenny had tears in her eyes. "Oh, Uncle Bobby, I'm so frightened. Dad took a new job a few weeks ago and he has acted differently ever since. He never tells me about his job, but I could tell he has been nervous lately." She wiped tears from her cheek with the sleeve of her shirt.

"It's OK, Honey," said Bobby as he reached out to comfort the girl. "I haven't seen Don in a few weeks. I've been busy getting ready for hunting season and he said he had changed jobs. Did he say why he quit the Pipefitters to move to the labor union?"

"He just said he was moving to the other union for more money. I don't even know what he does at work. All I know is he's some kind of high-powered negotiator for the unions. The only thing he told me was that he was changing jobs because they were going to pay a lot more money."

"Well, we don't have much to go on. Let's see if he will answer his phone." Bobby reached into his shirt pocket for his cell phone and pressed the speed dial number for his brother. It rang several times before going to voicemail.

"He's not answering, Jenny. I don't want to leave a message. If he's really in trouble and fearing for your safety I don't want to leave any trail for them to follow. Hopefully, he'll call us today."

"I hope so," said the teen.

"OK, we have to eat. Come with me. I'll get a fishing rod and we'll go down to the river to catch a salmon for dinner. Do you like to fish?"

Jenny smiled, "You should know. You taught me how to catch sockeye."

"Let's go catch one for dinner. We'll try to contact your father again later this evening."

Bobby chose one of the fishing rods from the shed beside the cabin and the two of them walked the short distance to the stream where the sockeye, or "reds", were running upstream to spawn. Half an hour later they carried the fish fillets back to the cabin where Bobby lit the BBQ grill and prepared the fish for cooking. Jenny set the table and found a can of green beans she opened and poured into a small saucepan to heat. Minutes later dinner was served.

"Fresh fish and beans, you can't do much better than that. In one of the Anchorage hotel dining rooms you would pay a hundred dollars for that dinner. Ours was free, but of course we had to drink Pepsi instead of white wine." Both of them chuckled at the remark. "Let's try to call you father again." The two sat on the small front deck of the cabin while Bobby dialed the number again with the same result as before. He looked at Jenny and shook his head. She hung her head in despair, holding back the tears she felt.

"I have some repairs to make on the cabin while I'm here. You can help me if you'd like."

"Perhaps later, but I have dishes to wash and a table to clean. I'll come out when I'm finished." She paused a moment, "Thank you for being so nice to me, Uncle Bobby."

"We're family, Jenny. We take care of each other." Bobby gave her a pat on the top of her blonde head. "I think we'll move on tomorrow. I have four more camps to inspect and clean up out on the lower Alaska Peninsula. I think I am going to drop you off in King Salmon while I take care of my camps. I have a friend, a widow, there and she can be trusted to take good care of you while I'm away. Your dad knows to contact her in an emergency when I'm on the Peninsula. You will be safe there until I can get back."

"Who is this lady?" asked Jenny.

"Her name is Lindsy Gibson. Her husband was a master guide in the early days. He's the one who taught me everything I know about the guide business. He's dead now, but he taught me how to fly, how to trap, how to follow a trail and most of all how to stay alive in the wilderness. He was my mentor and my friend. He married Lindsy when he retired and she's a super lady. You will love her."

"You make her sound like a wonderful person. I'm sure I'll like her."

"Your dad knows to send her a message if he needs me when I'm at camp. We'll head out to King Salmon in the morning. Do you want to fly up through Lake Clark Pass?"

"Oh, can I Uncle Bobby? I've never flown the Pass before. It would be fun — if the weather's good."

"OK then, let's get things packed up and finished tonight. I'll fix the shed roof while you finish the dishes and clean up the cabin. We'll get a good night's sleep and leave in the morning. Let's do breakfast in Iliamna. There's enough fuel to take us to King Salmon, and the fuel costs less there." Jenny was smiling with excitement now, her troubles temporarily forgotten.

Chapter 2

It was early the following morning when Bobby Halstead and his niece, Jenny, climbed into the Cessna and readied for takeoff. With preflight done and tanks checked, he taxied to the end of the short airstrip in front of the cabin. After checking the area for traffic and Jenny's seatbelt he pushed the throttle to the stop for takeoff.

Once he had safe altitude he began the 180 degree turn to the south and the entrance to Lake Clark Pass. In the past thousands of years, the glacier had filled the Pass, and it required more than 800 feet to cross. But today the glacier has retreated and 500 feet would get you through. For safety reasons Bobby climbed to 5,000 feet before letting Jenny take control of the airplane. The air through the narrow Pass is sometimes turbulent, although the weather was clear today with little wind. It was to be a pleasant flight through the pass to Lake Clark and on to Iliamna where he intended to have breakfast at the hotel.

Jenny handled the plane with skill, following the right side of the narrow canyon through the pass and out onto Lake Clark at the other end. She crossed the end of the lake near Nondalton a few miles from their destination and the Iliamna airport. Bobby, once again, took control of the plane, reported their position and asked for permission to land.

Permission was granted. They landed and the two on board were greeted by the flight service attendant who was familiar with this airplane and knew the pilot well. Bobby parked the Cessna in a transient parking spot from where he and Jenny walked to the hotel for breakfast. Several locals came to greet the guide they knew well, shake his hand and meet his niece. The visiting allowed Bobby to drink an extra cup of coffee.

An hour later they returned to the airplane to depart. Bobby advised Jenny, "You can fly on to King Salmon if you would like. Just stay inland of the lake's shoreline and on down the river. Stay at about 700 feet. We should see a lot of wildlife on the way."

Jenny handled the plane like a pro. They saw several brown bears as they traveled down the Kvichak River. During the flight Bobby wondered what Don had gotten himself into. He was hoping to hear from his brother when they reached King Salmon and the home of Lindsy Gibson. They flew down the north side of the river and admired the mid-summer scenery as they traveled on toward the small town of King Salmon. As they approached the airport Bobby took control and contacted the tower for landing instructions. Once he had them he used his cell phone to call Lindsy.

"Hello, Bobby. Are you in my neighborhood?"

"Yes, Lindsy, on approach to the airport now, can you pick us up?"

"Sure, but you say 'us.' Who's with you?"

"My niece, Jenny. I don't think you have ever met her. Gotta land now, see you when you get to the airstrip."

He taxied to transient parking and tied the airplane down. King Salmon is noted for being a bit breezy at times so Lindsy drove directly to where the Cessna was parked. Bobby loaded the luggage into the back of the truck and introduced the two ladies to each other.

"I've heard a lot about you, Ms. Gibson, from both Uncle Bobby and my dad. They both think you are something special." Jenny reached to shake the hand of the older lady.

"Speaking of your dad, where is he?" asked Lindsy.

"We should talk about that later at your place, Lindsy," interjected Bobby.

Ten minutes later Lindsy pulled into the driveway of her home. "Get your luggage inside, Bobby. You know where the spare bedroom is located. I'll rustle us up some lunch. You can help if you want, Jenny."

Jenny nodded and followed the older lady to the kitchen while Bobby stowed their bags in the spare bedroom they would use while in King Salmon. When he was finished and had made a stop in the small bathroom he proceeded to the kitchen where the ladies were setting food on the table.

"Have a seat, Bobby. Jenny, you pour the milk and have a seat. I'll be right there." Lindsy ran water in some kettles in the sink and returned to the table. "Now, tell me about Don."

"OK, Lindsy, but you can't breathe a word of this to anyone. I had a call from Don. He was whispering and asked me to get Jenny out of town immediately. He hung up before I could ask him why. I've tried a couple of times to contact him with no success. I was on my way out here to get the cabins ready for hunters when I got the call so I brought Jenny with me. I want to leave her here with you for a few days while I tend the cabins, if you will allow it."

"That doesn't sound like Don." Lindsy was deep in thought. "Sure, you can leave her with me. We can find things to do for a week or so while you do your business."

"Thanks, Lindsy, you're a sweetheart. I'll leave my cell phone with you in case Don calls again. I can call you each time I get near a phone down there on the Peninsula. I'm thinking it will take me about five days to get the cabins ready. I'm going to need five of the gas cans I left here."

Lindsy turned to Jenny, "My but you're growing up. How old are you now?"

"Almost fourteen," she replied.

"I think you and I will get along just fine, Jenny. We can drive around and see the sights in King Salmon and Naknek and visit a couple of the lodges down by the river. We'll figure out some things to do while you're here."

"Thank you, Lindsy. I'm really worried about my dad. I have taken care of myself since Mom passed away, so I'm used to being alone a lot. Dad has acted strange since he took that position with the new business he represents."

"I thought he was still with the big labor union. When did he change jobs?" she asked.

"Only a couple of months ago. He got offered a big raise and a promotion to change over to this big international labor union. He never said what was bothering him about the new job, but he was nervous all the time and told me not to answer the house phone. About a week ago he said he didn't like the new company or job and was thinking about quitting. He never said why, but he acted scared. I've never seen him like that." Jenny became quiet and stared at her sandwich.

Bobby broke the silence. "You'll be safe here with Lindsy. I won't be out there long and will check in as often as possible. Lindsy knows how to get a message to me if need be. No one, not even your dad, knows where you are, so you should be safe here. I don't like leaving you, but I have to get the camps ready. I'll be as speedy as possible and be back for you. We should hear from your dad by the time I return and then we can decide what to do next. You're a brave girl, Jenny, and with the help of Lindsy we'll figure it all out.

"I know, Uncle Bobby, I'm just worried about dad."

The following morning Bob Halstead loaded food, gear, tools, and cans of gas into the Cessna and headed down the Alaska Peninsula to his four camps scattered around his hunting /guiding area. It had always been relaxing to make this trip and do the work on his cabins, but it was different this time. Bob had never married and was used to being alone most of the time, but now he had Jenny in his care and no word from her dad, his brother, as to when this duty would end. This information about his being nervous with his new job was troubling. There was nothing he could do about it now, being in the Alaska wilderness and away from any communication source. He would have to finish his work and get back to King Salmon as quickly as he could.

He decided to start his work at his southernmost camp on the Sandy River in the shadows of Mount Veniaminof, an active volcano with a crater nearly six miles across. There is a large cinder dome in the center and a clear lake with a stream flowing out through the side of the crater. In the small valley the stream splits to flow both directions—to the Pacific Ocean side on the south and Bristol Bay on the north—attracting spawning salmon from both bodies of water.

Bobby's cabin was placed on a small barren ridge above Sandy River near an important caribou crossing. This cabin would require the most work because a bear had broken into the cabin by breaking the door down. The animal had taken most of the contents out of the cabin and left them scattered around the area. It was a mess. The one window in the cabin needed to be replaced, but for now, he would cover it with plastic and boards. He would try to finish this project in two days, repairing the window and door as well as gathering the mattresses and other furnishings to return them to the cabin. The days were long now, and he worked late to finish as much of the labor as possible. It was nearly eleven o'clock when he finally stopped to make some supper. The work was nearly complete and he was tired.

He had caught an Arctic char for dinner and was sitting on the front step to eat. A large brown bear came down to the stream looking for food but did not cross to the north side where Bobby was eating his dinner. As the bear wandered off in the other direction, he once again began to think about his brother Don and what was happening to him. Jenny had said her dad had changed jobs for a promotion and salary increase. She also noted he was nervous about his new position. All this was troubling to Bob, but there was nothing to indicate there was any danger involved. All he had was questions with no answers.

The night was warm, and he laid on top of his sleeping bag on the bunk he had rebuilt inside the cabin. He slept soundly and rose early the following morning. It was another sunny day and the sun was high in the sky when he awoke. Skipping breakfast, but making a pot of coffee, he continued to repair the cabin. His last big project was to attempt to make the door more bear-proof. It was almost noon when he completed the job and loaded his Cessna for the trip to the next camp about 20 miles to the north of Becharof Lake and just south of Meshik River. He finished the repairs and readied the camp by late afternoon and moved once more. The other cabins took one day each and on the fifth day he filled his tanks with gas from the cans he had brought with him and flew back to King Salmon. He loved the wilderness and didn't want to return to the civilized world and its problems, but it must be done.

Back in the transient area of the King Salmon airport he tied down the Cessna and went inside to call Lindsy for a ride to her home. Within minutes she was there to pick him up. He loaded the empty gas cans and trash bags into the back of her pickup.

"Has Don called?" he asked.

"No, and I'm worried. Don would never leave his daughter alone like this."

"I have a friend who is with the state troopers. He may be able to help me locate him. I'll call him when we get back to your place." Bobby was silent for a moment before asking, "How is Jenny?"

"She's fine, she is worried about her father, but she's doing OK."

Lindsy drove the rest of the way home in silence. Bob unloaded the trash and empty gas cans before entering the house where Jenny was busy fixing dinner for the group.

"Hi, Uncle Bobby, I hope you like sloppy joes," she called to him as he entered the house.

"Sure do," he called back before turning to Lindsy. "Where is my cell phone?" he asked.

She retrieved the phone from the charger. Bob turned it on and scrolled through the phone contacts for a number. Finding it he dialed and waited for a connection.

"Harrison," came the short answer.

"Tony, it's Bob Halstead. Do you have a minute to talk?"

"Sure Bob, what's up?"

"Hold on a second, Tony. I need to get outside for this call." Stepping outside the house, he resumed the conversation. "Hey, Tony, I'm concerned about my brother Don. I had a call from him and he was whispering into the phone, like he didn't want anyone to hear. He asked me to get his daughter, Jenny, out of town. He said it was urgent. That was six days ago, and I haven't heard from him since. I didn't know it, but he recently changed companies and is now working for some international labor union. Jenny says he was acting strange, like he was afraid of something. I was wondering if you could do some discreet snooping around and see if you can locate him."

There was a short silence on the other end before Tony spoke again. "I'll look into it, Bob. It sounds a little strange and out of character for Don. Is this a good number for you?"

"Yes, but I would rather that no one know where we are, at least for the time being," Bob replied.

"I'll get back to you as soon as I have anything. Keep your head down, buddy."

Bob ended the call and re-entered the house. "I'm starving," he called to Jenny.

"Come, sit down. It's almost ready."

Lindsy was already sitting at the table when Bob arrived in the kitchen.

"I have a friend checking on Don," he whispered to Lindsy. She nodded understanding.

Jenny came to the table carrying a large bowl of steaming pulled beef and sauce for sloppy joes. The buns were already on the table as was the steaming cup of coffee by his plate.

"You girls have been busy today," commented Bob.

"Lindsy and I figured you hadn't eaten much since you left here the other day, so I cooked you dinner. You have to eat a lot of it because I made a lot." Jenny was giggling now.

During dinner Bob told of repairing his camps and sighting the big brown bear at Sandy River. He also commented on being dead tired and in need of a good night's sleep.

"OK, Uncle Bobby. I won't make you wash dishes tonight."

Chapter 3

The Bristol Bay commercial salmon fishery was in its last days of the season. Bob Halstead had used the days to make day trips to several of his camp sites to do additional repairs and stock the cabins with supplies. It was early evening and he was about to sit down with Lindsy and Jenny for dinner when his cell phone rang.

"Can you talk a minute?" asked Tony Harrison.

"Sure," said Bobby as he exited the kitchen to sit in the living room for privacy. "Have you heard anything yet?" he asked.

"You may not have heard the news, but there is a report of a body found in a gravel pit near Palmer. It was just dumped there by someone. No clothing, no ID and beaten beyond identification. I think it's your brother, Don."

"Oh my God, where is the body now?" gasped Bob.

"We are reporting it to be at the crime lab for identification, but don't believe those reports. We thought he was dead when we found him, but he survived. Nearly all his bones are broken, covered with blood and battered beyond belief, but he is alive. He is still unconscious and we have him in Providence Hospital under another name. We're hoping he will regain consciousness and be able to tell us who did this to him. I'm going to need for you to come to Anchorage as soon as possible for a positive ID." Harrison paused in his report.

"I'm going to get a bite to eat and fuel my plane then I'll head your way. Meet me at Merrill Field at eight o'clock."

"Park your plane in front of my hangar, you know where." Harrison added his word of caution, "Be careful, Bobby. Don't rush things and get into trouble out there."

"Thanks, Tony, I will. The weather is clear and will allow me to fly direct, over the top of the mountains. It will be daylight all the way and I'll be cautious. See you at eight."

He hit the off button on his phone and returned to the kitchen. "I have to make a quick flight into Anchorage tonight. Something has just come up and I have to go to town. I would like to leave Jenny here with you, Lindsy. That is, if it's OK with you."

"It must have been an important phone call. Of course she can stay with me. We have more mischief to get into anyway. You go do your business and don't worry about us."

"Thank you, Lindsy, I'll stay in contact with you. Is there anything you want from the big city?" he asked in a quiet voice.

"No but load up on fresh vegetables when you come back. Good produce is hard to come by out here."

Bobby sat at the table to finish his dinner. He packed a small bag with clothing and shaving gear, hugged Jenny and had the ladies drive him to the airport. It took several minutes to do a preflight check and top off the fuel tanks. "I'll call you later," he said as he opened the door of the Cessna and climbed inside.

Once in the air he climbed to 8,500 feet and set a course direct to Anchorage. The sun was still high in the northern sky, the air was smooth and the engine was purring as it should. He had learned long ago these trips were long and seemed even longer when he was anxious to get to the destination. When he arrived he cut the engine in front of the private hangar of his friend, Trooper Lieutenant Anthony Harrison. Fifteen minutes later Tony arrived.

"Jump in, Bobby, I'll take you to the hospital," said Tony without further greeting.

At the hospital Tony led the way to the ICU unit where the unidentified victim was being treated. A nurse was at the bedside changing one of the fluid bags on the stand as they entered.

"There isn't much change, Lieutenant," she said as she left the room.

Bob stepped to the edge of the bed to look at the beating victim. "It's him, Tony. I see a scar on his neck. I gave him that scar. I hit him with my bicycle when we were about nine years old. I never would have recognized him otherwise. I've seen crash victims that weren't this badly beaten. What are his chances of survival? Have you heard?"

"I talked to the doctor earlier today. It's still touch and go. His heart is stronger this evening, but he has internal damage that hasn't fully been assessed yet. The doctor said he would give him about a 30 percent chance of making it. I wish I had better news for you, Bobby."

"Is there any progress on finding out who did this?" asked Halstead.

"Not yet. That's one of the reasons I wanted to talk with you in person." Tony took his notebook from his pocket and began to make notes. "You said Don had recently changed employers; do you know who he was working for now?"

"No, I don't, but he said it was some international labor union. You know he had been working for the local labor union until recently."

Tony made a note, "You said he seemed uneasy or frightened when you talked with him and he asked you to take his daughter away for her safety. Did he say anything else?"

"No, but he was really worried about Jenny's safety. I took her to King Salmon to leave her with Lindsy Gibson for a few days while I worked on my cabins on the Peninsula. I had tried several times to contact him with no luck." Halstead had a sudden thought: "Damn, Tony, did you find his cell phone?"

"No, we didn't. He was dumped in the gravel pit after he was beaten at some other location, but I see your concern. You think that if they still have his cell phone they may try to locate you and Jenny by tracking the number."

"I have to get rid of this phone right away," said Bob, holding the phone up in his hand.

"Give it here, Bob. I'll take out the SIM card. That should disable it until the phone company can replace it." Tony took the phone and opened the back where the battery pack was housed and removed the small subscriber ID electronic card. "You can talk with the phone company about using the same phone number and such, but I would advise you change it."

"If they're smart enough to know about the SIM card they may find me anyway. I advertise a lot and my number is on all my business cards and advertising. I think I had better go back and get Jenny. I need to get her out of Alaska and hide her." He stopped speaking once more, thinking, "Oh, God, Tony, let me have your phone. I have to call Lindsy and warn her and tell her about Don. She may think Don is dead and these employers may too, but Jenny may still be in danger."

Harrison passed his cell phone to Bob, "I guess you may be right, but when you finish give my phone back and let me call the trooper in King Salmon. I'll have him get Jenny and bring her here. That will give us a little time to figure out what to do to protect her."

Bobby dialed Lindsy's home phone. It rang several times before she picked it up. "Hello?" she answered.

"Lindsy, Bob Halstead. Listen carefully, you and Jenny may be in danger."

"Oh, Bobby, we just heard on the news that Don is the body they found in Palmer. Jenny is devastated."

"Lindsy, listen to me. Don is NOT dead. He was alive when they found him. The story is just a plant to protect him. The point is that Jenny may still be in danger. I'm going to take her somewhere safe. I don't know where yet, but Tony is sending the King Salmon trooper to your place to bring her here to meet me in Anchorage. Don't take any more calls and get her ready to move. The King Salmon trooper will come directly to your house to get her and bring here to me."

"Oh, that poor child, she is so distraught, but I'll get her ready to go right away. I'm glad Don is OK." Lindsy was sobbing now.

"Don isn't OK, Lindsy, but he is getting the best care available. I'll get a message to you as soon as I can. Now, get her ready to move, and remember, don't breathe a word of his being alive."

"Oh, you're right. I wouldn't have thought of that. I'll have her ready by the time the trooper arrives."

Bob handed the phone back to Tony. "She will have the girl ready when he gets there."

"Good, I just remembered the state twin engine plane in is King Salmon right now. Some senator is there to do some fish board hearings. I'll have them bring Jenny here to Merrill Field. Now, let's figure out where we're going to take her." Tony called the number programmed into his phone for the King Salmon trooper and informed him of the emergency.

Bob had been pacing the concrete apron of the hangar while Tony delivered his orders. "I have a good client in Harbor, Oregon I can trust. I think I'll take her there. He'll agree to care for Jenny for a while, I'm sure. Let's tie this plane down and then I'll call him."

The two men pushed the Cessna 185 to the tie down rings embedded in the cement and used straps to secure the plane. Bob took his bag from the plane and locked the cabin door. Together they waited for the airplane to arrive from the Peninsula. During the wait Tony arranged for Bob and Jenny to leave on the red-eye flight at midnight tonight. When he finished he turned to Bob and said, "We have to stop at the phone office to get help with your phone." Tony called an officer to meet them at the phone provider office. This officer was his electronics advisor and he knew what had to be done.

Bob was able to arrange for a new phone with the same number, without having to notify his clients. With a new phone that included the downloaded information and connections that had been transferred from his old one, he couldn't be tracked, although both phones had the same number. This had been accomplished in less than an hour.

The men were ready for a late dinner at a local Olive Garden restaurant. They had just finished eating when there was a call on Tony's trooper radio to inform him the aircraft was arriving at Merrill Field. They were only ten minutes from the airfield and arrived by the time the big twin engine plane taxied to the base of the tower where Jenny stepped out of the plane. She was excited to see her Uncle Bobby waiting on the tarmac.

She ran to him, throwing her arms around his neck. Jenny was sobbing and holding on to him for security. "Oh, Uncle Bob we heard the news that daddy was dead. I didn't know what to do and Lindsy and I just sat and cried. Now you say he's not dead. I just don't understand what is happening. Hold on to me, Uncle Bobby. I'm scared." She sobbed loudly and began to shake throughout her entire body.

"It's OK Jenny, we still don't know if your dad is going to make it and you should be ready for it if he doesn't, but he is getting the best care by the best doctors and the best hospital in Alaska. I think the chances of his recovery are good. Don't worry, I'll keep you safe." He pried her arms from his neck and turned her to introduce Tony. "This is my good friend Tony Harrison. He is a state trooper who is in charge of caring for your dad. He will be trying to find out exactly who it was that did this to him."

Jenny dried her eyes on her shirt sleeve and held out her hand to shake the hand of the big trooper.

"Thank you for taking care of my dad. Can I see him?" she asked.

"I wish you could, Jenny, but I don't think it's a good idea for a while. I think Bob is planning to take you away to a safe place tonight. But, as soon as your dad is well enough I'll let you know and you can visit him. I promise to keep you aware of how he is doing. Is that OK with you?"

"Yes sir, Tony, thank you."

"Are you hungry, Jenny?" asked Bob.

"No, Uncle Bobby. Lindsy and I had dinner just before they came to get me."

"Tony is getting ready to take us to the Anchorage airport. I'll bet he already has our tickets." Tony held them up for her to see. "We will be going out to Oregon for a while. You can't tell anyone about that, though."

"I understand, Uncle Bobby. It's to keep us safe." She had a somber look on her face.

"We should be going, Bob. I made arrangements for the two of you to bypass TSA and go directly to the gate. I'll be escorting you all the way to the airplane. I hate to remind you of this, but the folks we are dealing with have international affiliations and we must be very careful. Now, let's go to the airport. Your bags are in the trunk of the car. Jenny, you ride up front with me."

Chapter 4

The flight to Portland, Oregon from Anchorage was on time. Escorted by Alaska State Troopers, the two passengers boarded without incident after bypassing the security check. Once on the airplane Bob and Jenny settled in to sleep during the flight. Upon landing in Portland Halstead rented a car from Avis. The two were still sleepy but set out on the long trip to the California/Oregon border where the small town of Harbor is located on the Pacific coast of Oregon.

On the south edge of Portland Bob pulled in at a truck stop where the two ate a substantial breakfast. Back in the car, Bob found a local country music station to keep him awake and alert while Jenny pulled her light jacket over her shoulders and went to sleep once again. Arriving in the town of Harbor at daylight Bob looked at his watch and decided it was time to call his friend, a local city official.

A sleepy voice came on the other end of the line, "This is Vic," it said.

"Vic, Bob Halstead, we're in town. Tell me how to get to your place."

Immediately Victor Lamar came to full awake. "Bob, where are you?" Bob gave him the location. "Stay there and I'll be there in a few minutes." Vic drove to the meeting place and found the rental car. He didn't get out but only waved for Bob to follow. It was a short drive to Vic's home on the edge of town near the river and overlooking the harbor. At the house Vic unlocked the door and ushered them to enter before he made an official greeting. He grabbed Bob and hugged him tightly. "Good to see you, old buddy."

"Good to see you too, Vic." He turned to Jenny saying "I'd like you to meet my niece, Jenny. I'll tell you the whole story when we get settled in."

"Of course. Come on back and I'll show you to your rooms." A half hour later both Jenny and Bob had washed and cleaned up from the flight and met Vic in the spacious kitchen.

Vic was a short but muscular man with a black shadow of a beard. He had hunted many times with his favorite Alaska guide, Bob Halstead. Together they had claimed many trophy animals and fish all of which were displayed throughout the house. He was seated at the kitchen table and invited the new arrivals to join him.

"How about some coffee, Bob?" he asked.

"Black, but I don't think Jenny drinks coffee," he replied.

"Coffee it is, Bob. What would you like, Miss Jenny?" asked Vic in a pleasant tone.

"Do you have a small glass of milk?" she asked.

"Sure do, kiddo," he replied as he walked to the refrigerator. "OK, Bob, what's the story?" he said as he retrieved the glass of milk for Jenny.

Bob began to tell the entire story in detail. When he had finished, he sat quietly for a moment.

Vic had listened intently then turned to Jenny. "I'm sorry for your troubles, Miss. I want you to know you and Bob are welcome to stay here as long as you need. If you want or need anything while you're here, just ask. I guess there isn't much I can do to help, but if there is, you just say so."

"Thanks, Vic. I knew I could count on you. I had to find somewhere safe for us to stay until we work this out. My trooper friend, Tony Harrison, has your home number and will call when he has news. Right now both Jenny and I are worried about my brother Don. I don't want you to change your routine to accommodate us, but we sure do thank you for taking us in without an explanation. You're a good friend, Vic."

Vic turned to Jenny, "Do you like to fish, Jenny?"

"Yes, but I don't have an Oregon license," she said.

"Well, young lady, we'll get you one. Perhaps we can go out on the salt for a while if the weather is nice." And so the waiting began. It was up to Tony now. There was nothing for them to do but to keep Jenny safe from an unknown enemy.

Lieutenant Anthony Harrison had been busy gathering information about the supposedly dead victim who had been found in a gravel pit in the valley east of Anchorage. Tony had been to the site and combed it as well as he could and found nothing worthwhile in the way of clues as to who did this to Don Halstead. Tony had known both Halstead brothers for many years. The trooper had hunted many times with Bob and had been to many of his big game camps. Don had come and gone a few times during these hunts, consequently he was not as well acquainted with this brother.

Tony had been told that Don had recently changed employers, but no one seemed to know anything about the new company. It was a labor union of some kind, but the federal government had no record of its offices or who they represented. He had searched the computer for the address and phone number of the union, but none was listed. The name of the union, he had learned, was AmerAsian Labor Union. The computer search did not disclose any offices in the U.S., only a main office in Indonesia. The short profile he found said they represented mostly Asian laborers working all over the world. Many Asian seamen were members of this union. The headquarters was located in a plush high rise office building in West Jakarta. The given address proved to be in a prosperous business district. The maps and photos of the area showed this to be a very affluent housing area with worldwide business offices of many major international companies. He also realized there was a nine hour time differential and the offices were now closed for the day.

Frustrated with the lack of information available to him Tony closed the computer site and tried to think of where to look next for information. He reasoned that if they had offices in Anchorage and had hired Don Halstead the union must be licensed by the State of Alaska. He began to search the licensing commission sites for any listing for AmerAsian Labor Union. There was none listed, not even as a parent company of a licensed corporation. That seemed very strange indeed.

His frustration only grew as he attempted to determine where Don had been beaten before being dumped in the gravel pit near Palmer. Don had rented a house in East Anchorage. Tony had gone to the home, a small single-family dwelling with no garage, only a carport. He had ordered his office to obtain a search warrant for the property, but it had not been issued yet. He was sitting at his desk pondering his options when his telephone rang. It was Bob Halstead.

"Hi, Tony. I'm using that untraceable phone. Have you heard how Don is doing?" he asked.

"He's still in a coma. The doctor told me they were going to keep him that way for a while until some of the brain swelling and bruising begins to heal," he commented. "How are you and Jenny making out in sunny Oregon?"

"My old friend Vic Lamar is taking good care of us. I don't think anyone knows where we are. Jenny is holding up well, but I hear her crying at night and she asks if I have heard any news about her dad. I feel sorry for the kid." Bobby paused a moment, but then continued, "Have you learned anything new about what happened to my brother?"

"No, I haven't, in fact, I was just sitting at the computer attempting to track the company Don is working for, but I can't find anything. I'm beginning to wonder if this is a legitimate labor union or some kind of a mafia-style scam.

There is a nine-hour time difference, so I can't contact the Indonesian police to ask about the outfit. I checked with the Alaska Licensing Commission and found nothing. It's like they don't even exist. I wish I could talk to Don and get some answers."

"Have you talked with his old employer in Anchorage?" asked Bobby. "Someone there may know who they are and what they do."

"No, but that is where I'm headed now. Their offices are downtown on Post Road near the railroad depot. I can't delegate this investigation because I don't want anyone to know Don is still alive. It's a frustrating mess. I'll keep you in the loop, though. Keep your head down, old buddy."

"Vic is trying to keep Jenny busy and tomorrow is going to take us out on the salt water for some albacore fishing. My only problem is my guide bookings will soon need attention. I don't know how to deal with it unless I get a computer. I don't want to chance using the telephone. You can't tell who is calling." It was a problem Bob had been thinking about since they boarded the airplane in Anchorage.

"Well, you take care, Bobby. I'll copy this new number to my cell phone contacts and try to stay in touch. I'll let you know if there is any change in Don's condition."

"Thanks, Tony. Waiting is the hard part. See ya." Bob closed the cell phone and leaned back to think. A small notebook style computer would do what he needed to book clients. He could find that at a Walmart store. His thoughts were interrupted when Vic spoke to him.

"I think we should go out to dinner tonight, Bobby. We have a little oyster bar downtown that serves a great dinner. I like the fried oysters, but Jenny can have the fish and chips if she doesn't like them. What do you think, eh Bobby?"

"I think it sounds great, Vic, but you don't have to entertain us. I know you have things to do and we can fend for ourselves."

"You always take good care of me when I come to your camps. I owe you that much." Vic seemed in a jovial mood.

"How would you like to drive me down to Walmart?" asked Bob.

"Sure thing. What are you shopping for?"

"I need a computer notebook to keep track of my guided clients. I also need some more clothes. I'm sure Jenny will want a change of outfits, too. We can go to that oyster bar when we finish shopping, if you still feel like fish for dinner." Bob stood to search for Jenny and tell her the plan.

At the store Jenny took her own basket and began to shop. Vic and Bob took another basket and headed directly to the electronics department in the rear of the store where Halstead found a computer notebook that he thought would do what he needed. He paid cash for the device at the electronics counter and began to shop around for a couple of changes of clothing and underwear. They met up with Jenny near the check-out counters. To her credit Jenny had been conservative in her clothing selections. Bob told her to go the shoe department and select a pair of decent shoes and some canvas deck shoes to wear on the boat. The shopping had taken her mind off her father at least for a short time. She was having a good time shopping for the new outfits.

Once out of the Walmart store Vic drove to a small building near the marina. The parking lot was nearly full with more cars arriving behind them. They locked the car and entered the restaurant where they found a short line at the check-in desk. The aroma inside the café was wonderful and the food on plates carried by servers as they walked to a table looked delicious.

Vic, touching Jenny's shoulder offered, "All they serve here is fish, but you can have any kind you think you might like. Bobby and I are having fried oysters."

She looked up at the big man, "I like fish and chips. Can I order that here?" she asked.

"You sure can, little lady," he replied.

Once seated Bob opened the menu then turned to Vic and said, "There is no way for me to repay you for what you are doing, old friend. You can come and hunt with me any time you want, my guest."

"Thanks for the offer, but it isn't necessary. You have always treated me like I was special when I come to your camps. I'm happy to have the opportunity to repay some of that." The serious look on his face disappeared and he broke into a broad smile, "But, I'm happy to hunt for free, if you insist." He and Bob were both chuckling while Jenny looked up from the menu to learn what was so funny.

The trio ate a wonderful meal. The oysters were excellent, and with Jenny at the table they settled for iced tea with dinner instead of wine. It was late when they arrived back at Vic's home. Bob unloaded the purchases from the car while Vic helped him carry the bags inside. Jenny made several trips to the dining room to get her packages and take them to her bedroom where she removed the tags and studied her selections to pick an outfit to wear in the morning.

The fishing expedition was planned by Vic and Bob, but it was determined an early start was not going to be necessary. They were looking forward to a relaxing day.

Chapter 5

The next two weeks passed slowly for Bob Halstead and his young charge. They had taken day trips to California and the giant redwoods. They had fished with Vic for several days, but they were long and tiring ones. Jenny was becoming distraught without news about the wellbeing of her father. Bob had called Tony Harrison several times with no news available yet.

At the beginning of week two there was a call from Tony. "Hello, Bob. I just had a call from the hospital. They told me they were going to attempt to awaken Don today. They said they would call me when he woke up. I'm hoping to have another call this afternoon."

"Oh, that's good news. Jenny is having a tough time of it. Call me back when you hear how he is doing." Bob hung up the phone and called to Jenny. "Jenny, come in here. I have an update from Tony." He spoke loudly in order for her to hear him while she was in the next room.

She came running quickly to the kitchen, "Is he awake?" she asked.

Bob shook his head, "No, but they sent word to Tony that they were going to awaken him today. I don't know how responsive he will be at first, but at least things are changing and hopefully, for the better."

"Oh, Uncle Bobby, I'm so happy to hear this. Can we go home now?"

"Sorry, Jenny, not yet, it will likely be a few days before he's coherent and able to give us any information about what happened to him. Tony is going to the hospital to talk with him as soon as they will let him."

"I want to go see my dad, when can we go see him?" The question came from an excited Jenny.

"I don't really know, Honey. There may still be danger for you if we return. It's my job to keep you safe. We'll have to wait until your dad says it's safe for you to return. I need to get back to work, too, but I don't want to take any chances. Do you understand?"

She hung her head in sadness, "Yes, I understand, but I don't like it much."

"That's two of us, girl, that's two of us."

Later that same day Tony Harrison was in his office when the hospital called to inform him that Don was awake and speaking. The doctors were hopeful he would be able to talk with the trooper by tomorrow. He was told that Don's many broken bones were going to take at least two months to heal, but his mind was clear although his memory had not yet completely returned. Tony was advised he could see the patient tomorrow morning if he promised to make the visit short and without stress. He agreed.

His next call was to Bob, his second of the day. "Just got off the phone with the doctor and he will let me see Don tomorrow morning. He said I can't stay long, but I may get some idea about what happened. I just wanted to call and let you know he was a wake."

"That's good news, Tony. I'll pass it along to Jenny. I'll talk with you tomorrow." Bob breathed a huge sigh of relief as he hung up the phone and called out, once again, to Jenny. Bob relayed the message to the young lady, adding, "I think this calls for a celebration. How about you and I take Vic out to dinner this evening?"

The following morning Harrison finished his daily office chores before driving to the hospital in an attempt to interview Don Halstead to determine how he had been injured. At the hospital he was met by the doctor treating the patient. He gave Tony a short list of his injuries and his prognosis. He noted that Don's memory of the incident was still faulty and he could not remember most of what had happened to him. The doctor also stated Don would need to remain in the hospital under immediate care for at least six to ten weeks because of the severity of his injuries. Blood clots and internal bleeding possibilities were high on the list of health threats demanding that decision.

"You may visit for ten minutes, but please take care to avoid exciting him in any way. A nurse will stand by outside the room in case there is a problem. She will show you the way to the ICU. I'll be in my office on the next floor in case you have further questions." The doctor motioned for the nurse to escort the trooper to the ICU.

Another nurse was in the room changing a fluid bag on the IV pole when they entered. Don was awake, but very weak. He smiled when he recognized Tony as they entered. After changing the IV bag both nurses exited the room to leave the two men alone.

"Hello, Don," said Harrison. "Do you feel like talking a few minutes?"

"Sure, Tony," replied Don in a very weak voice. "Drag that chair over by the bed."

Tony reached out to grasp Don's bruised hand and squeezed it gently. "First of all, I want you to know Bob has your daughter hidden safely away from here. I talked to them last evening and let them know you were awake. They were excited to hear the news." The trooper moved the chair close to the bed and sat. "I have a lot of questions, but if you get tired I'll leave and come back another time. Can you remember what happened to you?" he asked.

"Just bits and pieces, but it seems to be coming back to me little by little."

"Can you tell me a short version of what happened?" Tony asked.

"I can't remember where I was when they took me. I just remember someone breaking down the door and knocking me out. I woke up in the trunk of a car, tied up. I don't know how long they drove me around, but it was a long time. It was still daylight when they drug me out of the car and began to beat me and ask me questions I didn't understand. I kept yelling 'I don't know,' but they kept hitting me and asking over and over."

"Did you recognize these men?"

"No, I don't think I ever saw them before."

"How many of them were there, do you remember?"

"Sorry, Tony, but all I can remember is there were at least four of them. I think they were all foreigners of some kind, Asian I think. Not Japanese, but from that part of the world."

"This new company you are working for, where is the office? I can't find them listed on any corporate register. I couldn't even find them listed with the State of Alaska."

"I know. I became suspicious after going to the office to start work there. They came to my old office when they interviewed me and offered me this job. They were all business and told me it was the same kind of work I was doing with my old job, but with a lot more salary. Being stupid and greedy, I took the job without looking into it first. They gave me a huge cash bonus for changing companies. I was excited to make the change. I was to be in charge of all of Alaska with an office in the suite of offices they had rented in a new complex in mid-town. I was blinded by the money and didn't follow up on learning about them."

"OK, Don, just a couple of questions and I'll let you rest. Do you have any idea why they did this to you?"

"Not a clue, Tony, not a clue. They asked who I was working for and I told them AmerAsian Labor Union, and they started hitting me with clubs and fists. They kept on asking who I worked for, but I had no idea what they were talking about. That's about all I can remember."

"Thank you for talking with me, Don. Right now, I think they still think you are dead. The papers reported a body found in a gravel pit, but I think

I'll put a guard on duty outside your room anyway. I don't want them to get another chance at you. I'll also call Bob and Jenny to let them know you are on the mend. Is there anything you want me to tell them?" Lieutenant Anthony Harrison, Alaska State Trooper, was indeed, worried for the safety of this man. He had been kidnapped and beaten severely without knowing the reasons for the act. There was a great deal more to this story and, Tony believed, Don was still in danger.

Tony left the hospital and drove his unmarked patrol car to the recently built office complex in mid-town. It was a very modern arrangement of offices with a parking garage on the first level to accommodate renters, employees, and visitors to the twelve-story building. He climbed the stairs to enter the large entry lobby and located the tenant directory. AmerAsian Labor Union was listed as the single occupant of the fifth floor of the new building structure. Near the rear of the lobby was a desk where a uniformed attendant was seated monitoring a bank of electronic security screens. The guard on duty was making an entry in his logbook and looked up as Tony approached.

"May I help you, sir?" he asked the man in the suit.

"Perhaps. I'm Anthony Harrison. I've never been in this building prior to today. Can you tell me what type of clients rent these offices?"

"I saw you reading the client board over there. You probably saw that there are a variety of businesses located in the building. There is a mix of domestic and international companies. Some are single office or suite renters while others may occupy one or more floors. The building is owned by a local corporation, and since this complex has nearly full occupancy the owner is considering construction of another one like it a few blocks from here on property they already own. I've worked here since they opened the building over two years ago. It's a good place to work and the renters all seem happy." The guard seemed friendly enough as well as being free with the ownership information.

"Who would I see to get a tour of the offices and ask about rates?" asked Tony.

"The general manager is Mister Garfield. His offices are down that hallway to the right. There is a sign on the door that reads Midtown Leasing Corp. Just go into the office and the secretary will make an appointment for you to see Mr. Garfield."

"Thank you. You have been very helpful." Tony smiled at the guard. "You say to go down that hallway over there, right?" He pointed at the hallway to the left of the desk.

"Yes sir, the office has a sign on the door. The secretary is Miss Carmody."

Tony turned to walk down the long well lighted hall, and the guard made a note in his logbook. He reached a large oak door with brass trim and fixtures. There was a sign on the glass denoting the offices of Midtown Leasing

Corp. and indicating the regular business hours and the general manager's name, Winston Garfield. He opened the door to enter and found a young, attractive, and busy receptionist. The sign on her desk said Willow Carmody.

She looked up from her keyboard as he entered. "How do you do, sir. How may I help you?"

"I spoke with the security guard and he said you could set an appointment for me to tour the complex. I may be interested in leasing an office space."

"Certainly, sir, and what is your name and your type of business?" she asked.

"My name is Anthony Harrison, but I would rather not mention my company just yet."

"That's fine, Mr. Harrison. Mr. Garfield does all that sort of introductions in the building. He is tied up today, but if you can come in tomorrow morning at ten he will be able to see you and give you a tour of the complex. Is that a good time for you?" she asked.

Tony mentally noted the furnishings, carpets and office equipment were all very new. There was just a hint of soothing music playing on the overhead speakers. "Yes, Miss Carmody. That will be fine. I'll be here at ten. If I'm interested after the introduction, I'll leave you my business card. Thank you," he said as he turned to leave the office.

Back at Trooper Headquarters Tony went directly to the office of the commander, Major Tim Gatsby to give him a verbal report of his visit to the hospital and to the office building where AmerAsian Labor Union was located. It was a lengthy meeting where the two planned a strategy for his meeting tomorrow morning with hopes of making some contact with the office of AmerAsian. He asked the major to have someone make him 25 business cards for the meeting. He suggested they use North Star Investigations as the name of his imaginary company. The major agreed.

"Do you think Halstead will be able to remember more details about his attack?" asked Major Gatsby.

"He said it's slowly coming back piece by piece, but the doctor said he may never remember everything."

"I agree with your assessment that the danger may not be over, and we should keep Don's identity secret for a while. The daughter is still hidden, is that correct?"

"Yes, she is out of state at this time, but with her father awake she may want to come back to see him. Don said these people threatened her safety and I don't believe that danger has passed. It's difficult to assess, not knowing what the threat and assault was about. I guess that's my job at this point—discover why."

"OK, Tony, do the paperwork and I'll have my secretary make you some cards for your new business." The major made a note on the pad on his desk as the lieutenant made his way out of the office.

Chapter 6

Back in his office Tony sat a few minutes with a cup of hot coffee he had picked up on his way to his small office in the rear of the building. It took him nearly two hours to compose his report. He was so intent on the report he had forgotten the coffee and it sat cold on his desk. He read the final draft of the report and satisfied with the document printed it out for his files. Realizing he was holding a cold cup of coffee he walked back to the small break room for a fresh cup before calling Bob Halstead. He sipped the coffee before sitting down in his office chair to dial the telephone. A dispatcher came in at that moment with a small box of business cards in her hand.

"The major asked me to make these up for you, Tony. Will they do the job for you?" she asked.

Lifting the lid of the small box he took out one of the cards and studied it a few moments. "North Star Investigations; it has a nice ring to it. They look good. Thanks."

She gave him a small wave of her hand and left the office. Tony continued to study one of the business cards while sipping his hot coffee which was half gone by the time he sat down at his desk.

His first call was to the hospital to check on Don Halstead. The nurse on duty said he was doing better but had been given pain medications to allow him to rest.

His next call was to Bobby Halstead to report Don's condition. It was a short call to Don's brother who was planning to take Jenny out for dinner this evening.

"I have a busy day tomorrow, Bobby, so I won't call you any more today. Don is very alert and looks good considering his injuries. They have him sedated in order for him to rest this afternoon. I'll call again tomorrow after I try to speak with him again. I'm going to be busy in the morning following up on a lead here in town. Talk to ya later," he said as he hung up the telephone.

Tony came into the office the following morning wearing a gray blazer, black slacks, and an off-white shirt with a black silk tie. He hoped his attire would portray him as a successful businessman when he went downtown for his appointment to see what kind of offices were in the building where AmerAsian Labor Union had their offices. The early morning was spent with his daily duties in the office where he met briefly with the major, drank too much coffee and waited for the prearranged time to visit the office of Mr. Winston Garfield.

Miss Willow Carmody greeted him with a broad smile as he entered the outer office. "Good morning, Mr. Harrison. Go on in, Mr. Garfield is expecting you."

Tony left one of his new business cards on her desk and smiled back at her, "Thank you, Miss Carmody."

Inside the main office Garfield offered him coffee which he declined due to the amount of caffeine he had already consumed during the morning. Garfield had a packet prepared for his possible new client and handed it over after shaking hands with Tony. It took several minutes to outline the types of offices available in the complex and he quoted rates per square foot for each style of office.

"I only give you these quotes in order for you to understand each of the several styles of offices I can show you this morning. All the lower floors are completely leased, but, as you will see, the upper floors are equally accessible to your clients. Do you have any questions before we start our tour?"

"No, Mr. Garfield. I think you've covered everything, however while we are viewing the offices I would like to take a look at one of your full-floor office arrangements. I'm not interested in an entire floor at this time, but our business is growing very quickly and I may need to expand the offices within a very short period of time. Is that possible?"

"Of course, Mr. Harrison. The only full-floor complex at this time is on the fifth floor and I'm quite sure they wouldn't mind if we stop and look into their offices for a moment." Garfield arose from his plush chair to lead the way out of the office, down the hall and to the elevators. The first stop was floor seven. Garfield used a large master key to open the first office. "This is the basic office with, as you can see, a desk and waiting room for your secretary/receptionist and incoming clients."

Tony looked around the outer office thoughtfully. It was less plush than the one Mr. Garfield occupied, but very nice. Garfield led the way to the inner office where the view was spectacular, looking over most of the surrounding structures and the Alaska Range of mountains across Cook Inlet. This morning was a perfect morning for the tour when Mount Denali was visible, lit by the sun with a blue sky behind the snow covered mountain.

"I'm impressed with the view," said Tony.

"The view is the reason we went with the glass walls on this side of the building. This is the main office in this suite. From the outer office you have access to two smaller offices and a break room with an attached restroom. In your packet you will see that this office is a few dollars per square foot for more than the same offices on the other side of the building; however, the view over there is also wonderful with a view of the Chugach Mountains. Except for the view the offices are identical." Garfield walked to a wall of cabinet doors and opened one near the window wall. "This stack of shelves, as you can see, has a small bar or snack bar. The rest of the doors," he opened one, "are your private filing cabinets. All are lockable for private access."

Tony looked into all the cabinets, genuinely impressed with the office. "I like this office, but my partners may not want to spend the money on the view. I, of course, will try to convince them this would be an ideal office space." He opened the packet Garfield had given him while downstairs and noted the difference in cost. "There is quite a difference in rate, I see."

"Do you think you would be satisfied with this office arrangement?" asked Garfield.

"Yes, I do, but as I said earlier, we are expanding and would like to look at those offices you mentioned. Is it possible to do that now?"

"Of course, Mr. Harrison, follow me."

Tony followed Winston Garfield to the elevators and rode down to the fifth floor in silence. When the doors opened he saw a long hallway and several people moving from office to office.

"This is the AmerAsian Labor Union complex. I really don't know much about their business activities but they employ a lot of staff. I'm told they are a world-wide labor union. They told me they represent mostly Asian laborers around the world. He said most of these laborers are in service employment. They work on ships as laborers, cooks, stewards, and the like. I had never heard of them before they leased our offices. Most of the folks working in the offices seem to be Asian and I don't understand what they are saying when they converse in the halls. They don't use the English language. The main office is across the hall. We can go inside if you like, these are public offices."

"Is it possible to look inside this office? I'll try not to disturb anyone working inside." Garfield led the way as they entered the outer office. Tony stopped inside the door and looked around at the number of people passing through the office, most carrying file folders and not speaking.

"May I help you?" asked a voice from behind the receptionists' desk.

Tony smiled at the lady who looked to be Filipino. "Oh, no thank you. I'm just touring the office complex. I'm thinking of renting an office here."

"Would you like to speak with Mr. Wei?"

"I don't want to put him to any trouble, but that would be very nice."

"No trouble," she smiled again and dialed the inner office.

A moment later a small, well-dressed, Asian man came out of his office. "Ah, Mr. Garfield," he greeted. "What may I do for you?"

Garfield was obviously embarrassed. "Sorry to disturb you Mr. Wei. I was just showing Mr. Harrison our office complex. He is interested in office space on the seventh floor."

Wei turned to Tony saying, "Ah, Mr. Harrison. I am Ang Wei, administrator of this division of AmerAsian Labor Union. Would you like to come back to my office for a visit?"

"Thank you, sir, but we didn't come to interrupt your day. I was just interested in the option of expanding our offices if the business continues to grow at its present rate." He reached into his shirt pocket for a business card to give to Mr. Wei.

"Well, then, I will leave the two of you to discuss your business. Feel free to stop and see me anytime." With that short statement he turned to go back into his office.

"I think we had better go back to my office, Mr. Harrison," said Garfield reaching for the door handle and clearly uncomfortable with the moment.

The two men rode the elevator back to the first floor to return to Garfield's office where he made a final pitch to Tony. Tony said he would do his best to convince his partners they needed the office with the view and get back to him. He took the packet of papers and left to return to his own office at trooper headquarters.

Inside his own small cubicle he noted that corporate executives have much nicer surroundings than those of public safety officers. He spent the bulk of the day composing a report on his morning activities and his encounter with Mr. Ang Wei. The AmerAsian Labor Union had a great many people working in their offices, all of whom seemed to be of Asian descent. Once again he wondered how they were able to operate a corporation in the State of Alaska without registering it with the state. He decided to speak with the major before contacting someone at the Alaska Department of Commerce. He picked up the phone to see if Major Gatsby had time to see him.

"Sure, Tony, come on over. I'm curious to hear how your appointment came out."

In the major's office Tony handed him the copy of the leasing packet Garfield had given him. "I've decided you should lease the office I looked at as my new office. What a view! Mount Denali from the office window. It is spectacular."

"It would be nice for you, Tony, but the governor would never approve of you having an office with a view better than his." The major looked at the packet. "I see the price is equal to the view," he commented.

"I was able to talk Garfield into stopping on the fifth floor where Amer-Asian has their offices. It appears most of the employees are of Asian descent and the conversations I overheard were all in a foreign language. The head guy over there came out of his office to meet us and spoke perfect English, although he was also Asian. I had no hint of what they were doing in the office, but everyone seemed to be busy."

"Did you ask him about his business activities?" asked the major.

"No. Garfield became very nervous when this Mr. Ang Wei came out to see what we were up to. I thought it best to say nothing other than introduce myself and leave the office. I do have a question on that thought, though, Major. I want to contact the state Commerce department and see why AmerAsian Labor Union is not listed as a corporation licensed by the State of Alaska."

"I read the report you submitted, and I was curious about that myself. Go ahead and follow up on that and get back to me when you learn anything."

Tony stood to leave the office. "Thanks, Major, I will."

In his own office Tony found his state offices directory and looked for the number for the Alaska Department of Commerce. He dialed the long distance number in Juneau.

"Hello, Department of Commerce, this is Lou Anne. How may I direct your call?" It was a friendly voice on the phone.

"This is Trooper Lieutenant Anthony Harrison in Anchorage. I am looking for information about a corporation operating in Anchorage, but I am unable to locate any licensing for them. I would like to speak to the director of the Division of Corporations and Businesses about it. Is the director in so that we could discuss my concern?"

"Please hold and I'll see if the director is available." There was a click and a long pause before she came back on the line. "Mr. Weber said he will speak with you, Lieutenant, please hold while I transfer your call."

"Hello, Lieutenant Harrison, this is Director Adam Weber. What can I do for you?"

"Hello, Mr. Weber. I'm investigating a case involving a corporation doing business in Anchorage. I have been unable to find where they are registered with the State. I was wondering if you could help me out."

"I will if I can. Which corporation are you referring to?" asked Weber.

"It's the AmerAsian Labor Union. I can't find it listed on the corporate register."

Weber chuckled. "You are the second officer to contact me about this same corporation. May I ask what type of case are you investigating?"

"I can't give you any details, but it's probably assault with intent to commit murder. I would appreciate it if you didn't tell anyone that fact."

"Oh, my gosh, Lieutenant. I'll send you what you need right away. Give me your contact number. The file is rather thick and I will send it electronically.

I can tell you this corporation is shadowy at best. AmerAsian Labor Union is the local name of the corporation. The parent corporation is IndoAsia. Between you and me they're being investigated by ICE (Immigration, Customs, Enforcement). You need to call Officer Greg Beason at the ICE office. The two of you may be investigating the same case. Write down this number to reach him."

"Do you know what Beason is investigating?" asked Harrison.

"Off the record it's slavery, sex trafficking, kidnapping and possible murder, but you didn't hear that from me." The volume in Weber's voice had dropped to a very low level.

Tony wrote down the phone number given on his desk pad. "Thanks for the information. He certainly sounds like someone I should talk with. Please send me that other info as soon as possible."

Before calling Beason he walked into Dispatch to alert the secretary to the large file being emailed to this office by the Department of Commerce. Back in his own office he dialed the number for Greg Beason. The call was answered by a receptionist in the ICE office. She forwarded the call to Beason.

"Hello, Lieutenant Harrison. What can I do for you?" he asked upon answering.

"I think we need to meet face to face and talk. It could be about a case we are both working," said Tony.

Beason's voice became very official. "Where do you want to meet?" he asked.

"Is it possible for you to come to my office at trooper headquarters?"

"What time?" was the short reply.

"Come on over," said Tony, "I'll have fresh coffee by the time you get here."

Chapter 7

Through the intercom the receptionist notified Tony of Beason's arrival. Tony walked to the front and escorted the visitor to his office. They shook hands and Tony asked Greg if he wanted coffee. He said he would pass until later. Beason offered him a thick file folder.

"This is our case so far. We really don't have a case because we have no witnesses. It usually begins with someone wanting to leave the sex trade, but before we can establish the complaint is legitimate the witness disappears. Our intelligence division informs us that this happens all over the world. They have offices collecting union dues and finding members employment, usually in sea-faring positions, as laborers. Many are young women wanting to get to Europe or America. These ladies come from China, Indonesia, many island nations of the Pacific and, I guess, anywhere they can find a helpless woman to exploit. The only common ground in all these cases is the labor union. Each country has a labor union with different names, but they all funnel cash back to the central offices at IndoAsia in Jakarta, Indonesia. All this information is pure speculation from trying to solve how and why the women vanish after they seek us out." Greg was in his chair shaking his head. "It's really frustrating."

While Greg had spoken Tony was scanning the folder in front of him. "This is an unbelievable number of cases. You say these ladies all disappeared after coming to you with a complaint and wanted to get out?" inquired Tony.

"Mostly, yes, and it isn't isolated here in Alaska. This is common all around the world, mostly in port cities of the Pacific. We have cases from Mexico and South America as well as all around the Pacific. There are several from right here in Anchorage. We try to keep these cases quiet. How did you get a case like this?"

"This one is a little different," Tony began. "I have a good friend, a big game and fishing guide. We've been friends for years. His brother worked for one of the local labor unions as some sort of business agent; pretty high up in the union. He had called his brother in Soldotna to tell him he had taken a job with an international union for a lot more pay. Several days ago he made a frantic call to his brother to ask him to get his daughter out of town. He said he was afraid for her safety. When the line went dead my friend Bob went to his brother's home to get the daughter and take her out of town. A couple of days later someone reported a body in a gravel pit near Palmer. It was Bob's brother, Don. The man wasn't dead, but very close to it. He was taken to the hospital in Anchorage as a John Doe. The hospital called me and the case was opened. We have continued the story that the person in the gravel pit was dead and have been keeping him sedated in the hospital since. Bob took the daughter out of state for safety. I tried to find out about his new employer and met with dead ends. I don't want the people who did this to learn that Don is still alive."

Greg blew out a long breath. "Well, Lieutenant Harrison, you have just jumped into a bog of quicksand. I think we should work together on this for both our safety sake. These people kill anyone who gets too close to them. You have something no one has ever had before, a live witness. I think you should contact the brother to let him know there is a real danger here for the daughter. If they are the ones who beat the witness so badly then I think they will go after the daughter and put her in the trade."

"At this point I think you're right. Come with me and we'll talk with the major to get this joint effort approved." Following a brief discussion, the major was in agreement on teaming up. Being a practical man, he was more than willing to accept the help of another investigator he didn't have to pay out of his budget.

Back in Tony's office they discussed a plan of action and arranged for a sharing of intelligence. Tony suggested it would be to both party's advantage to hear what Don had to say if he was conscious enough to speak with them. Greg agreed and the two men rode to Providence Hospital in Tony's unmarked patrol car.

In the ICU unit they spoke with the nurse caring for Don. She said he was doing better but was still on pain control meds. "He's awake right now. You can go in and see him, but please, don't stay long." The television was playing as they entered the room. Don smiled when he saw Tony. "Hi there Tony, who do you have with you?"

"Hello, Don, meet Greg Beason. He is now working with me on your case."

"Sorry, I can't stand up or shake hands, Greg," explained Don.

"We can get reacquainted again later when you get out of here. I'm with ICE and have been investigating your labor union for some time. Do you feel up to answering a few questions for us?" asked the federal agent.

"If I can. I still can't remember everything." He turned his head to face Tony. "I did remember that there were four men in the group that picked me up and worked me over. They were all Asian, not Chinese, but Asian looking. They all had fists as hard as a Kung Fu master. They kept asking me who I had talked to about the union. Every time, I told them I hadn't talked to anyone. Then they all hit me again and again. I don't remember them calling each other by name and I had never seen any of them before."

"Where did they take you to beat you?" asked Beason.

"I don't know but it looked like a parking garage. I was blindfolded, but during the beating the mask slipped a little and I could see cars and trucks parked inside." Don winced as he tried to adjust his position in the bed.

Tony asked the next question, "Don, I know you only worked there a short time, but did you ever hear anything about young girls disappearing?"

"Funny you should ask about that. My secretary warned me that I was about to be taken away and beaten. She said she had seen this happen to some of the young union girls and they were never seen again. When she warned me I got on the phone and called Bobby and asked him to get my daughter away. A couple of minutes after I called, they pulled me out of my office, loaded me into a van and drove me somewhere to ask me questions and beat the tar out of me. That was the last I remembered until I woke up here in the hospital." Don was becoming weak from talking.

"So, they took you out of your office. Was your office on the fifth floor of the new office building in mid-town?" Tony asked.

"Yeah, it was, end of the hall to the left of the elevators." He was getting weaker with every word.

At that moment a nurse entered, took one look at Don and ordered the two visitors out of the room.

They sat in the patrol car while it was parked in the lot. Both men were attempting to make sense out of the information they had just heard. Greg was the first to speak, "I hate to ask you this, but do you suppose someone at the union offices got wind of my investigation and thought Don was an informant?"

The question startled Tony, "I didn't make that connection, but I believe you could be right. Something made them want to take drastic measures and it had to be something with dire consequences. I'm beginning to think it was a wise move for Bobby to take little Jenny out of state to hide her. They would have known from his employment forms that he had a thirteen year old daughter. They could have snatched her and put her on the streets in some foreign country. That's a scary thought."

"I have connection with the witness protection program and I think I can arrange for them to be placed in a safe house somewhere. What do you think about putting Don and his daughter into that witness program when he gets out of the hospital? He'll need a safe haven until this is wrapped up and the union directors are put away."

"That's a good idea, Tony. Let me go to work on that aspect and I'll get back to you. From past experience I would not let Bob and the girl stay in one place for an extended length of time. These people have worldwide connections and we don't know where they will appear next." Greg Beason was looking into the eyes of the trooper. "Do you want me to see what I can do in that regard?"

Tony rubbed his chin while thinking. "I think we had better ask Bobby what he wants to do. Let's go back to my office and call him."

On the way into the little office they stopped and poured themselves a cup of much needed coffee The trip had generated a lot of new information and created a lot of new problems. Once inside the office Tony picked up the phone to call Bob's cell phone number.

"Yeah, who's this?" asked the voice on the other end.

"Bobby, it's Tony. I'm putting us on speaker phone so you can talk with me and my new associate, Greg Beason. He's with ICE and is working the same case as I am." Tony hit the speaker button. "Can you hear me OK?"

"I hear you just fine, Tony. What's going on?"

"First I want you to meet Greg. He's an investigator working on another aspect of this case for the federal government."

"Hello, Bob, Call me Greg. We just came from the hospital and a visit with your brother. He had some interesting information for us."

"Good to meet you Greg. If Tony says you're OK then I'll be happy to meet and talk with you. What about this new information you got from Don?"

It was Tony who offered the answer. "Don said his secretary warned him about them coming to get him, that's why he called you. As it turns out your quick response to Don's request to move Jenny may have saved her. It seems these same folks are in the slavery and sex trade. It is suspected they buy and kidnap young women all over the world and distribute them through the labor union. If they get hold of Jenny there is no way to know where she could end up or what she could be forced to do."

"Oh, my dear God, I didn't realize how big this thing was," Bobby exclaimed. Then he went silent for a moment. "What do you want me to do?"

"Greg has connections with the Federal Witness Protection Program. We wondered if you would like us to arrange a spot for you and Jenny?" asked Tony.

"Do you think they will find us here?" asked Bob Halstead.

"It would be difficult, but with the connections they have around the globe they might get lucky," said Greg.

"Can I have some time to think about it?" asked Bob.

Greg was nodding at Tony who answered. "Sure, Bobby, you think about it. Just be aware of your surroundings at all times. Greg will check with his agency and make arrangements in case you decide to take him up on the offer. By the way, how is Jenny holding up so far?"

"She's a trooper. She wants to go back and see her dad, of course, but I explained it might be too dangerous right now. I think she understands."

"OK then, Bobby, you get back to me if you even have a hint of a problem. Good luck, guy."

Greg was staring at Tony as he hung up the telephone. "I hope he doesn't get into any situations out there. He's a long way from help."

"You need to meet with Bobby. He's a big game and fishing guide. He knows how to take care of himself," said Tony.

The witness protection program is a good idea, Tony. Let me go to work on that aspect at my office and I'll get back to you. It's been great working with you on this case. I hope we can bring it to a successful end." Greg stood to leave.

"Stay in touch and I'll let you know if I learn anything new from Don." Tony was making notes on his desk pad as Greg walked away. After making his notes Tony walked to the office of Commander Gatsby to bring him up to speed on the case and its new developments. It had been a productive day.

Chapter 8

Bobby Halstead sat alone for a long while, thinking about what to do next. He had responsibilities to his own guiding business and the clients already booked who would be wondering where he was and why he wasn't there to take them fishing. He had passed on his July clients to other river guides, but with August on the way and silver or coho salmon season beginning it would require being there to fly them to remote spots and his camps on the Alaska Peninsula. After several minutes he stood and walked to the back yard to speak with Vic Lamar with whom he and Jenny had been staying. He found Vic pulling weeds near the rear fence in the yard.

"Hey Vic, can we talk a minute?" he called out.

Vic stood, rubbing his aching back. "Sure, I need a break. Get me a beer, will you?"

As he walked across the green, grassy yard, Bobby stepped into the kitchen to grab a beer to take back for his friend. Returning to the back porch he handed the can of cold brew to Vic who downed most of it in one drink without removing it from his lips.

"Ahhhh, that's good," he said, wiping the moisture from his mouth. "Now, what is it you want to talk about?"

Bobby dropped into a chair and looked up at his friend. "I just had a call from Tony and another guy, a federal officer with ICE, who had just come from visiting Don. Don gave them quite a bit of information. It turns out this is an international sex and slave trade cartel. They operate all over the globe.

The federal officer said it may not even be safe for us here. His agency is going to try to find a safe house for us, but I'm running out of time and have to get back to fly clients out hunting and fishing. Coho season is beginning on the Alaska

Peninsula and bear hunters will be showing up soon. I just don't know how to handle this problem. I can't leave Jenny, and I can't neglect my guide business with the fishermen and the hunters without losing the season and the major portion of my income for the year. It looks like I've painted myself into a corner."

Vic put his empty beer can on the table between them. "It's going to be a tough decision, Bobby. That little girl needs you right now, but she needs her father more. Perhaps what you say about these criminals being an international cartel is true—she may not be safe here for long. If you have to go back to take care of business, you know I'll protect little Jenny with my own life. But you also know those are not my decisions to make. I do have one thought, though."

"What's that, Vic?"

"What if you called Lindsy Gibson and asked her to come down here to stay with Jenny. Once she's here and Jenny has a female companion we could go on a road trip in my motorhome and travel around America. It would be difficult for them to find us since we won't have a schedule and it would be educational for Jenny. That would leave you free to take care of your guiding business and we could make it last a couple of months if need be."

Bob Halstead was dumbfounded. "You would do that, Vic?" he asked.

"Of course. You have given more than that would cost in hunting and fishing trips over the years. It would be a good way for me to repay you. Besides I like Jenny. It would be fun to travel with her and Lindsy, although Lindsy does talk a lot." He was smiling at Bob.

"Boy, you sure got awfully drunk on one beer," said Bob.

"I just want to help you out, Pard, and I don't know a better way to do it."

"Let's give Jenny a vote in this." Bob was emotional and relieved the offer had been made. He stood to go inside the house to call Jenny.

The three of them discussed the situation at length while sitting in the shade on the back porch. Jenny brought up the problem with her going back to school, but both Vic and Bobby determined that the trip would be a good education and she could do other classes on line in order for her to maintain her grade point average, which was very high. After nearly an hour of discussion it was decided to call Lindsy to ask if she was willing to participate in this venture.

With Bob's call to Lindsy, she agreed to come as soon as the commercial fishing season closed and she shut down her commercial set net site near Naknek.

"Let me know when you want to leave and I'll have a ticket waiting at the PenAir counter for you. Pack light and we'll find new travel clothes for you when you arrive."

Bob was surprised at how quickly this had come together to leave him free to go back and attend his businesses. He decided it was time to call Tony to let him in on the plan.

Tony was about to leave his office when the call came on his cell phone. "Hello, Bobby. What's up?"

Bob explained the plan. Tony could think of no reason the plan couldn't work and agreed to go along with it, provided that the travelling trio would need to let both Tony and Bob know where to find them for safety reasons. These were not common street criminals and had vast resources at their disposal. They devised a safety net that could be activated through any state police office in the United States. Tony also said he would discuss this with Greg Beason and he thought it would be possible to add nationwide federal help if it was needed to protect them. Bob was relieved that Tony agreed with the plan. Now it was possible to return home and go to work as soon as Lindsy arrived.

Bob reasoned that he would not be in any danger while he had his airplane and was working on the Alaska Peninsula. Being in his home territory had definite advantages. He planned to take extra precautions while in the wilderness. As a rule he carried only a large pistol in a Cross Draw holster located on his center chest. This trip he would also carry a .40 caliber Smith and Wesson semi-automatic pistol in a holster on his hip. He always had a large caliber rifle in the airplane to discourage bear attacks but now planned to take extra ammo for the .375 Winchester. He tried to make a list of the things he usually took on these trips. Weapons of war were never on his list, until now. He keyed up his computer to contact his soon to arrive clients. His activities took the entire afternoon and early evening. Vic was the one to bring him back to his present surroundings when coming to ask what time he wanted dinner.

"Sorry, Vic, I guess I was pretty engrossed in getting back to business."

"Jenny and I decided it was getting late and we're grilling some burgers in the backyard. Jenny is making a coleslaw salad to go with the burger. Are you about ready to eat?"

"Yes, I am," said Bob as he power downed and closed the lid on his laptop. He looked at his wristwatch, "Wow, it is getting late. Sorry, I didn't realize the time."

"Lindsy called and said she's ready as soon as you have tickets," relayed Vic.

"It's an hour earlier in King Salmon. I'll call PenAir and make the arrangements for her. Where should we meet her on this end?"

"Medford, Oregon would be the most convenient, but we can go anywhere. We'll take the motorhome so we can overnight anywhere without running up the national debt."

"Thanks Vic, I'll see what the agent at PenAir has to say. Go back to your cooking and I'll be there as soon as the plan is in place and I give them a credit card number."

It was nearly nine in the evening when dinner was finished and the dishes were washed. Jenny was tired and went to her room to go to bed for the night. Bob turned to Vic, "Would it make you unhappy if I made arrangements to return to Alaska when we pick up Lindsy? I have a lot to do and need to get back."

"I'm sure it will be fine. I know how much needs to be done to make ready for your clients. In fact, it would save me a couple of hundred miles of driving." Vic was sad to see Bob leaving with so much uncertainty looming ahead, though.

"I'll make all the arrangements first thing in the morning. My first order of business is to contact a travel agent who can arrange a flight for me at the same time Lindsy arrives in Medford. Do you know anyone?" asked Bobby.

"Yeah, I do. Call Milestone Travel and ask for Marcie. In fact, we can drive down to the office if you would like. She always does my travel arrangements when I come to Alaska. It's the only travel agency left in town since everyone does their own arrangements on the internet."

After breakfast the next morning, Vic drove Bob and Jenny to the travel office to make the arrangements. Three hours later they returned to Vic's home with tickets in hand. Lindsy would arrive in Medford at 1:35 p.m. on the day after tomorrow and Bob would leave Medford at 6:28 the same afternoon. He was to fly directly into King Salmon from Anchorage. He would have no checked baggage, only a small athletic bag with shaving gear and his two medications inside. The long summer daylight hours would give him ample time to fly his Cessna back to Soldotna where he would land on his unlighted airstrip at his home. He felt he could relax with Lindsy and Vic looking after his niece and keeping her safe.

There was much to be done and preparations made to accommodate his clients who would begin arriving a couple of days after his return. Luckily, he had prepared all his camps prior to fleeing to safety with Jenny.

In Anchorage Ang Wei, director of the Anchorage office of AmerAsian Labor Union, called for a meeting with his head security officer, Li Tan. The meeting was to be in Ang's private office. Li Tan appeared to be a total contradiction of himself. He was short, five feet six inches, weighed nearly 200 pounds, and wore a well-tailored suit. The weight he carried was all muscle. The scar near his right eye was a souvenir obtained during a world championship fight in Hong Kong many years ago. The man never raised his voice and seldom moved quickly. He was a very strange man, indeed.

Ang Wei motioned for Li to sit in the large leather chair in front of his desk. "One of our people, a janitor at the newspaper, has reported a strange occurrence. He overheard a reporter mentioning that it was strange that he had not been able to learn the identity of the body found several days ago in the gravel pit in Palmer. He said he had called the trooper office and they informed him the body was still in the Medical Examiner's office in Anchorage. The reporter thought it strange the autopsy had not been completed as of yet and no cause of death established. The reporter attempted to get more information but was stonewalled by the troopers. He asked who was in charge of the investigation and was told it was Lieutenant Anthony Harrison."

"What makes this so strange to you, sir?" asked Li Tan.

Wie reached into the small index box on his desk to retrieve a business card. He handed it to Tan. "Read the name on the card. He came to this office a few days ago under the pretense of wanting to rent office space. I met him in the outer office. I want to know if these two men are one and the same person. If so, we must find a way to end his curiosity."

Li Tan studied the business card. The name on the card was Anthony Harrison and his business was private investigations. The telephone number had a cell phone prefix. "I will look into it, sir. Is there anything else?"

"No, that will be all, but I don't want any loose ends. Do you understand?" said Ang Wei.

"Of course, sir," said Tan as he stood to leave the office with Tony's business card in his hand.

In his own office at the far end of the hallway Li Tan summoned his three assistants. Each man was dressed in a suit, but none as perfectly fit as the one Tan wore. There was no small talk as they waited for the last man to arrive. Once the four were all present, Tan asked them to sit at the conference table to discuss the immediate problem. They sat and waited while Tan outlined the potential problem.

"If this is, indeed, the same Anthony Harrison, it means we have loose ends to rectify. Chang, I want you and Hua to learn what happened to the body from the Palmer incident. Chang, I want you and Aluan to determine if the man on the business card and the Lieutenant on the Alaska State Troopers are the same man. If you can get a picture I will take it to Mr. Wei for identification. I am sure the business agent we took care of is really dead, but we must make certain. If he is not, we must remedy that problem. If the businessman and the trooper are the same man we must see to it he has an accident. This is a priority which threatens our company and our dealings here in Alaska. Do you have questions?" he asked.

There were none. The four men stood to attend their respective tasks. Chang and Hua decided they would attempt to learn who transported the body from the gravel pit in Palmer to the Medical Examiner's office in Anchorage. Chang and Aluan returned to their own office and, using the number on the business card, called North Star Investigations.

Tony answered the small cell phone with the printed label attached, "North Star Investigations. "This is Detective Harrison. How may I help you?"

"I have a missing relative I would like to have you attempt to locate. Do you do that kind of investigating?" said the voice on the other end of the line.

He wrote down the number of the caller listed on caller ID. "Yes, we do, but our office isn't open yet. Is it possible to meet somewhere to talk about the case?"

"Of course, could you meet me at the Red Robin restaurant in Muldoon? We can get a booth and talk privately."

"When would you like to meet?" asked Tony.

"Perhaps around two this afternoon, after the lunch hour rush?" replied the voice.

With the arrangement made, Tony walked to the major's office to let him know there was a bite on the bait. Major Gatsby listened to the plan, nodding approval, but when Tony finished the major said, "I don't want you to go out to that meeting without backup. You know as well as I that these are dangerous people and if this is one of the attackers you could be in danger."

"I'll agree to that but tell them to keep back and out of sight. I think these are professionals and I don't want to spook them off." Inside, Tony was happy to have the backup.

Chapter 9

It was shortly after 1:30 that afternoon when Tony, with two trooper investigators following, drove to the east side of town to meet with the caller at the Red Robin restaurant. He had no idea how he would recognize his caller but figured the caller would come to him when he entered the restaurant. At five minutes to the hour he climbed out of his car and entered. Near the entry door he was met by a well-dressed Asian man looking serious.

"Are you Anthony Harrison?" asked the man.

"Are you the one who called me?" replied Tony.

"Yes, I'm Mr. Chang, Arnold Chang." The man spoke with almost no accent. "Shall we get a booth and have coffee?" he asked.

"That's a good idea, lead the way." Tony followed him to a booth near the back wall of the dining room. He sat across the table from Chang.

"My family and I are looking for a relative who has disappeared. None of the family and none of his friends have seen him in more than two weeks. We are not rich people and I must first ask, what are your rates?"

"Simple investigation without extra expenses is six hundred dollars a day. I will take any information you can give and follow up with the resources we have available. Our firm has been successful in locating missing persons. Does the price seem justified to you?" asked Tony.

"Yes, it seems very fair. We have exhausted all our own abilities and feel we must get professional help; however our budget will only allow for ten days of investigation. I hope you can bring him home in that length of time."

"I will need his personal information and a picture of him, if you can get me one." He reached into his shirt pocket for a business card to give Chang.

"This has my number if you need to contact me for any reason. I will need your number for the same purpose."

Chang handed Tony a card with a number on it. "This is my office. My secretary will answer the telephone. Give her your name and she will put you through to my desk. I thank you for taking my case, Mr. Harrison."

Tony stood and took money from his pocket to leave on the table to cover the coffee. "I'll get back to you as soon as possible, Mr. Chang. The two men walked out of the restaurant together. Outside an Asian tourist was taking pictures of the front of the restaurant and seemed to be muttering in Chinese. Tony stopped in order to avoid running into the man. The man apologized and bowed before stepping out of the way. Chang said something to him in another eastern language and walked away.

Tony walked to his car and climbed inside. His radio crackled on the personal contact channel. It was one of the men covering him. "Hey, Tony, those two Asians are together."

"I suspected that. I think the second guy took my picture." Tony started his patrol car, driving away and searching his rearview mirror for anyone following him. "Did you get their photos?" he asked.

"Sure did. I'll check them against the national archives and see if we can find them," said the officer that had taken the pictures.

"You may have more luck with Interpol," commented Tony. "I'm going back to the office."

The next two days were busy, but not exciting for Tony and his associates. At midday he decided to call Bob Halstead in Oregon.

"Hey there, Tony, you just caught me. We are leaving for Medford right now. I'm flying to Anchorage and from there to King Salmon where I left my airplane. I have clients waiting for me to pick them up in Kenai. Do you have any good news to report?"

"No, but I was about to drive to the hospital to see Don. I won't tell him where you are or that you are on your way back to Alaska. Give me a call when you get here."

"Thanks for the call, Tony. I'm going directly back to Kenai from King Salmon and thankful I got the camps set up before I left town. I'll call when I get home. I need to get to Anchorage to see Don and will call you tomorrow."

Bob carried his athletic bag to the motorhome where Vic and Jenny were waiting. The engine was running when he climbed aboard. It was a two-hour trip to Medford and his delays cost them the extra time they would have had before Lindsy's arrival. On the way to the airport Bob explained to Jenny that he would call her as often as possible. He also said he would let her father speak to her if he was up to it. It would depend on his physical condition when he got to the hospital.

Vic parked in the outdoor lot and the trio walked to the arrival gate where they met Lindsy and picked up her luggage. There were hugs all around along with some good natured banter. It was decided they had time to leave the airport to find a decent restaurant for dinner. Vic would drive Bob back to the airport departure gate and drop him off after dinner.

Bob slept nearly all the way from Medford and the three and a half hours to Anchorage where he changed planes to board a PenAir flight to King Salmon. The sleek little plane made the flight in about two hours. He walked from the terminal to his Cessna, carrying his athletic bag. It took only a few minutes to preflight the plane and start the engine. He always kept a rifle stashed in the plane and made sure it was in place before taking off toward Lake Iliamna and the flight to Lake Clark Pass. It was nearly three hours from the time he walked from the King Salmon terminal until he was reporting in to Kenai Air Traffic Control. After landing he taxied directly to the fuel pumps where he bought fuel and checked the oil level in the plane. He taxied once more to the tie down in the transient parking area. He exited through the Kenai passenger terminal and found a taxicab idling in front of the terminal. It was late and he was completely exhausted by the time he reached his home. He fell into bed and slept soundly until his phone rang at seven in the morning.

"Halstead," he answered sleepily.

"Are you taking me and Lance out to camp today, Bob?" asked the voice. Harold Porter and his partner, Lance Pierce, were the clients he was to meet this morning to take them to the camp on the west side of Cook Inlet.

"Where are you now, Hal?" asked the guide.

"At the hotel here in Kenai," he replied.

"I'll be there in thirty minutes to take the two of you to breakfast at Louie's."

Half an hour later he stopped the engine on his big Dodge pickup and got out to help the men load their gear into the back. Everyone said hello and shook hands before Bob drove to the restaurant for breakfast.

An hour later they had loaded the gear into the Cessna 185 and strapped in for the ride to the camp. The sun was bright and the air smooth as they crossed the nine miles of open water in the single engine airplane. Over the west shore Bob dropped to five hundred feet for the trip to the little airstrip at the cabin. It was fairly early and he wanted to show them any bears that might be headed to the river for breakfast. They spotted six big brown bears as they crossed the low, alder-filled landscape en route to the cabin. There was a moose grazing on the edge of the small airstrip requiring Bob to buzz the animal and clear the path for a safe landing.

Settling the clients into the cabin and giving the instructions about visiting bears and moose as well as warning of the hazards of the muddy stream bank took nearly an hour and a half. Bob said he would check on them daily. He also told them they had cell phone service in this area and he could be reached at any time. Once satisfied the two men were safely accommodated, Bob took off, heading directly to Merrill Field in Anchorage. On the way he called Tony to meet him at the trooper hangar.

Bob parked his Cessna in the transient parking near the old control tower and waited for Tony. The two were going to the hospital to visit Don. He couldn't help worrying about his brother and niece, Jenny, and being concerned they both could be in grave danger. Fifteen minutes later the trooper arrived. Bob walked around the front of the car to get into the passenger side before speaking. The two men shook hands.

"Good to see you, Tony. Is there any new information you can tell me?" asked Bob, displaying a worried look.

"The investigation is continuing, but there really isn't anything new. Don has remembered a couple of things that helped and he may remember more as time goes on." Tony turned the car around to head toward the hospital. "By the way, how is the girl, Jenny?"

"She's worried about her father, but I have tried to keep her busy and not give her much time to think about it. I called Lindsy Gibson to come down and stay with Jenny. She and my friend Vic are taking her on a road trip, just in case they find it necessary to become a moving target. We figured if this continued until after the school year started she could claim this as an educational experience, you know, visiting historical sites around the United States. If she has someone looking to do her harm, she will be a little more difficult to find. Besides, I had clients coming and had to find a way to get back to take care of them."

It was less than ten minutes to the hospital parking garage. The two men walked into the hospital and made their way to the ICU wing where they were met by the nurse caring for Don.

"Hello, Lieutenant, your friend is out of his room at this moment. He has been taken down to the pool by a therapist and his helper. The doctor thought it was time for him to begin moving some of his injured muscles. They have been gone for almost an hour and should be back any time now. Can I get the two of you some coffee?"

"We could sure use some, Nancy. By the way, this is the patient's brother, Bob," explained Tony.

"Pleased to meet you, Bob. You two go into the room and I'll bring you each a cup." She turned to walk to a small break room secluded behind the nurse's desk. "Call me Nancy," she said as she walked away.

Bob and Tony had finished their coffee when the therapist and his aide rolled Don back to his bed. He was sitting up in a wheelchair but held in place with a wide web belt. Don smiled when he saw his brother. He was in obvious pain.

"Hey there, Bobby, when did you get in?" he asked. "Sorry I can't reach out to shake hands."

Bob was nearly in tears when he saw how damaged his brother's body actually was. "We can make up for the handshake later. Jenny sends her love, Bro."

The conversation was halted while the two attendants lifted Don into his bed and helped him get comfortable. The nurse had returned to assist with settling him into bed.

Nancy said, as the therapist and aide took the chair out of the room, "I just got word from the doctor that they are going to move you out of ICU and to a room in the recovery wing. You will be in a private room with a private nurse and a security guard. Your friend Tony, here, ordered the extra help. I don't know if he will pick up the bill for the dancing girls you ordered, though." Moments later she finished adjusting his bed and monitoring machinery, waving as she left the room.

"How is Jenny?" asked Don once they were alone.

"She's just fine. She sends her love," answered Bob.

"I had a strange call yesterday and I think it may be some of the group who did this to you," commented Tony. "During my investigation I went to the labor union offices and met a man by the name of Wei. I think he's the boss of the place. Later I had a call asking to hire the fake investigator I said I was when I made an appointment to see the offices. I met with the man at a local restaurant and he had a friend waiting outside to take a photo of me when we left, I think to learn who I really am. My backup guys in the parking lot took pictures, too. We're running them through a few other agencies to see if we can learn who they are and what kind of characters they really are. They could learn my identity and blow my cover."

"I still can't tell you why they did this to me, Tony. I don't know anything about the union except what they told me. I do know Mr. Wei is head of the local office and has a lot of power. He answers to an office in Jakarta, Indonesia. That is where the world headquarters is located. That Anchorage office in the new building is the headquarters for the entire United States and Eastern Pacific territory. Until this happened, I only did work answering correspondence and arbitrating some minor local disputes. The members seem to be hotel maids, busboys, dishwashers, window washers and such. At sea they are only laborers, not seamen or longshoremen. Other than that I don't know much." Don was obviously tiring.

"I'll try to find out more, Don. Get rested up. We're glad to see you up and moving a little." Tony wanted to leave and allow Don to rest.

"Bobby, come back and visit again soon, please." There were tears in Don's eyes as he spoke.

"I'll be back, Don. I have clients to take out to my hunting camps. I took a fisherman to the west side camp yesterday. I'm going to get busy, but I'll be here anytime I can. Let me know if I can bring you anything." Bob, too, was feeling the emotion.

"Let's go find some dinner, Bob. I'll bet you haven't eaten all day." Tony could see the sadness in his friend. "The best steaks in town are at O'Sullivan's on Fifth. Does that sound good to you?"

"I hadn't stopped to think about it, but a steak would be great. I can't have a toddy with you because I have to fly back home tonight."

Bob and Tony both relaxed a little during dinner, sharing small talk and eating the best steaks in Anchorage. It was late when Bob climbed into his Cessna for the short flight to his own small airstrip. The sun had gone down by the time he readied for bed. It had been a long and tiring day.

Chapter 10

Early the following morning Li Tan met with his four enforcers in his office. Many things were discussed, but the most important to Li Tan was the identity of the man who visited the office in the previous days. "Mr. Chang," called the leader. "Have you identified the stranger who came to this office? Was it the same man Mr. Chin met at the restaurant?"

"Yes, in both cases, sir. We were able to take some photos at the restaurant and compared them to the video surveillance footage from here in the offices. Without any doubt, it is the same man. He is Lieutenant Anthony Harrison. The name on the business card is his real name and he is indeed an investigator, but for the State of Alaska. He must have some reason to be investigating this office to go to so much trouble as to have those business cards printed." Chang was concise in his speech.

"Have you learned the purpose of his visit?" asked Li Tan.

"We can only speculate at this point. We have discussed it and there is only one thing we can be sure of and that is the death of the business agent. We believe they have identified the body and are looking into his background as part of the investigation," replied Chin.

"Is it possible the business agent is alive and not dead as you supposed?"

"We checked for a pulse after he was no longer able to answer questions. We found none. We waited for several minutes, watching for any sign of life, but there was none. I think it is impossible he was alive." Chang felt certain the business agent was dead when they left the scene at the gravel pit.

"Did any of you put a knife in his heart to be certain?" asked Li Tan.

"No sir, we did not," replied Chang.

"Then, it is possible the man was alive after all. Not making sure of his condition was a very bad mistake. If, for some reason known only to the gods, he did survive and is able to recover enough to speak it could lead back to this office. That is unacceptable and we must rectify it if it is true. Check all hospitals for an injured, unidentified person of his description who was brought in soon after you were finished with him. The newspaper account states an unidentified body was recovered from that gravel pit. That same article could give you a description and a date and time of the recovery. You should start there. I will report to Mr. Wei."

Li Tan was not looking forward to meeting with Mr. Wei and delivering this possibility. He used the office phone to call the receptionist to make an appointment for himself with Mr. Ang Wei for 20 minutes on an important matter. The secretary made the call and reported back, "Your visit is scheduled for one half hour from now, sir."

The head of security checked the time and used it to prepare his presentation to the boss. Minutes later he entered the outer office to check in with the secretary who had scheduled him. As he talked with the secretary, her telephone lit up and beeped. She answered. When the call was completed, she hung up and looked up at Li Tan, "You may enter now, sir," she said.

Twenty minutes later he exited the office with a solemn scowl on his face. It was a look not often seen on the scarred face of the head enforcer. Tan returned to his office for a few minutes of private reflection. His meeting with Mr. Wei had not gone well. Ang Wei was not one to recognize failure at any time. He was a man very used to dealing out extreme measures to those who failed.

Li Tan had been a world class martial arts fighter until one hot and humid evening in Saigon, Viet Nam he was in a bout with the reigning world champion. The fight was going in favor of Tan when a group of men working for a gambler who had bet heavily on the champion, stormed the ring and cut the face of Li Tan with a machete. The injury was such that he could not continue the bout and lost his chance at the world title. Ang Wei was at the bout, seated in the third row from the ring. He had bet heavily on the challenger, Li Tan. After the bout was stopped and Tan was taken to his dressing room Wei sent his aide to learn of the seriousness of the injury. It was determined Tan had lost sight of his left eye and the gash across the eye and down his cheek was sewn shut.

Some weeks after the fight Wei once again asked his aide to contact Li Tan to offer him employment with his security team. Tan was an educated man, soft spoken, with an imposing muscular physique. His martial arts training had given him all the knowledge he would need for the position he was asked to take. In the short years since the boxing bout, he had been moved to the head of the security unit for the Eastern Pacific offices of AmerAsian Labor Union.

Once he had regained his composure, Li Tan summoned his four associates to a meeting. He took the seat at the head of the conference table and closed his eyes to meditate until the others arrived. The four enforcers filed into the room and sat, saying nothing until Li Tan opened his eye to scan the room. "Chang, what did you learn at the hospital?"

"The newspaper reporter didn't know any more than what was in the article. We checked with the medical examiner's office and they gave us a song and dance about not being allowed to divulge the information. At the hospital we talked with a nurse from the ICU who told us that there was a man of that description in the unit. She also said he was being moved to a recovery unit. She wouldn't say anything about his injuries but did say he was improving. She also said the man had a brother who came to visit him. I have learned this brother is a big game and fishing guide. I searched our man's employment files and found no brother listed.

We looked him up on the internet and he seems to be a very popular guide. He owns at least five permanent cabins at camps stretching all the way down the Alaska Peninsula. He has clients in his fishing camp on the west side of Cook Inlet and, according to his advertising, brown bear hunting is about to start and he will be required to have guides with each bear hunter. We also learned the guide and our company business agent are friends with Anthony Harrison, an Alaska State Trooper. We are still working to learn more, but we were called back for this meeting." Chang closed the paper file folder in front of him and nodded at Li Tan.

"Very good Chang. This meeting will be short and you may continue your investigation. I have been given specific orders by Mr. Ang Wei. We are to complete this business immediately. He is angry that this entire episode has gotten so far out of hand. His orders are to dispose of the business agent at once. There are to be no more excuses. Therefore, I want you, Chang, and you, Mr. Aluan, to complete the task and get word back to me by eight o'clock this evening. That will be all. However, Mr. Chin and Mr. Hua will remain here for another meeting. I have a task for the two of you." Chang and Aluan stood and were leaving while the other men moved closer to the head of the big conference table.

Once the others had left the room Tan spoke to Chang, "I want the two of you to learn what you can about this brother. Since we have been unable to find the daughter of the business agent I suspect the brother has hidden her somewhere. It is not necessary to eliminate everyone whose name comes in contact with us; but I want this to end without witnesses. If we fail I suspect we will meet the same fate as those we are dealing with. It has gone bad from the very first and we were unable to get any information from our business agent. Errors must stop. That trooper coming to this office is a signal that we are no longer anonymous. You must deal with it or we shall be dealt with. Any questions?" asked Li Tan. There were none.

Chang and Aluan drove directly to the hospital from the office meeting. There was no conversation during the drive, both men knowing the outcome in either completing the task or not completing the task would likely be the same for these two enforcers. If they completed the task they would likely be killed or arrested; if they did not succeed they would surely be killed by the very ones they worked for.

"We must attempt to accomplish this task without gunfire in the hospital. The nurse said they were going to move the patient to another unit today. Perhaps we will be able to use this as a cover to contact the patient." Chang checked his semi-automatic pistol while he talked.

"That is a very good idea, Chang," said Aluan as he drove into the hospital parking lot. "You try to find us some scrubs and lab coats and a gurney. I will meet you on the ICU floor when I locate the room where he is to be taken. We may be able to get this done while moving him and be gone by the time he is found."

"Good plan. I will also attempt to find a couple of clip-on name tags to look official. Give me twenty minutes to meet you." Chang spoke as they walked into the hospital.

Inside they parted in different directions, going about the task at hand. Aluan went directly to the elevators while Chang found an employee locker room where several employees were changing clothes. The first two lockers he opened were not in use, the third was used by a large and heavy individual. The third locker, however, yielded success. Inside were several sets of scrubs, green in color, cloth shoe covers and hair protection. There were protective masks in the common area of the locker room. This was, obviously where personnel from the operating rooms changed clothing. He found a laundry bag and put another set of clothing inside for Aluan. He had been unable to find any identification badges. As casually as possible he made his way to the ICU unit on the fifth floor. Aluan was waiting in the anteroom outside the unit. Without a word he took the bag from Chang and went into the men's room to put on the medical garb.

In the hallway outside the elevator area they found a gurney they needed. It had been used to transport a patient, but that would not be a problem for this room change. The two men pushed the gurney down the hall to the nurse's station and asked for the room number for the patient they were asked to move.

"Let me see your room change order, please," asked the nurse at the desk.

"Sorry, but our supervisor said it was already arranged," said Chang.

"Let me check with my supervisor," said the nurse as she turned to enter a small office behind the front desk.

Through the open door Chang could see the nurse he had spoken with in the food court downstairs. He turned around so he would not be recognized. The nursing supervisor stepped out of the office to speak with the two orderlies and immediately recognized both of them. "I'm sorry, sir, but you will have to have a written order to take the patient," she said to the men.

"We have other patients to move and this would interrupt our schedule," said Chang. "Now, please give me the room number."

The nurse was not to be intimidated. She returned to her small office and pressed the security alarm on her desk. Within seconds two security men came into the unit. A third entered the unit by the time the first two reached the nurse's station.

"What's the problem?" the guard asked the nurse.

"These men want to move a patient and they have no written orders. They also have no identification on them. They came here with an ER gurney when they should have just taken the patient in his bed. None of this is correct."

The lead security man turned to Chang, "I think you men should come with me to my office. We need to get to the bottom of this."

"Of course, sir," said Chang as he motioned for Aluan to follow. They walked out of the ICU area closing the door to the anteroom as they left with one guard leading the two men and two more security men behind.

In the waiting room outside the secure ICU the lead officer turned to say something to Chang who stuck him in the throat with a hardened set of knuckles. At the same time Aluan spun around to kick the next officer, knocking him unconscious. The third guard was reaching for his radio when Chang kicked him in the knee causing him to fall. Once on the floor Chang kicked him in the head. Now the two men returned through the security doors of the ICU. The head nurse saw them reenter the unit and again signaled for emergency response from security.

Chang and Aluan immediately were behind the desk gripping the head nurse painfully by the shoulder. "Which room," Aluan demanded.

"I won't tell you," replied the frightened nurse. The second nurse was cowering behind the desk.

"Don't hurt her," said the second nurse. "I'll show you, just don't hurt her."

Chang was about to release the supervising nurse when the doors burst open and a flood of security men entered with guns drawn.

"Release her and get on the floor," shouted the first uniformed officer, his semiautomatic pointed directly at Chang. The security men marched toward them. When they were close to him Chang released the nurse and slapped the gun from the officer's hand.

Aluan made a dive for the sliding firearm. As he reached it, he rolled but too late. There were six shots fired, one by Aluan the rest by security officers.

The gunshots brought more security men as well as doctors and administrators coming to assist. Aluan and Chang lay on the floor, both dead from gunshot wounds. The second nurse was hysterical, but the nurse supervisor, though still shaking, was able to explain what had taken place.

The head security guard ordered his men to secure the area and keep spectators out. His next order was for the nurse to contact the state trooper office and report the incident. She had spoken with Trooper Lieutenant Anthony Harrison many times and reached for his business card on her desk.

Tony answered the phone. "Trooper Harrison," he said.

"Lieutenant, this is the nursing supervisor in the ICU at Providence. We have just had an incident and shooting in the unit. We need you here right now. The men who came are dead, shot by security. All this started when some men, pretending to be nurse's aides, came to get your friend from ICU."

Tony was shocked, "I'll get my team moving and I'll be there in five minutes. Try to have everyone back away from the scene, if you can."

"Security is here, they shot the men. Your friend is still in his room." She informed Tony.

She hung up the phone and fell into her desk chair, the adrenalin rush now leaving her totally drained, weak-kneed and shaking horribly.

Chapter 11

Lieutenant Anthony Harrison took the call which had been forwarded to his office desk phone. When he heard the words 'shooting at the hospital ICU' the trooper immediately ran to the office of the major to report. He was on the phone with dispatch regarding the same report. Overhearing his orders to send all available units to the scene of the shooting Tony said, "I'm on my way, Major. Send the forensic team to meet me there."

The major replied, "Will do," and waved him on.

At the entrance to the hospital Tony leapt from the car, leaving the red lights flashing. He ran inside to the elevator bank where a security officer was holding the door, waiting for him to arrive. On the fifth floor he made his way to the ICU where the doors were open and another security officer was standing and keeping the onlookers away. Tony walked the hall with long, swift strides. He could see the bodies on the floor. Both the duty and the head nurses were in the small office to keep them from contaminating the shooting scene.

At the desk he was stopped by the chief security officer. Tony knew the officer from previous disturbances in the hospital. "My team is right behind me, Fred. Give me a quick rundown on what took place."

The chief of security pointed to the men on the floor and gave a brief account. "I don't have any idea why they came to get this patient." said Fred.

"I think I do," replied Tony. "The patient they came to get is a crime witness. We have him here as a John Doe for his safety. Somehow they got word he was here and probably came to finish the job they thought they did in a gravel pit near Palmer."

Fred looked at the trooper with questioning eyes, "You mean you know who the patient really is?"

"Yes we do, but this is the very reason we were so secretive. We can talk about all that later. Right now we need to get my team in here to document the scene. They should be on the way up as we speak. I want to talk with the head nurse, if she'll let me."

"She's in her office behind the nursing desk. We asked her to stay there until we cleared the scene out here. Go ahead and talk with her and I'll take care of the details for your men."

Tony stepped into the small office and asked the nurse to come out into the hall. They walked behind the nurse's station to the far end of the countertop. He had never known her name, though they had spoken several times. Her name tag, he now noticed read EMILY. "Emily, how is my friend?" he asked.

"I haven't had time to talk with him, but I checked on him after the guns were fired to make sure he was OK. He said he was and I haven't had time to get back in there since. Security asked me to wait in my office."

"Let's both go check on him," said Tony.

When the two entered the room Don was looking out the window. His head snapped toward them when he heard them enter, visibly frightened.

"Take it easy, Don. It's me, Tony. The excitement is over. You can relax."

There were tears in his eyes, "I was afraid I couldn't protect myself. I thought I was a goner." Don spoke with a shaking voice.

"Everything is good now, Don. There will be a lot of activity in the hall for a while. My men are doing the investigation. Are you alright now?" asked Tony with genuine concern.

"Yeah, Tony, I'm good. I just felt so helpless, not being able to move or help myself."

"Both the bad guys are dead in the hall. Hospital security officers took them out when they went for one of the officer's guns. I'm going to have you moved to a secure wing and leave a trooper on guard until you get out. I haven't called Bobby yet. I thought we could both talk to him if he answers his telephone. Are you up for it?"

"Yes, but you will have to punch in the numbers on the phone. My arms still aren't working," said a relieved Don. "One more thing, Tony. Please don't let Jenny know what happened here today."

Tony motioned to Emily it was OK for her to go back to her desk while he continued to dial the number for Don's brother, Bobby. It only rang twice and was answered by the guide.

"Halstead Guide Service," he answered.

"Bobby, this is Tony. I have you on speaker phone, and I'm here with Don."

"Hey there Bobby, how goes it?" asked Don.

"Hey, Don, good to hear your voice, are you doing OK?" asked Bobby.

"Yeah, I'm fine. There was a little excitement here in the hospital today, though."

"Is that true, Tony?" asked Bobby.

"Yes, it is. We haven't identified them yet, but two men came after Don a little while ago. Security confronted them because the nurse didn't like their looks and she asked security to check the two men out. There was a fight and the two Asian men tried to take a pistol from one of the officers. Security officers shot both men. My team is cataloging the scene now. They never got to Don's room, thanks to a sharp and courageous nurse."

Don turned toward the telephone. "Where are you now?" he asked.

"At my place. I'm loading the plane to take a couple of clients and my assistant guide to the Wildman Camp. A half hour from now you wouldn't have been able to reach me. I'll come visit with you when I get back tomorrow. Thanks for the call."

Tony put the phone back in his pocket. "I'm going out to arrange your new accommodations. All the voices in the hall are my troopers and the hospital security team. Relax for a while. If you need anything at all I'll have Emily get it for you."

The gathering of evidence and the documenting of photos, security video tapes and statements from those present, both staff and onlookers, were all listed on evidence forms and placed in the custody of a designated investigator for safekeeping. The process took most of the rest of the day. Once the scene had been documented the two bodies were sent to the medical examiner's office. It was late afternoon when Emily, the nurse in charge of the ICU, was allowed to call housekeeping to clean and restore order to the area. Two additional nurses were called to serve the needs of the patients in the wing who had received only minimal and necessary care during the time of the incident and investigation. By the time all the troopers and security staff had made their way out of the hospital the entire staff was totally exhausted.

Trooper Harrison returned to his office to give a brief report to the major. Once that was done he went into his office to complete the report and coordinate the entry of evidence into the secure storage locker. The time was nearly midnight when Tony left the office to get some needed rest.

The afternoon had been busy for the offices of Mr. Ang Wei and Mr. Li Tan. News of the shooting in the hospital had been announced on the radio with little detail other than to say two Asian men had been shot and killed when they confronted hospital staff. The radio announcement also stated the altercation took place in the ICU area of the hospital which, in any hospital, is a secure area where casual entry is not allowed. No other details were available.

Li Tan had summoned the remaining two enforcers, Mr. Chin and Mr. Hua, to his office where he ordered them to learn as much about what had happened as possible. The radio report had said there were no other injuries reported. If that were true it meant Chang and Aluan had failed to complete their task and another attempt would be necessary. This new attempt, however, would not be as blunt as the one attempted by the first two men sent from this office. "We must gain more knowledge and use more stealth in this new attack, but we must succeed without fail or we will all be made to pay the price and I fear our corporation will be at risk. We cannot allow this to happen."

A plan was devised to gather information and possibly hire spies in the hospital in order to find a point when the AmerAsian business agent would be vulnerable. He ordered Chin and Hua to be speedy, but to be careful. "The protectors of our prey will now be wary," cautioned Li Tan.

It was nearly ten the following morning by the time Bob Halstead had flown from the lake on the lower Alaska Peninsula. He had set up his assistant guide and two clients in cabins, opened the main lodge house and made certain all would be well at the camp until he returned. He bid his clients and assistant guide farewell and took off from the airstrip aside the small lake, climbed to 9,500 feet for a direct flight over the mountains to his home on the Kenai Peninsula. On the way he contacted Tony Harrison who convinced him to change course and fly directly to Anchorage. Bob checked his fuel and calculated the time difference for the flight and decided it was safe to make the change. Two hours after the call ended he landed at Merrill Field in Anchorage where Tony was waiting.

"Take me to the hospital, Tony, I want to see Don."

Tony nodded agreement and gave Bob the details of the attack at the hospital as they traveled the few short miles to the hospital. After Tony parked, they walked quickly into the hospital and directly to the elevators. "We moved him to a more secure unit on a different floor. I have a guard posted on his room to stop any unwanted visitors," said Tony.

"Has Don been able to say why these men want to harm him?" asked Bob.

"He told me he didn't know why. He claims they kept asking him questions he knew nothing about. He told me he didn't know any of the people or situations they questioned him about. This attack at the hospital has him really frightened because he is lying in a bed with no way to defend himself. I don't blame him, but I have tried to reassure him of his safety," Tony said as they reached the designated floor.

There were no visitors seen in the hallway as was usual on other floors.

Halfway down the hall there was a uniformed guard stationed at one of the doors. It was the room occupied by Don Halstead. When they entered Don was sleeping. He was now without IVs hooked to his arms, but electronic monitors were still in place recording blood pressure, pulse rate, oxygen retention and inhalation rate.

Tony stopped to speak with the guard at the door before following Bob into the room. As he entered he saw Bob with his hand on his brother's shoulder in a gesture of comfort. The scene was heartwarming and he stopped near the doorway to observe the moment. After several seconds Bob pulled a chair to the bedside and sat. The movement disturbed Don who then opened his eyes to see the men in the room with him. Startled at first, he calmed when he realized it was his brother and friend, Tony.

"Hey, Bobby," said Don in a hoarse voice.

"How are you doing, Don?" asked Bob.

"OK, I guess. You probably heard about the men coming to the ICU to get me. Damn, Bobby, I'm still scared."

"I have given this a lot of thought and we can't do anything until you are well enough to be mobile. Once you get to that point I'm going to get you moved out of the state to somewhere safe and somewhere both you and Jenny can live without fear." Bob now had tears on his cheeks.

"I'm going crazy, Bobby. I can't defend myself. All I can do is lie here and take whatever someone wants to do to me. It scares me to death. It's all I can think about." Don's emotions were getting the best of him.

Tony patted Don on the shoulder, "We underestimated the men we're dealing with, Don. None of this is your fault. Your job now is to get well. I'm keeping an armed guard on this room for as long as it takes. Not many people in the hospital know you're in this wing and you don't appear on the general list of patients. Hospital security is aware of the situation and is prepared to respond to this room within 30 seconds of an alert by the guard on duty or the supervising nurse."

"I have a bunch of hunting and fishing clients to move around in the coming weeks, so I won't have time to come visit much. If you want anything you call Tony. I've never wanted a season to be over, but this year my heart just isn't in it. You will need the time to heal and get some physical rehab before you can be released. I'll check in as often as possible." Bob tried to reassure his brother he was safe but didn't think it worked very well.

"Sorry, Bobby, but the medications are putting me to sleep again. Come back and see me, OK?" Don's eyes were heavy and his voice fading.

Bob and Tony stepped from the room and walked toward the elevators. "It's pitiful to see him this way, Tony," said Bob.

"I understand how you feel, but there really isn't anything either of us can do right now. He needs the time to heal. Once he can move his arms and stand again he'll regain his old confidence. He's just feeling helpless right now and honestly I'd feel the same way." Tony spoke as they walked out of the hospital. "How would you like to have some lunch before you fly home?"

"I'd like that, but I will have to leave immediately afterwards to get ready for more clients due in tomorrow. I have some fishermen at my cabin on the west side of the inlet and I should fly in there on my way home." Bob took off his cap and rubbed his hair and shook his head. "I usually look forward to clients and making my rounds of the camps, but this thing with Don has me sidetracked and is making it tough for me to stay focused on my business."

"There's an Olive Garden restaurant not far from here. Is that good for you?" asked the trooper.

"That will be great," replied Halstead.

After lunch they returned to the parked Cessna. They said their goodbyes as Bob made his preflight check. He needed to fuel his plane before continuing his flight to the west side cabin and then home. The warm afternoon sun and nineteen hours of daylight made the flight enjoyable. When he arrived the client in the cabin had several fish fillets in a cooler for Bob to take back with him for freezing. He had enough food and indicated he might want to stay a few extra days if the cabin was going to be open. Bob said it was and offered it for half price to him because he was a good and loyal customer. After loading the fish in the plane Bob waved and started the engine for the flight back to his home airstrip and the chores of prepping for the next group of clients. This was the ritual every day all through the fall season each year.

Chapter 12

It was mid-afternoon by the time Tony returned to his office. He stopped in the breakroom to pour a cup of coffee before beginning work on his daily office chores. When he entered his office he saw a large packet with a thick file folder inside on his desk. The return address was the local ICE office. Opening the file, he found sub-files from several other government agencies and countries. There was a cover letter written by Greg Beason. It basically said "The enclosed files should help you understand our concerns regarding AmerAsian Labor Union. Call me if you need clarification on any of the material."

The top file marked ICE was documentation of the many complaints and inquiries regarding the number of missing persons connected with the Union. The majority of the cases were women of all ages, mostly young, who had taken employment in menial jobs on ships of many nations with the intent of traveling to some other country and getting off the boats to seek employment in that country. Their intent, as a rule, was to send money home to the family. What had happened in many of those cases is the women had boarded the ship but were never heard from again. These missing person reports were generated in nearly every country along the western shoreline of the Pacific Ocean. The common thread in these reports was the employer who had hired them.

The labor union was not actually the employer of these people but collected union dues from them and assigned them to the job requests from companies worldwide. These requests were for many kinds of laboring jobs. Among them were janitors, hotel maids, gardeners, and ship cleaning personnel. Aboard ship they lived with the crews and worked on tanker ships, cargo ships and passenger ships. The pay for these positions was much more than that paid to onshore positions. The work was usually hard and dirty. Many younger people in that part of the world chose this as a way to leave their country and immigrate to more prosperous places in the world where they could make enough money to send cash to families back home. Alaska was one of the favorite places to seek work. Fish canneries were always hiring and they paid good wages.

Tony read the entire ICE folder without touching his coffee. He understood how the thought of a job with good wages and a chance for free passage aboard ship to some more promising places would encourage many workers to sign up. It took most of the afternoon to read about the number of hires, types of hire and what was promised by the union. It was far into the file when he began to read of the union hire numbers of people who were off on their adventure and never to be heard from again. Most of the inquiries were made by families of these missing individuals.

Another interesting factor was the many young girls on the list of missing persons. With no OSHA or other protective agencies the age of hire ranged from as young as twelve, although most of the young workers were fourteen to eighteen years old. Also startling was the sex and ages of the missing persons. Some were male, but the vast majority were young females, ages twelve to eighteen. The numbers, too, were startling. In the ICE file dealing with persons destined for the United States, there were thousands of names. For the past two years alone there had been more than three hundred names added to the list. To Tony, these numbers were shocking. He reached for his phone and dialed the number for Greg Beason.

"Immigration and Customs Enforcement; this is Officer Beason. How may I help you?"

"Greg, it's Tony Harrison."

"Hi there, Tony. Did you get the files I sent you?"

"Sure did, Greg, thank you. I didn't realize just how widespread this problem was. I have only read the ICE file and haven't started the others yet."

"Those will shock you even more. The Interpol file is really scary, but the one to look into is the one from a special unit from Japan. In Akishima, Japan there is a school that teaches law enforcement personnel from all the countries in the near and far east. It is the third largest police academy in the world and was established in 1962 by the United Nations. The name is UNAFEI, United Nations Asia Far East Institute. Nations from Japan to the Middle East send their instructors there to learn different methods and tactics. The instructors, in turn return home to teach the police officers in their own countries. They are as modern and knowledgeable as the FBI Academy or the Interpol Academy. In recent years they have begun to study the files you have in your hands. I sent these files to you in order for you to grasp just how big this problem really is. You are dealing with extremely dangerous people, Tony."

"I'm beginning to realize that. I recently went undercover to the AmerAsian Laborers Union offices in Anchorage and met the big boss. His name is Ang Wei. I got the impression everyone around him was scared to death of the man."

"As well they should be. You'll see when you finish reading the files." Greg was chuckling.

"I don't know if you heard, but they made an attempt on my friend, Don. Two company enforcers went to the hospital ICU and tried to take him out. The supervising nurse buzzed security as they began to fight and one of the enforcers attempted to grab a security officer's gun. As the enforcer pointed the gun at the security officer another guard shot and killed them both. I spent all day yesterday at the hospital investigating the shooting. Don is OK, frightened out of his mind, but he's OK. We moved him to a secure wing and have a 24-hour security guard stationed on his room." Tony didn't mention Bob Halstead in his short report.

"No, I hadn't heard about it. We need to get together again soon to talk about this. I'm being summoned to a meeting. I'll talk with you later. Good to talk with you, Tony."

Tony hung up the telephone and leaned back in his desk chair. His back ached and he needed to get up and walk a little. He decided one more cup of coffee would be good right about now. He needed to make final entries in his daily log before leaving the office for the day. Back in his office he made the necessary entries and sipped his coffee. He looked at the thick files on his desk and decided the one marked Interpol was the next file he should read. Downing the last drop of coffee he picked up the file and turned out the light in his small office, tucked the file under his arm and went home for the day.

Not a drinking man, tonight Tony made an exception. A Glenfiddich Scotch whiskey and water was his choice along with a ham sandwich for a chaser. He bit into the ham and mustard sandwich, wiped his fingers on a napkin and opened the file.

This file read very similarly to the ICE file, but the locations were all over Europe and the British Isles. The Interpol file also noted a difference in the reasoning behind the disappearances in a few special cases. For example, young girls were sold to wealthy clients. A footnote read that at first it was believed the buyers were only wealthy Arabs, but later determined there were many buyers from other factions including all of Europe. This fact was disturbing to Tony as he read about recovered bodies and only two recovered live girls. This was amazing because of the number of missing young women on the lists.

From the bits and pieces learned from the hundreds of cases a pattern was formed as to how the operation worked. All young girls wishing to find employment were given union numbers upon payment of the union dues. Jobs were assigned as they were made available. This meant the handlers had a current inventory of young girls any time they were asked to provide one. The handlers would read the preferences of the client and find the most desirable candidate. When selected, the candidate was given liquor, drugs, and money to make them willing to go with the client. At that point few of the young girls were ever heard from again. The few bodies recovered indicated that when the client tired of the purchase he merely disposed of them. It was not known if any were used in other tasks such as housekeeping or any menial tasks but it was assumed many of them were still alive and working for the client somewhere or sold to other wealthy clients with the same tastes in entertainment.

There were individual cases documented where a girl had reappeared, usually by arrest, in some prostitution operation somewhere in the world. Some surfaced as brides of, usually, much older men in some far-off country. In all the cases it was clear the labor union, no matter the individual union name, was in the human trafficking and slavery business. It was also clear there were a great many enforcers on the payroll.

Tony thought about the army of thugs employed by the traffickers and marveled at the amount of money it would take to fund such an operation. Worldwide this would, by nature, be a multi-billion dollar operation. He realized that if Ang Wei was the supervisor of this Eastern Pacific headquarters of the AmerAsian operation he was a very big cog in the wheel.

Don had remembered there were at least four and possibly five men in the group who abducted and beat him. Tony reasoned these could be part of the worldwide labor unions' army of enforcers mentioned in these reports. He was beginning to understand the warning given by ICE Officer Greg Beason.

He sat a long while attempting to digest all the information he had read today. There was still one report to read, and he knew it would add pieces to the picture he was starting to visualize in his mind. Finally he gave up. It had been a long day and he had another in store tomorrow.

Lieutenant Anthony Harrison was in his office early the following morning. He was setting the daily assignments and roll call. The mandatory supervisory duties were enough to keep him busy, but he wanted to expand his time to read and evaluate the final report in the packet from UNAFEI. He checked the time and called the major's office to share his findings with his commander.

Major Tim Gatsby listened to the lengthy report his Lieutenant was giving. He made many notes and asked many questions during the session. When Tony seemed to have finished his report he just shook his head. "This is the biggest case and the most bizarre case in the history of the troopers. How do you plan to go about investigating a case that stretches around the world to, probably, a hundred countries?" he asked.

Tony thought about it for a moment, "I know we don't have the resources to investigate the labor union on a world scale, but we have a responsibility to investigate an attempted murder of one of our United States citizens. With your permission, I want to ask Greg Beason to help in the investigation. He has the resources and manpower as well as the financial wherewithal to investigate where we cannot." Tony leaned his elbow on the major's desk. "Can we do that much?" he asked.

The major was smirking, "Yes, Lieutenant, we can pursue that route. However, I'm not giving you permission because of your sarcastic comments. I'm giving you permission because it now falls within the policies of the department. I should take you off the case because you're too personally involved with the victim. If I note your attitude is being influenced by your involvement, I'll take you off the investigation. The reason I am allowing you to stay on it is because I know you; you would do it on your private time without supervision. Now get back to work and forget this conversation ever took place."

"Thanks, Major, I'll try to curb the attitude," said Tony as he stood to leave the office.

In his own office he picked up the phone to call Beason at the ICE office on the other side of town. There was no answer, but the voice mail recorder kicked on.

"Greg, Tony. We need to get together right away. Ask your supervisor if we can work together on this then get back to me." He hung up and went back to reading the UNAFEI file regarding the labor union.

From the file he learned that many Japanese citizens had been supposed victims of the human trafficking scheme through labor unions. They listed AmerAsian, Mediterranean, Laotian and Atlantic labor unions. Each of these individual unions was a subsidiary of an international labor union. Each had a headquarters office similar to the one in Anchorage with a very powerful manager like Mr. Ang Wei. And, each office had a small security force, usually five or six men, all skilled in martial arts and all with ultimate authority to deal with any problem.

An hour later Greg returned his call, "What's up, Tony?" he asked.

"Can you come to my office for a meeting? What I want to discuss we can't talk about at the restaurant."

There was a short pause by Greg, "I can't make it before two. I have a court appearance. Will that be soon enough?" he asked.

"Just fine, Greg. I want to discuss working this case with you. The major finally gave me permission and since my friend is still in danger. I think this a necessary step. You may want to clear that aspect with your boss."

"Sounds good. I'll clear it with my supervisor before I come over. I hope we can work together on this. We each have resources the other doesn't. See you at two."

Tony felt good about the turn of events and checked the time. Three hours, enough time to get some lunch and check on Don.

Chapter 13

Li Tan was seated in the office of his boss, Ang Wei, who sat behind his own huge desk, scowling over his wire rim glasses.

"Do you have a plan to rectify this problem?" asked Wei.

"Yes, sir. Since the incident, the hospital has moved the patient and there are armed guards everywhere inside the complex. I plan to revert to the original plan and find the daughter. Once we have her the business agent will comply with our every wish. We will keep watch at the hospital, but we are attempting to find the girl. Once the immediate problem is solved we can sell the girl for a huge profit. She is thirteen years old and attractive according to reports from those who know her."

"Where is she now?" inquired Wei.

"We have been unable to locate her, but we are looking. The former business agent has a brother and we suspect he took her away, perhaps warned by the father."

"What is your plan to find the girl?"

"The uncle is an Alaska registered guide, and the fishing season is open and bear season is about to start. We believe he will be taking care of his clients during this time. The girl could possibly be with him, but I think he has someone looking out for her," replied Li Tan. "The guide should be easy to find and we are looking now. Once we locate the brother we will learn the location of the girl. The hospital will eventually release the patient and we will use the girl to gain the information we seek. He did not fear enough for his own life, but I believe he will fear more for the life of his daughter."

"Do you need to replace your two men?"

"Yes, but I need experienced men with knowledge of Alaska and America. I have no time to train anyone right now." Li Tan knew the boss was planning to bring on his replacement in the event he was unable to put an end to this problem very quickly.

"You have one week to find the girl. I also want to know when the hospital plans to release the agent. You will have until then to resolve this incident that occurred at the hospital." Ang Wei looked at the notes on his desk before concluding. "That will be all, Li Tan."

Li Tan returned to his office to ponder the situation, determined to find an answer that would reaffirm his status at the company. It was mid-afternoon when the answer came to him. He called Ang Wei on the interoffice telephone.

"Yes, Li Tan, what is it?"

"I would like to change my decision about outside help. I have come up with a plan, but it will require special assistance. I need two men with hunting experience and at least one of them will need to be a pilot certified and licensed to fly a small airplane. Can we find such men?" asked Li Tan.

"I am sure we have such men available. I will get back to you within the hour," replied Ang Wei.

When Bob Halstead returned to his home to prepare for another trip to the Alaska Peninsula, he had a long list of items to get for his next client. Most of the camp gear and necessities were on hand, but this client was a city dweller and had no boots or clothing suitable for the rugged conditions of tundra lifestyle. The client had given him a list of things he was to provide including shoes, boots, coats, heavy shirts, and socks. The client was bringing a suitable rifle and assured Halstead he was a decent shot with the weapon. Bob would test that statement before they left the Kenai Peninsula.

The following day he found it was time to bring the fishermen back from the west side cabin. It was late morning when he flew across the inlet to the cabin on the river. When he arrived the fishermen had the cabin cleaned and gear piled near the runway. Bob was impressed at the way the men left the cabin and surrounding sit clean with no trash blown by the wind in the surrounding bushes. After finishing the cabin inspection, he closed the door which he seldom locked and returned to load the Cessna for the trip home. There were two duffle bags, four large plastic coolers, tackle boxes and fishing rods in long plastic cases. Before the engine was started, the fishermen were chattering excitedly with stories mostly about the huge brown bears wandering near the cabin and fishing spot. The pilot checked on fastened seatbelts then started the engine and taxied to the end of the grass airstrip for takeoff. As if to say goodbye to the fishermen a large, blond brown bear walked to the middle of the runway and stood on its hind legs looking at the idling airplane. The scene only lasted a few seconds, but the memory of this act would last a lifetime for these two fishermen.

Once back at Bob's home the men helped unload the gear and carry the coolers to a small out building where Bob had a clean room suitable for cleaning and processing the fish for freezing. The two men helped with this process before giving Bob a healthy tip and thanking him for a wonderful trip. They would spend the night in Kenai and catch a flight home tomorrow afternoon. Bob was to bring the frozen fish and their fishing gear when he came to pick them up for the trip to the Kenai Airport. It was decided that the three of them would have dinner together at Louie's Restaurant that evening.

After dropping the men at their motel he used the time to shop for the incoming client. His season had begun and there was little time to waste on social events. He purchased a small duffle bag for the clothing he had bought for the incoming client, packed it for the trip, fueled the Cessna, completed his logbooks and came into the house to check his phone recorder.

One of the calls was an inquiry about a bear hunting trip for two to the Alaska Peninsula with a number to return the call. It was an Alaska (907) number. Bob dialed.

"Lyle and Morris Consulting," said a pleasant voice.

"Yes, this is Bob Halstead. Someone at this number left a message inquiring about a bear hunt?"

"Oh yes, Mr. Halstead. It was Mr. Lyle calling. Please hold while I connect you."

A moment later a man with a deep voice answered. "Clyde Lyle here. I've heard of your guide service and wanted to ask about availability for a hunt for two, me and my partner, this season."

"I'm booked up for the entire season, but I have one booking that may cancel for health reasons. It will be four weeks from now in my camp on Wildman Lake. The man who booked the hunt has had health issues and advised me he may not be able to make it. Would that work for you?" asked the guide.

"Four weeks, hmmmm. That would be the second week of September?"

"Yes sir, but if you accept I can't confirm the dates until I hear from the other client. He's an older man who has just had a heart attack and I don't think his doctors will let him go on the hunt," explained Halstead.

"I'm interested. Can you give me some rates and tell me what I need to bring, what kind of terrain, and what kind of weather I might expect to see?" asked Lyle.

For more than thirty minutes Halstead explained the terms, the hunt, the assistant guide, equipment needed, the camp accommodations, what kind of weather to expect, transportation, care of the hides, and many more points that would interest a hunter. From the conversation Bob determined this man was an experienced hunter.

"All this sounds like a hunt I want," said Lyle. "How soon can I expect to hear from you about this cancellation?"

"I'd say a week to ten days. I realize that doesn't give you much time to prepare, but it's the only open spot that I might possibly have this season. If you don't think it will work for you I can give you the names of some other reputable guides on the Peninsula and in Kodiak."

"I'll be waiting to hear from you. Let me give you my private number." Lyle gave Bob his cell phone number and thanked him.

Bob made several notes in his appointment book about the call as well as the phone number. Inquiries of this sort are a part of the business and almost never turn out, but this one seemed genuine. He was making notes when the phone rang again. It was Vic Lamar.

"Howdy, Vic. Before you start talking don't tell me where you are. If I don't know I can't tell anyone."

"How the heck are you, Bobby?" asked Vic.

"Getting busy around here. In fact, I was just on the phone with another client," informed Halstead. "How is Jenny?" he asked.

"She wants to speak with you, and I'll give her the phone in a minute. I just called to check in and let you know we're OK and having a great time. How goes it with you and Don?"

"Don't tell Jenny, but they tried to get Don in the hospital. Two hit men were killed by hospital security. Don's been moved out of ICU and into a more secure unit. A security guard is posted at his door. Don's doing fine and getting stronger each day."

"Lindsy says to tell you hello. She says you're not to worry about her or Jenny. The three of us are just fine and having a good time."

"Are you OK for money or anything else?" asked Bob.

"We're doing just fine. Like I said, don't worry about us. Here's Jenny wanting to talk to you."

There was a short pause. "Hi, Uncle Bobby, how are you?" she asked in her teenage tone.

"I'm great Jenny, but you can't tell me about the trip over the phone. You understand. I just want you to have fun and learn about America. By the way your dad is improving every day. He still has a lot of healing to do, but the doctors say he will be able to leave the hospital in about six or seven weeks." Bob didn't go into detail but wanted to ease her mind about the condition of her father.

"Oh, Uncle Bobby, I'm having such a good time and Lindsy and Vic are so sweet to me. I want to thank you for all you are doing for us." She had started with a giggly voice and ended on a quiet note.

"I love you Jenny. Have a wonderful time." There wasn't much more to say to the girl.

Vic came back on the phone, "That's about all for now, Bobby. We were just checking in with you."

"I'm glad you did. I'm going to start getting insanely busy, Vic. The next six or eight weeks will be hectic. I probably won't be in phone range most of the time. All my camps are going to have clients and I'm going to have to personally guide some of them as well as spend the rest of my time checking on the other camps and my assistant guides. You know how it goes."

"Yes, I know how it goes. Take care and be safe. See you soon, Bobby. Bye." With that Vic hung up, knowing that time is what Bob Halstead had to sell and it was precious.

The next ten days were hectic for the guide. Halstead had taken three new clients to the cabin on the west side, brought in supplies, and instructed the three men on the proper way to catch and care for the fish once filleted out and placed in the coolers. He said he would be in and out in order to take the fish back to his home and prepare them for freezing, ensuring good quality salmon for the table at the end of the trip. Upon leaving he flew around the area to scout out the huge brown bear he had seen on a previous trip. He spotted several smaller bears on a neighboring tributary but no sign of the big boy.

Back at home he was enjoying a rare evening alone. He had grilled some salmon and fresh corn, drank a copious amount of iced tea and settled in to watch the late news when his phone jingled. It was the client who was in doubt about his being able to come on the hunt he had scheduled.

"I'm getting worse, and the doctors advised against me attempting the hunt. I'm sorry, Bob, I don't mean to let you down. Keep my deposit as a thank you for indulging an old timer." They chatted a little longer before hanging up. Bob thought a moment and went to his desk to find the number for Clyde Lyle.

When Clyde answered Bob wasted little time telling him there was an opening for the hunt the two men had spoken about. "I just had a cancellation and wanted to let you know the hunt is available for you and your friend if you still want to take it."

"That's wonderful, Bob. Sign us on for the dates," said Lyle. The men spoke for a long time about the essentials of the trip. Bob said he would furnish everything needed except personal clothing and firearms. There would be fishing gear at the camp and the lake was good for salmon and Arctic char; char being the most beautiful fish and silver or coho salmon the scrappiest. A couple of hours of fishing would be good recreation in the remote camp.

Lyle agreed to all the terms and gave Halstead a credit card number to pay for all the fees. Bob went back to his chair, poured another glass of iced tea and changed the channel back to the local news. It is not often he made a profit on a canceled hunt, but this one had become very profitable. When the news program ended he turned out the lights and locked his door. It would all begin again in the morning.

Clyde Lyle called his partner on the hunt, Dick Morris. "We're on for the trip two weeks from today," he said to his partner. Both men had been on many hunts together all around the world. It was a great diversion from the line of work they were in as security personnel for an international labor union.

Chapter 14

Clyde Lyle called his new supervisor to report. "Dick and I are on the schedule for two weeks from today. All arrangements have been made. We need to have a meeting to decide how you want to handle the operation."

"Good idea, Mr. Lyle. My office tomorrow morning, nine o'clock," said Li Tan, now pleased with the direction the situation was headed.

The following morning the two men entered the office at the appointed time, and the receptionist announced them. Li Tan came out to greet the men, whom he had never met before today.

"How do you do, gentlemen? I am Li Tan. Please come into my office where we can speak freely."

The two men followed him into the office and were pointed to the large leather chairs near the front of the large desk where Li Tan seated himself. "Now, gentlemen, I want to hear your plan. Keep in mind there is no room for error; it must not fail."

The larger of the two men spoke first. "You must have not heard of us. I am Clyde Lyle and my partner is Dick Morris. We have hunted all over the world. I am a licensed pilot and Dick flies as well. You will tell us what outcome you wish and we will do our best to accomplish the task. We never fail."

"There are two dead men who recently told me the exact same thing. I expect careful planning. The guide you will be hunting with is the brother of a man we have failed to kill. He was the new business agent for this office. We suspected he was passing information about our business to the international police. He was taken to a place near Palmer and questioned. He was beaten severely without revealing any information. He was beaten until it was presumed that he was dead, but he survived. There was an attempt from this office to finish the task while this man was in the hospital, but the men sent to take care of it were unable to get past the hospital security staff. Both men were killed before completing the task. We believe this problem will soon lead back to this office and that is unacceptable. There must be no more loose ends." Li Tan was not used to making such lengthy statements.

"We don't leave loose ends, Mr. Tan. Exactly what information do you want us to extract from this hunting guide?" asked Lyle.

"The business agent has a young daughter. We wish to find her and have her put into service elsewhere. The business agent will never say anything to the authorities as long as we hold his daughter. We believe the guide has hidden the girl. We need to find her as quickly as possible. It is your task to do just that. Once we find the girl we begin to eliminate the evidence, you understand?" Once again Li Tan instructed his new enforcers.

"Yes, we do understand," said Morris. "We will need any reports and background you have on both the brothers. We have two weeks to prepare and we will need all available information we can find. It is up to you to get that information to us. We will also need topographical maps of the area in which we will be working. FAA (Federal Aviation Administration) maps of the area are the preferred ones, since we will likely be using them to escape from the scene in the guide's airplane. Once we report back to you with the information you seek, we will return to our office in Asia. If we need further information or supplies we will contact you."

Li Tan was not used to being addressed in such a manner and resented the impertinent speaker, Dick Morris. "You will fulfill your duties as I have instructed and report back to this office when you have completed the task. Your methods are of your choice, but I want complete success with no exceptions."

Both men stood preparing to leave the office. "We always succeed, Mr. Tan. If we need anything we will contact you." With that the hunters exited the office.

Lieutenant Tony Harrison was in his office finishing his morning assignment duties when his telephone beeped. "Trooper Harrison," he answered.

"Hello Tony, it's Greg Beason. Have you gotten through the information packet I sent you the other day?"

"Oh, hi there Greg, yes I did and I'm on the last of the folders in it. I agree we need to work together on this. I have a lot of questions to ask you. When can we get together?"

"That's the reason for this call. I wanted to ask you the same question. Do you have some time this morning?" asked Greg.

"For this I do, yes."

"My boss gave me a, sort of, free hand in this case. How about I get there around eleven?"

"Good I'll be finished with my daily routine by then. See you at eleven." Tony hung up the phone with genuine excitement in his chest. This could be the biggest case he had ever worked. He reached into his desk drawer to bring out the entire folder. When he finished with his daily stuff he would tell the major of the meeting to be held at eleven.

He was about to leave the building when he stopped by Major Gatsby's office. He explained why Beason was coming to the office, but he would have to go to the courthouse to deliver several case reports to the District Attorney's office.

When he returned to the trooper offices Beason had been admitted and was sitting in Major Gatsby's office chatting with the boss. As he walked by the door the major asked him to step inside with him and the ICE agent.

Tony put out his hand to greet Greg Beason as he entered the office. "Good to see you, Greg," he said.

"You, too, Tony, the major and I were just discussing the case. I have some new info from Interpol I think will interest you."

"It's nearly noon, how about I treat the two of you to lunch before you get too busy to eat?" asked Major Gatsby.

"We'll go anywhere for food," joked Greg.

Upon returning from lunch Greg and Tony went directly to Tony's small office. The file folders were still sitting on the desktop. Greg was carrying another thick folder under his arm. "This is another folder from Interpol. It details some of the cases they are investigating. They include kidnapping, prostitution, slavery, forced marriages and many, many murders. It seems when they are no longer useful the labor union eliminates a lot of workers. It also outlines what is known about the union's international parent company of the labor union. This is a ruthless organization."

For the rest of the afternoon they sat in Tony's office making notes about anything that could relate to Alaska from the international cases. It was interesting that one of the officers on the international board of directors for the parent company was Mr. Ang Wei.

"It is mind-boggling when you understand the scope of the crimes. The reason it becomes so difficult to investigate is there are so many jurisdictions involved. My organization, ICE, comes across many related cases, but we have never put all the cases together," said Greg.

"What do you mean about jurisdiction?" asked Tony.

"You would never think all these different cases could be related, but just take immigrations for instance. We go to the port to check on the crew of a ship docking from Asia somewhere. It could be from any of the countries overseas. We have discovered live birds in luggage. We have discovered precious gems—emeralds, rubies, diamonds, and sapphires—stashed in the lining of suitcases, duffle bags and boxes when we check them. And we aren't the only agencies to do so. Precious stones coming into this country are usually finished and cut. In Europe they catch more stones than we find, but usually they are raw stones. We assume the reason for this is that there are so many stone cutters in Europe and very few in America. We didn't realize the differences until we read the notes from Interpol."

"You said you find small animals. Why would they smuggle animals and birds? Is there that much of a market for them?" asked Tony.

"You can't imagine. Down south they nab folks with all sorts of animals from South America to be sold to pet stores. Exotic animals are a big trade. Here in Alaska we've taken rare birds, small animals, and even snakes. Animal trade is a huge business and since we've restricted so many of the rare animals they're worth a great deal of cash.

Don't get me wrong, that's only one faction these people bring into the country. We get drugs, plants, anything of value including people. The point is that the people we find with the goods are only the carriers. They're sent by much larger marketers. We, as well as Interpol and UNAFEI, think the labor unions use the members to smuggle the goods into every country in the world. This isn't just a penny ante scheme, it's a big business." Greg leaned back in his chair and stretched his back.

"So, what you're saying is that this labor union is part of an international crime syndicate?"

"That's exactly what I'm saying," commented Greg. "We didn't realize what was really happening until all the world police agencies began to compare cases. The computer has helped us a lot. It recognizes similarities and when we put in cases from Europe and Asia with ours, we found a common denominator, international labor unions and all their subsidiary company offices around the world, including the one right here in Alaska."

Tony scratched his head, "Well, getting back to my case, what is your opinion on why our friend Don Halstead was kidnapped and beaten?"

"I don't know for sure, but my guess is that he was suspected of being a spy for the police. I wish he could remember what they were asking him the night they beat him so severely. Reading the files I find that the labor organization works hard at eliminating witnesses." Greg stretched again.

"Let's get some coffee and take a break. I need to think a minute." Tony stood and motioned for Greg to follow.

Ten minutes later they were back in the office where Tony asked, "Tell me, Greg, do you think the union would take Don's daughter, Jenny, to use for leverage to get information?"

"I don't want to be an alarmist, but that is the kind of tactics they use all over the world. If they could find the girl they would be sure Don would be an obedient servant and never say a word. I also believe he would never see his daughter again. Those are the tactics they use wherever they operate." Greg sipped his coffee. "The problem is we have no proof of any wrongdoing, only guesswork."

"Now you're beginning to frighten me!" Tony was thinking, "If any of your supposition is true they may try to get to Don again in addition to attempting to locate Jenny. Let me ask you, do you have any suggestions as to how to stop them?"

"That is the question that has perplexed every police organization in the world for a very long time. In one sense you have an advantage. You have a real crime and a witness. I don't think the union is very happy about any of those things and will try to correct their mistakes. You're sitting in a very dangerous position." Greg was closing his folder and looking across the desk at the trooper.

Tony looked down at the legal pad on his desk, "I've made a lot of notes here. I am convinced you're right about the outcome. Do you have time to come with me to Major Gatsby's office and do a recap for him? I'm going to need help in finding a solution to a problem no one else has been able to solve. I could use your help."

"Sure, Tony, but I must caution you. These are very powerful people with spies everywhere, perhaps here in your offices. You should be cautious about speaking to anyone about this information. The men kill without any remorse at all and your name could be added to their list at any time. I believe Don is still in danger as well as the daughter. You once told me Don's brother hid the daughter. If that fact gets to the enforcers at the labor union he, as well as the daughter, are in danger. I can't impress on you enough as to how dangerous this outfit really is."

Tony nodded in agreement and reached for the telephone to ask the major for a meeting NOW. He agreed and the two men walked to his office carrying the files and legal pad of notes made by Tony. The meeting was a long one, lasting into the evening hours. Major Gatsby agreed with the assessment of the two men in his office and offered any help he could supply. He also agreed the information was to be kept confidential, even from office personnel.

At the end of the meeting there were more questions than answers. All three agreed more thought was needed and they would begin again in the morning. It would be a long and restless night for all three men.

Chapter 15

Bob Halstead was loading his Cessna 185 to be ready to take the last fishermen of the season to the cabin on the west side. He was nearly finished when they called to say they were on the way to the Kenai Airport where they were to meet him. The guide informed them he was almost ready to take off and would be there in thirty minutes. He loaded the last of the supplies into the airplane and did a quick preflight check. After starting the engine and while it warmed, he made a note in his logbook. It was a short flight to Kenai from his private airstrip and he was there at the terminal in fifteen minutes, parking in the transient parking area and walking to the terminal.

Inside he was met by two men carrying large duffle bags and long rod holders. The logo on his baseball style hat introduced them. "You must be Bob Halstead," said the first man.

"Yes, sir, I am. Are you ready to go fishing?" he asked.

"We sure are," replied the second man.

"OK, let's get your gear out to the airplane and do some paperwork, then we'll be off to the camp. It's only a 45-minute flight across open water and we will be climbing to 5,500 feet to be safe. Once on the other side of Cook Inlet we will drop down in order to see any bears that may be out and about. Do you have your fishing licenses?"

"We picked them up last night," said one of the men.

The three men carried the gear out to the plane where Bob carefully loaded everything into the back seat and baggage area of the plane. Once the gear was loaded Bob asked to see their licenses and entered the numbers on his logbook. He questioned them about the gear they had brought as well as the types of tackle they planned to use. Both men had fished silver salmon in the past and were prepared for the venture.

One man climbed into the back set with the gear and strapped in while the other slid into the passenger seat in the front of the plane. The flight was smooth and sunny as they crossed the open waters of Cook Inlet. Bob dropped to 700 feet once on the other side and took a direct route to his cabin on the river at the foot of the hills behind the tidelands. Several bears were spotted on the short flight. Bob circled over the cabin to check the runway and surrounding area for wildlife. He made a picture perfect landing and taxied to the front of his cabin.

Before unloading the plane he took the men into the cabin to show them the accommodations and give them the opportunity to ask last minute questions. He helped get the gear carried into the cabin and asked if they wanted him to demonstrate his fishing techniques. Both men laughed at the guide. "We fish over 200 days a year, Bob, we can manage."

Now Bob was laughing with them. "You will have cell phone coverage here in case you have an emergency. I have bear hunters out in some other camps and I won't be available most of the time, but I'll stop and check on you as I'm going by. Keep your fish in the coolers and I'll pick them up on each trip and take them to my place, vacuum seal them, and put them in the freezer. By doing it that way you will have good quality fish to take home with you at the end of the trip. Any questions?" he asked.

It was early in the day and he had planned to fly down the Alaska Peninsula to check on his hunters. The entrance to Lake Clark Pass was only a few miles to the south. He climbed into the shiny white with blue trim Cessna 185. Bob was always relaxed when he was flying. It was the best part of his days.

There are three huge lakes on the west side of the Alaska Range mountains: Iliamna, Brooks and Becharof Lakes. Each of them is nearly as large as one of the Great Lakes in the contiguous United States. As he passed over the mountains he maintained altitude to fly a direct route over the three large lakes. This route saved almost a hundred miles of flying distance. Once over the large Becharof Lake he began to drop altitude and view the countryside. Near Wildman Lake he called his assistant guide.

"Are you in camp?" he inquired.

"Just got in from the morning hunt. Where are you now?" asked the assistant guide.

"About five minutes out. See you in a few minutes."

On the ground at the camp Bob, with the aid of his assistant guide, poured avgas into his tanks for the return trip. Once done they all went into the main lodge for coffee. "Having any luck?" asked Bob.

"We have one hide for you to take back and today we spotted another good bear. I think we can get up on him in the morning, early. He had a caribou down and didn't pay much attention to us as we scouted him. He's on that knob near the foothills by the stream. As you know there isn't much cover out there and we will need to take the long way around on the other side of the high ground."

"Sounds good. Is the hide fleshed?" Halstead asked his guide.

"Yes, we did that last night after dinner. These men are pretty good at it. They never cut the hide even once. I didn't know if you were coming in today so I salted the hide and rolled it up."

"Have you seen any other hunters in the area?" asked Bob.

"No, but there has been one airplane scouting the area, a de Havilland Beaver. It's white with green and black trim. I've seen it before. It might be the guide from Bear River."

"It sounds like his plane, all right. Do you need anything?"

"No, just one more bear. I hope to fix that tomorrow morning," replied the guide.

Bob turned to the two hunters. "Which one shot the bear?" he asked.

The taller of the men answered with a huge smile, "I did."

"I'm going back to town now. Do you want to stay with your partner or go back to town early?"

"I'll stay with Bix. You have a great camp and I like the fishing, too. If Bix gets a bear tomorrow I'll help dress it out and flesh the hide. Thanks for the offer, though."

"OK, congratulations on a good bear hunt. Let's load the hide and I'll get out of here. I have a long flight back." Bob turned to his guide, "By the way, Ned, I filled that vacated slot for two weeks from now. There will be two hunters. They seem to be experienced and should be good clients."

"Thanks, Bob, I'll help you load up and see you in a few days."

Bob had another camp on the shores of Upper Ugashik Lake and he wanted to stop and check on the hunters at that camp on his way by. He talked with the guide on the radio before landing. The guide said he and the hunters were too far from camp to meet with him but would see him on his next trip. Halstead flew on over the camp, but was unable to locate them near the camp so he continued on, high over the lakes once again and over the mountains to Cook Inlet heading toward his home where he must package the hide he was carrying for the freezer.

It had been a very long day of flying and he was extremely tired. He decided to eat a leftover salad from his refrigerator rather than go to town for dinner. The sun was still high in the sky when he showered and crawled into his bed.

He awakened early the following morning knowing he had a full day of flying and delivering supplies to his camps. His first order of business after refueling was to fly to his west side camp to check on his fishing clients and bring their fish back to his freezer. The round trip took a little more than an hour with another hour caring for and packaging the fish for freezing. He had finished and was cleaning up after the project when his phone rang.

"Bob Halstead Guide Service," he answered, his hands wet from cleaning the fish table.

"Hey Bob, it's Tony. How is the season going so far?"

"Busy, busy, busy," replied Halstead.

"I don't mean to take a lot of your time, Bob, but this is important. Is there any chance I can get you to come to Anchorage this morning?"

"How important is it, Tony? I have to go down to my camp on Becharof Lake today."

"It's very important, Bob. Could you come up here on your way to the lake? I really need to talk with you face-to-face." The tone in Tony's voice ensured the importance of the meeting.

"OK, Tony, I'll be there in an hour." Bob could not imagine what could be this important, but Tony would never have insisted had it not been necessary. "I'll meet you at the fuel pumps." Bob finished loading the needed supplies and climbed into the front seat. He started the engine and watched the gauges; everything seemed normal and he took off still troubled by the urgency.

Tony was sitting in his patrol car near the fueling station when he arrived. The trooper motioned for him to come to the car as he stepped out of the Cessna. He walked to the car and climbed into the passenger seat.

"What's going on, Tony?" he asked. "Has something happened to Don?"

"No, Don is fine. I've been working with a federal ICE agent for the past few days and we've uncovered some things that you need to know about. First of all, I think you and Jenny are in a great deal of danger. The labor union your brother went to work for is a worldwide human trafficking organization. They deal in prostitution, slavery, murder and selling young girls. As near as we can figure out they suspected Don of being a spy for the police organizations investigating them. That investigation is active all over the world in at least fifty countries. They're ruthless and have their own hired assassins as enforcers. We have been able to piece together enough of a scenario to have real fear for you. We believe they may attempt to find Jenny and take her out of the country as leverage to keep Don quiet. If they get their hands on Don he will disappear." Tony looked over at Bob, "Now you know why I wanted to see you this morning."

"That seems a little heavy-handed to me. Do you really think it's that serious?"

"We think they suspect Don of being an agent for one of several police agencies, based on investigative information by Interpol, UNAFEI and U.S. Customs and Immigration Enforcement. The illegal trade they do is estimated to be in the multi-billions of dollars. They have a lot to lose. I've doubled the guards on Don's hospital room and isolated the rooms near his. I know you said you didn't know where Jenny is, and that is a good thing, but we think they will come after you in order to find her. I called you to meet me in order to impress on you how much danger you are in and to tell you to be armed at all times. We don't know how or when, but we are convinced you are a target. You should screen every client, every person you meet on the street and be especially watchful of anyone you have never met or seen before. You're too mobile and I can't protect you." Tony was at a loss for words to make the situation real to Bob.

Bob thought for a few seconds, "All the clients scheduled for the rest of the season are repeat customers and have hunted with me before." Then he suddenly thought of the replacement customers coming at the end of next week. "Hold on, Tony, I take that back. I had a cancellation and two men I don't know have booked the trip. I've talked with them on the phone, but never met them. They seem to be experienced hunters, though." He thought for a few more seconds. "Do you think I should cancel them?"

"It probably wouldn't do any good. If they are the ones looking for you, they will know where and how to get to you. Is there any way to have your assistant guide stay with you at all times while they're with you?" Tony inquired.

"I suppose I can do that; there are two hunters and I planned to guide one of them personally," replied Bob.

"I sure wish there was a way to have someone else in camp with you two."

"Hey, Tony, perhaps there is. I have an old client and friend in Oregon who would be perfect for the job and I think I can talk him into coming up as a backup."

"I think it would be a good idea, though I don't like the thought of putting some untrained person in a dangerous situation. I wish I could be the one to back you up, but I was seen in the labor union offices. I could be recognized." Tony scratched his chin. "I can ask the major for someone to go to camp as a cook or something. With budgets like they are I don't know if he can allow it."

"Let me call my old friend Vic Lamar and see if he is up to the trip. I trust him and he's been to camp enough to know his way around. He's an older man, but he has guts and smarts. I'll call him tonight when I get back from Becharof Lake. Which reminds me, I had better get moving or I won't have time to finish with the client I have over there. I talked with the assistant guide yesterday and they should have a bear down this morning. I'll be home tonight, but it will be late when I finish with the hide and take care of the airplane. I probably won't call you before morning."

"I'll be expecting your call, Bob. Remember, be wary of anyone you don't know." Tony was staring at Bob. "I can't impress that on you enough. These men are dangerous."

Both men opened car doors and stepped out to walk to the Cessna to fuel the plane and do a preflight for the three plus hour trip down the Alaska Peninsula to the camp on Becharof Lake.

Chapter 16

The day being perfect for flying and the trip long, Bob had a lot of time to think about what to do about the threat Tony had described. Being middle age, Bob knew threats but few came from dangerous human sources. This one was different and not only threatened him, but his niece as well. It seemed real considering these people doing the threatening had already severely injured his brother Don. It didn't sit well with him to do nothing about protecting himself or his family. It was time to go on the offensive, he thought.

He again flew the direct route across the big lakes to his camp on the lower end of Lake Becharof. The assistant guide and the client had just returned to the camp with a very nice blonde bear hide. The three men unrolled it and did a cursory fleshing and salted the huge hide. A preliminary measurement read nine feet four inches squared; a very nice bear indeed.

The client said that since he had been successful in his hunt he had just as well ride out with Bob when he returned to Kenai. Bob had brought a few supplies which were unloaded at the camp and replaced with the personal gear of the hunter. Bob instructed the assistant guide to clean up the camp to make ready for the next clients which were due in two days. The client spoke with the assistant guide before boarding the airplane and slipped a nice tip into his hand during the conversation.

Bob had loaded all the gear and the hide along with camp trash and disposables. He did his best to maintain a clean camp at all his locations. After pouring fuel into the airplane from cans in the rear compartment it was time to load his passenger and return to his own airstrip at home. He climbed to 8,500 feet for the eastward path over the lakes and mountains. The clear sky made it a spectacular trip through the glacier covered mountains.

Upon landing on his home airstrip he and the client unloaded the airplane and went to town for dinner at a local restaurant. It was early when they came back to the hangar to begin the final fleshing of the bear hide and making it ready to send to the taxidermist. Bob and the client discussed the trip and he was assured by the man he had a wonderful hunt and confirmed he would return one day for another hunt. Perhaps he would bring his son who would soon be old enough to enjoy a similar hunt.

The client stayed with Bob for the night and was taken to the Kenai Airport the following morning with a stop at Louie's Restaurant for breakfast. Once the man was checked in at the airport Bob began to make a plan to have Vic Lamar come to Alaska and watch his back.

"Are you where you can talk without being overheard?" Bob asked Vic on the phone.

"Give me a second to get outside," commented Lamar. Half a minute later he came on the line again.

"What's up, Bobby?"

"Things are getting complicated around here, Vic. Apparently some threats have been made against me and I need someone to watch my back. Do you want the job?"

"I guess Lindsy can drive the motorhome and care for Jenny. How soon do you need me?"

"By the end of the week if you can get here that soon, buddy. I have two clients coming whom I have never met. Tony seems to think they may be connected with the bunch that beat Don and left him for dead. He let me in on some international investigations and I believe him about how dangerous they are. I've been running around looking over my shoulder without a plan. I don't like being on the defensive. I want to be ready to take the offensive. There are two men in this party and as I say, I've never met either of them. If they are the men and are as dangerous as Tony thinks they are, I'm going to need more eyes I can trust. I plan to carry a sidearm as well as a backup gun. I have weapons you can use, too."

"Damn, Bobby, I've never seen you spooked like this before. I'll let Lindsy know what's happening and catch a flight into Kenai. I'll let you know the schedule as soon as the flight is booked." Vic had now become worried about both Jenny and Bob's safety and wellbeing.

"Tell Jenny not to worry. Her dad is coming along fine. Also, tell Lindsy to get a move on and go to some new location just to be safe," advised Bob. "I'll try to have everything ready to go when you get here. We will be hunting at Wildman Lake camp."

"I'm on it, Bobby. I'll call when I know the schedule. See ya."

The next several days were filled with collecting supplies, filling avgas cans, flying to the west side to pick up the last of his fishing clients at the camp there. He cared for the fish and put them in the freezer to be shipped later. He collected all his fishing rods and put new line on each reel to be ready for next season. Once done he stored the fishing tackle in a small shed behind the big shop he used as a hangar for the Cessna.

The weather was holding fair and clear as well as warm. The early fall season would bring rain and low visibility making flying more difficult. None of that worried him as it was an annual event he had learned to cope with a long time ago. What was worrying him at this point was the unknown factors. Who were these men he must look out for? What did they have in mind to do to him? Would they try to harm Don once again? There were only questions with no answers.

One question he did find an answer to was how to justify Vic Lamar in camp. He decided Vic was to be the designated cook and camp caretaker. This addition would make his assistant guide very happy as he was the one keeping the camp clean and making all the meals for the clients.

Finally, Vic called to tell him he would be in Kenai late tomorrow evening. Jenny and Lindsy were content to travel and see the sights without Vic wanting to take charge and give directions. The two girls giggled and tee-heed with each other while Vic packed for his trip. They were more than happy to drop him at the airport and be rid of his bossy nature.

Bob was at the airport waiting when Vic's plane arrived. He had brought a carry-on and a large checked duffle bag of gear.

"You didn't bring any firearms in the bag, did you Vic?"

"No, but I know the weather and I brought rain gear as well as some winter clothing in case we are caught in a storm out there. I just wanted to be prepared. You said you had weapons here anyway. Are you serious about packing sidearms all the time?" asked Vic, skeptical of the necessity for doing it.

"That will be our conversation this evening at the house. I need to fill you in on how dangerous these men will be. At this point I really don't know if the new clients are the men I'm expecting, but they are the only strangers on the list and were last minute bookings. Until we find out I think we need to be very cautious."

After dinner the two men poured a rare drink of top shelf liquor and discussed the many cases Tony had mentioned as well as what the police around the world suspected in regard to the operations of the labor unions. It was late when they turned out the lights and turned in for the night. Tomorrow would be another busy day of flying supplies to the camps. Each day was filled with transporting guides, clients, supplies, hides, fish and meat taken by clients. The rest of the week went quickly.

The last day before the new clients were to arrive, Bob took time to change the oil and filter on his Cessna. While working inside the cowling he inspected every fitting and wire to be sure there would be no unforeseen mechanical problems. It was late morning when Bob called Vic to give him a hand loading the final items on the airplane.

"OK, Vic, I've gathered some firepower to take to the camp. I've made a list of where to stash the guns." He gave a copy of the list to the older man. "I have a 9mm semi-auto I'm stashing in the airplane. I'll put it, along with two clips, in the map pocket in the side of the pilot's seat. There are three shotguns with a box of 00 buckshot for each one. The first one I want you to hide in the broom closet in the kitchen near the cook stove. The second one I want stuffed into the rafters at the rear of the outhouse. The third one I want you to stash inside your cabin, maybe under the mattress of the spare bunk. I want you to carry your sidearm at all times. You know where I keep the hunting rifles and ammo. The point of all this is that we should never be far away from a weapon for protection. You will be the camp cook and caretaker and will have free run of the camp. It will be your job to keep an eye on these two clients and to watch my back. The assistant guide has no idea what's taking place and I don't want to worry him unless it becomes obvious these are the men out to get me. Any questions, Vic?"

"I was wondering if we were going to take any precautions. I think you have it well covered. When do we leave with these supplies?"

"Right away, I'm giving you one last chance to change your mind. Are you still in for the long haul?" asked Halstead.

"I'm in Bobby, and I'm glad you are taking the threat seriously. Let's go to work."

The two men climbed into the Cessna and took off for the long flight to Wildman Camp. Once in camp the assistant guide helped to unload the supplies and re-fuel the airplane. When everything was offloaded and carried into the lodge Bob shook hands with the two men and once again climbed into the pilot seat.

"I'll see the two of you tomorrow around noon if they arrive on time. Is there anything you want me to bring from town?" asked the guide.

The two men standing on the ground near the plane shook their heads as Bob closed the door and motioned he was starting the engine. His plan was to fly into Anchorage, meet with Tony and go to the hospital to see Don.

Tony Harrison met Bob at Merrill Field once again and the two men drove to the hospital with Bob telling the trooper how he was preparing for the arrival of his new hunting clients. Once in the room with his brother he was pleasantly surprised at the progress Don was making in his recovery. He was sitting up in a wheelchair when they arrived. His left arm was in a cast holding his arm rigid, but the right had only a short cast on the lower part of the arm and he could move both his arms now.

"Dang, Don," exclaimed Bob. "Another week and I'll be able to take you to camp."

"They still have me on some pain meds, but I feel almost human. Tony tells me you have been busy this season and have kept your camps full the entire time. That sounds good. You can pay my hospital bill." All three men laughed.

"Have the doctors told you when you will be able to get out of here?" asked Bob.

"They say three or four weeks if I continue to heal as I have been doing. Since I don't know how well I will be able to get around I haven't tried to make any plans about leaving the hospital. I'm anxious to see Jenny, though." Don spoke in a quiet voice as if he were unsure of his future.

"I'll have my camps shut down by then, Don. I plan to take you to my place for a while until you are strong enough to make it on your own. Tony says they're investigating who did this to you and to put them out of business and keep it from happening again." Bob and Don had always maintained a close relationship.

"Is there any new information about who did this to me?" asked Don.

"I've been working with some other police agencies and making a little progress, but I can't say we have them in our sights just yet." Tony didn't want to divulge any particulars of the investigation.

The men visited a while longer until Bob said it was time for him to get home and refuel the Cessna for tomorrow. He would be taking new clients to the Alaska Peninsula for a guided bear hunt. Tony drove Bob back to the airfield and watched him climb into the small airplane.

"Do you want me to come down to your camp to check on you, Bob? The state will buy the gas for my patrol if you want to be checked up on."

"No, I don't think so, Tony. I've told you about my plans to keep safe and have a backup plan. I shouldn't say this, but if these men make a move on me and Vic I'll show them no mercy. They have already injured Don and I'm not going to let that happen to me or my crew. I don't plan to make the first move, but if they do, I won't read them their rights. It will be tundra justice."

"If it were anyone else I'd warn them about that kind of talk, but I've known you long enough to be sure you'll be justified in whatever measures you use. Good luck, pal." Tony pushed the door closed and waved at the pilot, still worried about his friend's safety.

It was late evening when Bob finished fueling the airplane and checking oil for the long flight tomorrow. He was hoping these men were who they said they were and only there to hunt brown bear, but he knew he must keep his guard up and be ready for anything. Tomorrow would be a long day with an early start. A full night's sleep would make it easier. He took a last long look at the sky and the world around him before going into the house for the night.

Chapter 17

The next morning Bob flew to Kenai and parked in the transient parking area at the airport. He walked inside the terminal and found a cup of coffee at the small coffee shop near the lobby. The turboprop passenger plane from Anchorage taxied to the terminal, and Bob went out to the lobby to find his clients. He took a seat near the baggage belt and waited. It didn't take long before he spotted two men wearing high dollar outdoor clothing from one of the sporting goods chains. Both men were in good physical shape and well groomed. They were searching the lobby for someone when Bob approached them.

"Are you Clyde Lyle and Dick Morris?" he asked.

"Ah, yes we are," answered the larger of the two men. "You must be Bob Halstead."

"Yes, I'm Halstead," he said as he put out a hand to shake. "Are you fellas hungry after your long flight?"

"We could sure use something to eat," replied the other client.

"OK, then, let's gather your gear and take it to the airplane. Then we'll go over to Louie's Restaurant for some breakfast." The men stood by the conveyor belt waiting until all the bags and gun cases arrived. Bob found a small four-wheel cart to haul the load to the Cessna parked a short distance from the terminal. Once the airplane was loaded and locked, they found a cab in front of the terminal and rode to the café a few blocks away.

At breakfast they discussed payment for the hunt, a schedule of what to expect and answers to all the many questions the men had. It was plain to see these men were really big game hunters. The discussions went on all through breakfast until Bob called another cab to take them back to the airport. He had been assured they both had hunting and fishing licenses as well as non-resident bear tags.

Clyde Lyle, the larger of the two men piled into the rear seat and strapped in while Dick Morris slid into the right front seat of the plane. Once they were strapped in and comfortable Bob climbed into the pilot's seat, checked the area and started the engine. He slipped on his headset and called for clearance for taxi and departure. Kenai is a small airport but has a long runway and a control tower. This time of the year the prevailing winds are out of the south making it necessary to taxi to the far north end for takeoff. Once clear of the traffic area he turned north and began to climb for altitude to fly over the nine miles of open water he must cross to get to the Alaska Peninsula.

Bob planned to take the scenic route, at low levels in order to allow his passengers a chance to see any animals in Lake Clark Pass and on to the south past Lake Iliamna, Becharof Lake and over the open tundra on the north side of the Alaska Range mountains, many of which are active volcanoes.

Both of the men were wearing headsets in order to have conversation while flying. Bob spoke into his microphone as they flew south pointing out many scenic and historic sites along the way. He was able to point out a few caribou, moose, and a couple of brown bears along the way. The flight took almost three hours to reach the camp at Wildman Lake. He buzzed the field once before landing to alert his camp crew of their arrival.

Halstead shut down the engine on the Cessna and opened his door. The assistant guide, Ernie, and Vic were walking toward the small plane. Bob helped the two passengers to the ground and opened the small baggage door in the plane's fuselage. Ernie waved a hello and immediately began to unload the gear stowed in the compartment. When Vic stepped under the wing to help, Bob began introductions.

"Hey, Vic," he said as he turned to the two new men, "This is Clyde Lyle, and this is Dick Morris."

Vic shook hands with the new arrivals. "The man over there is our assistant guide, Ernie, and this old goat is the camp cook and caretaker, Vic Lamar. Don't let his old appearance fool you he can still cook, even though he is too old to pack." Everyone laughed at the remark. Ernie continued to unload gear from the rear compartment while the introductions and chatting went on.

"Clyde, you and Dick will be in cabin number two. That's the second one in the row from here. There are bunks made up and I'll have your gear sent over right away. The outhouse is that building over there at the other end of camp. The bigger building alongside is the washhouse where you can shower and wash up. Try to be judicious, but not stingy with the water. I have to start the generator to pump water into the tanks."

Bob pulled the gun cases from the rear seat area and gave them to the hunters. They waved at the crew and walked toward the cabin they had been assigned. Bob called after them.

"The big blue building is the lodge building where I will be staying. If you need me, I'll be there. Vic stays there, too, but Ernie is in the number one cabin next to you fellas. Settle in and come on down to the lodge. We can do some fishing after a while. We can't fly and shoot on the same day by state law, so I'm going to fly out to scout for bears this evening. I can take either or both of you with me if you want to take a look."

"Thanks," said Morris as he waved and turned to walk to the cabin, saying "I think we will both go with you."

Once the hunters were out of earshot Bob turned to his men. "OK, guys, let's get the fuel stashed and finish unloading the rest of the gear. Is everything ready here?" he asked turning to Vic.

"Just like you had it planned, Bobby. All the weapons are stashed like you wanted, along with the ammunition for each of them. The camp is cleaned up and ready. Ernie is a wonder in camp. You need to keep him around."

Turning to Ernie Bob said, "I know this is more fuel than I usually bring, but this is one time I don't want to run low. Do your best to pile it into the shed. Did Vic give you a rundown on what to expect?"

"Yeah, he did, Boss, but I want you to know I'm not comfortable with the way this is playing out. I'm on your side all the way, but I'm not anxious to get into a gun battle out here."

"For what it's worth, Ernie, I don't expect a gun battle. They want some information from me and I think they will try to get me alone and beat it out of me. My only advantage is the two of you and the fact they don't know I suspect them. And, they may not be the men after me at all. Just go about your duties as always and don't worry; be aware, but don't worry."

Vic spoke then, "I gave Ernie the little 9mm as a pocket gun to go along with the big .44 Mag he carries. I got my .44 on my belt and the .45 auto under my shirt in a shoulder holster. The other 9mm is strapped on my right ankle. I've got more guns than Wyatt Earp."

"OK guys, this is it. I hope they are just hunters, but if not we're ready for them. Let's go to the lodge and start some dinner." Bob didn't want them to know he was as wary as each of them. "Have you seen any game around the camp?" he asked.

"We hardly ever see caribou down here anymore," said Ernie. "There was a big cow moose downstream by the little swamp. She walks through camp every couple of days. She don't have a calf this year. I've seen a few bear tracks, but the bears only pass through at night and don't hang around much. Ptarmigan are plentiful on the other side of the lake, and that old red fox has a den over there," he pointed across the runway, "and is raising a couple of kits."

"You're a good man, Ernie. I'm proud to have you as my guide. Now come on and help me tie the airplane down and we'll get the stuff to the lodge. I suspect the hunters will take a nap for a while and we should do the same. I'll take the hunters and scout the area this evening. The weather is supposed to hold for another week, and that's a good break."

"We been gettin' frost the past few nights, Boss. If it rains next week we could get some snow." Ernie was speculating on his version of a weather report.

An hour later the three men lay down to nap for a few minutes before dinner and the evening activities. Fishing for Arctic char in the little lake was great fun and the fish were good to eat for breakfast. Bob woke a half hour later to the sound of pots and pans rattling in the kitchen outside his bedroom door.

He stepped into the dining area and found a fresh pot of coffee brewing on the stove. Vic was busy adding seasoning to a pot roast on the stovetop. Life in this large base camp was very luxurious indeed.

"The hunters are up and moving," said Vic without looking up to see who was in the kitchen. "Ernie is still asleep."

Bob chuckled at the cook and walked outside where there was a large spotting scope on a tripod set up to scan the area. Through the scope he saw several fox and parka squirrels (Arctic ground squirrels) on the surrounding tundra. Looking up toward the mountains he scanned the foothills for bears. On a rise to the east he saw a sow with two yearling cubs crossing the river. The lack of visible game was not unusual for this time of day and more should show themselves as evening approached. As Bob looked at the countryside through the scope the two hunters walked to where he was standing.

"See anything?" asked Lyle.

"Not much." Bob swung the scope in the direction of the sow and cubs. "There's a sow with cubs up the river. Take a look."

Both hunters took turns glassing the bruins until they went out of sight at the top of the rise. "That was exciting," said Morris. "I'm encouraged to see game this close to the camp."

"A shootable bear probably won't come that close to camp, but we'll go out and take a look after dinner. How about it? Do you want to catch some fish for breakfast?"

"Oh, yeah, that would be great," both hunters agreed.

Bob led the way to the small gear shed alongside the lodge building and found two suitable rods and lures to use on the fishing expedition a hundred yards behind the lodge. Fishing was good and they caught and released a large number of char before keeping four nice fish to clean and bring to camp for breakfast. The generator was running to supply water and electricity in the lodge during the evening meal. This also allowed the refrigerator to cool down and preserve the fish in fresh condition overnight.

With dinner and the regular conversation out of the way Bob took the two hunters to the airplane and strapped them into their seats for the evening reconnoiter. The flight lasted just over an hour and several suitable bears were spotted. There were three bears closer to camp, but the larger ones were a little higher on the foothills. The first was a huge blond boar digging for parka squirrels. The second one was higher up the hills in a stand of alder brush. He was large, more than nine feet, with a thick coat that was shiny dark brown. It would make a great trophy. Back in camp the two men settled on who was to hunt which bear. Lyle wanted the bigger bear while Morris was satisfied with the smaller one, but lighter color bear.

Bob agreed to guide Lyle on the quest for the big bear while Ernie would lead Morris to the other one. Bob gave directions to both bears to Ernie who understood exactly where the bears would be. Ernie set upon the task of gathering the gear needed for the trek they would begin in the early morning hours. The group would be hiking together for most of the first two hours then they would split up to pursue the individual bears.

The following morning the men readied for the long hike up into the hills when Vic came to Bob to ask if it was alright for him to tag along with him and his hunter. Bob was thinking about it when Clyde Lyle, who had overheard the conversation, said, "why not, Bob? If I get the bear he can help skin the hide and help us pack the hide and skull back here to camp."

"OK, Clyde, if it doesn't bother you it doesn't bother me. I know Vic and he's a good hand in the field." He then turned to Vic Lamar, "It looks like you're going along, Vic. Get your pack ready."

Since it had been a dry summer they would only need leather field boots for hiking. The one stream they would need to cross had a spot where boulders had been placed for just such occasions. Minutes later the five men began the trek up into the hills. At the point they needed to cross the stream they parted company with Ernie and Dick taking the south bank further up the incline.

Bob, Vic, and Clyde crossed over on the rocks in the stream and continued to climb up the low hill ahead. An hour later they topped a small rise where they used binoculars to scan the brush-line further up the hill. They saw no sign of the bear from this first lookout and continued to climb upward toward the alder patch. Bob kept the group behind the rise in the ground to avoid being spotted by the bear if he was still in the area. It was nearly eight o'clock in the morning when they stopped to glass the alders again. This time Bob spotted the bear digging out a parka squirrel at the edge of the brush. The bear was more than four hundred yards away and the men decided to keep below the rise in the land and get closer and a little above the target.

Excitement was beginning to build in the small group as it does with any devoted hunter spotting his prey. Bob gave Clyde instructions on how they would continue up the hill and said they would have a chance to glass the bear one more time before they would set up to shoot. Keeping low they hiked another two hundred yards up the hill where there was a small stand of willow trees for cover. They glassed the area once again. The bear had moved out a short distance into the open.

"I guess it to be about two hundred yards, Bob. Should I take the shot from here?" asked Clyde.

"You can if you want, but if we stay behind this knob we can get about fifty yards closer for a better shot. That .416 Remington of yours is a great bear gun, but it doesn't perform well at distance. I think you should wait for the shorter shot, your choice."

Lyle thought a few seconds, "You're the guide and know the terrain. I'll take your advice. Let's go."

As they walked closer to the target Vic dropped further back and out of sight of the bear. Bob and Clyde carefully peeked over the little rise in front of them and gave Clyde a view of his target. This is the moment every hunter hopes for, and Clyde Lyle was a true hunter. He studied the target with his binoculars, placed his pack on the ground in front of him, checked the cartridge in the chamber, clicked off the safety and aimed the rifle at the huge bear. Bob watched closely as the hunter prepared to shoot. Yes, he thought, this man is a real hunter.

Chapter 18

Bob studied the busy bear with his rangefinder binoculars, "One hundred thirty-seven yards," he informed his client. "Wait for a heart shot and hold dead on the target spot," he whispered. Clyde never let his eye come away from the view through the rifle scope but nodded slightly in agreement. With Bob watching through his binoculars, Clyde kept watching the bear, waiting for it to turn slightly for a better heart shot. He was patient, holding steady on the target. Bob had seen clients get shaky or lose their nerve and freeze at this moment in the hunt, but this man was cold as steel while waiting for the right time to pull the trigger and make the kill.

Still digging for the parka squirrel the bear turned slightly to his left giving Clyde the perfect shot. He placed the crosshairs just behind the bear's right leg and eased pressure on the trigger. The .416 Remington roared, slamming the bear in the chest. The bear felt the bullet before he heard the shot. The startled bear, feeling the pain in his chest and not knowing the cause stood on its hind legs and bent to bite whatever had struck him. There was nothing for him to bite and he dropped to all fours.

"Hit him again, Clyde. We don't want this big guy getting into the alders," said the guide. Again, Clyde nodded while looking through the rifle scope, pausing and at the right second sent another round into the bear's chest, breaking the right shoulder in the process. The bear went down, heaving heavy breaths. Clyde now looked up from the rifle, grinning like a schoolboy. "My first Alaska brown bear," he said proudly.

Bob reached out to shake the client's hand. "And he's a nice one, too. Congratulations, Clyde. We had better wait a few minutes to be sure he isn't going to get up when we approach him."

Now Vic was atop the little rise to view the kill. "Wow, Clyde, you got a nice trophy. I think he's bigger than the one I got a few years ago." He reached into his pack and dug out a bottle of water to hand to the hunter.

Clyde Lyle took a long drink from the plastic bottle without speaking, but when he finished drinking he smiled broadly saying, "I've hunted all over the world, tigers, lions, elephants, cape buffalo and all kinds of animals, but this tops anything I've ever done. Thanks, guys, for a great hunt."

The three men sat drinking water for several minutes before moving to the bear which had not moved a hair since the second shot. Finally, Bob said, "I guess he isn't getting up, Vic. Let's go over there and take a look, cautiously, mind you. I think it's picture taking time on the Alaska Peninsula."

The three men moved toward the bear with caution. Bob was the first to approach the animal. He slipped his rifle from his shoulder and pointed the barrel at the huge head of the beautiful bear, poking the tip of the barrel into the closed eye of the trophy. It didn't flinch. Bob pulled a large hunting knife from his belt and made the first cut of the skinning process, deep enough to ensure the bear was, indeed, dead. This is when the bragging rights were verified and the pictures that would amaze the client's friends for years were taken.

All three men dropped their packs and the skinning process was begun. It took the expert skinners nearly an hour to remove the hide from the carcass. Vic did most of the skinning of the hide while Bob spent his time removing the skull and placing it in his pack to carry back to camp.

"I haven't heard your pardner shooting," Bob said to Clyde as they loaded the heavy packs on their backs.

"Don't worry, Bob. Dick is a good hunter and an excellent shot. If they get within range he'll own that blond bear." All three men laughed at that.

It was afternoon when the men returned to camp and began to process the hide for storage. It is said the fun is over and the work begins when the trigger is pulled. Today would verify that statement. At four in the afternoon Dick Morris and Ernie came into camp with another hide to be fleshed and salted. After dropping their packs the two men sat on the bench in front of the meat house drinking bottled water. Morris drained the entire bottle before speaking.

"Man, I'm beat. That bear wouldn't stand still and let me shoot him. We hiked over hell's half acre to get within range. That Ernie knows the countryside and he knows his bears. We finally got a shot and that bear dropped like a rock." He picked up another bottle of water and drank half of it. "I usually don't like getting my game the first day of the hunt, but in this case it was worth it."

"I'm glad you had a good hunt, Dick. I've been thinking about tomorrow. When the hides are ready to ship, we can fly into King Salmon and put them on the plane for you. Once that's done I can move you and the crew to a tent camp I use north of the Mulchatna River near Jack Rabbit Hills. There aren't many caribou left out there, but they sometimes come to the Hills this time of year. If you two want to buy non-resident tags in King Salmon I can move you and the crew up there and give you a couple of days hunting caribou. How does that sound to you to finish out your trip?"

The two hunters looked at each other and grinned. "That sounds like a bonus trip to me," said Clyde.

"Me, too," remarked Dick. "How far a move is it?" he asked.

"I'll take the two of you to King Salmon and you can overnight at the hotel and get tags. I'll then come back here and move Vic to the camp which is a little over an hour northeast of King Salmon. Vic and Ernie can close the camp while I take the two of you to town and ship your hides and get the skulls measured and sealed by Alaska Fish and Game in King Salmon."

"Sounds good, let's do it," said Clyde with Dick nodding agreement.

"OK, let's finish with the hides and get some dinner. Vic and Ernie can start to close the camp while I take the two of you to town."

"I guess I had better help you fuel up for the trip," said Vic.

While Ernie prepared dinner of fresh char, Vic helped Bob pour fuel into the Cessna. The chore gave the men a chance to talk privately.

"What are you thinking?" asked Vic.

"They seem genuine enough, but I still have to be careful. They may only be waiting for a chance to get at me. They are real hunters, for sure, but that may only be their cover story wherever they go."

"I agree, Bob," said a suspicious Vic. "I don't think we can take a chance just yet."

"I want you to get all the weapons you hid and pack them to take to the Hills. I'll move you up there and come back to King Salmon to get the hunters. You've been to the tent camp and know the layout. Do the best you can to be ready for anything." Bob was uneasy about the move, but still didn't know if these men were the killers after him to get information about Don.

Bob and Vic loaded the airplane with all the gear for the two hunters as well as the hides and skulls they needed to have sealed and shipped. Vic stood near the Cessna as the passengers were strapped in for the trip to town. "I'll be back in about three hours to get you and the rest of the gear to take to the Jack Rabbit Hills camp. Ernie can stay here and finish closing the lodge for winter and I'll pick him up in a few days."

Vic waved at the men as Bob closed the door and started the engine. The flight to King Salmon was smooth and uneventful. The hunters helped Bob take the trophies to the Fish and Game office for sealing and registration. From there he sent them to the hotel in a taxicab but kept their hunting gear in the Cessna to take with him to the camp in the Hills. After refueling, he took off toward the northeast on a direct course to the tent camp. Once at the camp he opened the larger of the tents and put all the hunting gear and guns inside. This chore took only a few minutes and he was back in the air on a direct flight to the Wildman Lake camp to load the camp gear and necessities they would need for a caribou hunt. He gave final instructions to Ernie, strapped Vic into the right front seat of the Cessna and took off on a direct course to the tent camp where they would spend the night preparing for the arrival of the hunters the following morning.

Before landing at the tent camp he flew around the area looking for any caribou in the vicinity. There were several small bands of animals in the immediate area with some good bulls mixed with them. The hunters should have a good hunt here before ending the trip and heading back home.

Once the airplane was tied down for the night Bob and Vic began to stash weapons around the camp in the event they were needed. Finally, very late in the day Vic cooked up a dinner of steak and eggs with hot coffee to drink. The last chore of the day was to walk to the stream to fill some water cans for camp water—washing dishes, bathing, cooking, and cleaning. It was late when they climbed into their bunks and sleeping bags.

The sun was high when Bob awakened and checked the Cessna for the flight to King Salmon to pick up his hunters. "I plan to be back in about three hours, Vic. I plan to eat breakfast in town, refuel and get back here. I'll fly them around to familiarize them with the area before landing. Do you want anything from town?"

"Nope, I have everything I need. Get back safe," said Vic.

Once back in King Salmon Bob called the men on his cell phone. "Have you had breakfast yet?" he asked the hunters.

"No, we were waiting for you. I'll buy," said Clyde. "I have one call to make before we come down to the restaurant."

Again, he fueled the plane and made a preflight check before walking the short distance to the hotel dining room just down the street. Breakfast was hearty and tasty as well as time consuming. Plans for the day were made while eating, both men stating they were anticipating a good day of hunting tomorrow since they would be flying today and not allowed to hunt.

It was another sightseeing trip back to camp flying low and seeing much game—moose, bears, and caribou. The bears were catching spawning salmon on the smaller streams along the route to camp. They spotted a dead caribou on a low knob where four wolves were feeding on it. The wolves ran for cover as the plane approached.

Bob showed the men several small bands of caribou in the area and recommended one little bunch with two very nice bulls. "Remember, caribou live out here and you will never be invisible to them. I would advise you to take the first clear shot you can get. I'll be guiding you out there, but you will have to decide which shots to take. Let's just lie around camp this evening and relax. We should clean the rifles after all this travel, though."

"Let us get settled into our accommodations and we'll meet with you and settle all the details. Which tent is ours?" asked Clyde. "After getting squared away, we have some things we would like to discuss with you."

"The first smaller tent is yours. Vic and I will share the bunks in the cook tent. Go ahead and get ready and we'll unload the plane and fix dinner." Bob talked as he walked toward the cook tent with his arms full of camp supplies he had brought from town.

The two hunters carried their personal gear to the second tent in the short row and went inside. Bob motioned for Vic to follow him inside the cook tent.

"This may be the time for them to act. They're acting a little strange and just now said they wanted to discuss something before we settle in for the evening." Bob spoke in a low voice, nearly a whisper. "It may be nothing but my suspicion but be ready for anything."

Vic glanced at the doorway and pulled his sidearm to check the clip. "I'm ready, Bob," he said.

The sun was low on the western horizon when they finished dinner and leaned back to relax. Vic got up from the table and began to clean the dishes and kitchen.

"Let's go outside and talk, Clyde," said Bob in a casual tone. The two hunters and Bob went outside into the cool evening air. Bob had set up a spotting scope in the clearing in front of the cook tent and placed a makeshift bench near it. He stepped over to the scope and peered into the lens, scanning the tundra around the western side of the camp.

"Well, Clyde, what were the things you wanted to discuss?" he asked.

Clyde came to where Bob was seated and sat alongside him. Dick drifted past the spotting scope and moved a little to his left, still in earshot, but strategically out of physical range. Bob had been in enough encounters to recognize the move.

"I want you to know what a great time we have had hunting with you, but there is another matter we must discuss with you now. It involves your brother. Dick and I have no interest in harming you or Vic, but we need to know where your niece is at this moment." Clyde spoke in a calm and quiet voice.

"My niece!?" shouted Bob in order to alert Vic.

"Yes, your niece. Your brother has information we need and we will use her to influence him to talk. We know he is in the hospital in Anchorage under guard. Please, Bob, give us the information and we will not harm you, Vic, or your brother to say nothing about the little girl, Jenny."

"I don't think you two are in a very good position to be demanding anything from me. It's a long walk home." It was an empty threat but gave Vic time to move to a vantage point near the doorway of the tent.

At that point Dick drew a handgun from a holster under his outer shirt.

"Dick doesn't have much patience, Bob. Just give me the location of the niece and we will leave you to walk home."

"Sorry Clyde, you know I can't do that." Bob was staring into the eyes of his nemesis.

"Oh, I think you'll talk, pal," said Dick now pointing his semi-automatic at Bob's leg.

"Go ahead and shoot. Who will fly you out of here?" said Bob through clenched teeth.

"You don't understand, Bob. I'm taking your airplane and leaving you here, alive or dead it makes no difference to us. Alive would be better for both of us. Tell us where the girl is right now." Clyde was losing patience now.

"Not a chance, pard," said Bob.

Clyde looked up and over to his partner, "Shoot him in the leg, Dick."

Dick moved the weapon slightly to the right and placed his finger on the trigger.

Vic took this movement as the threat moment and moved into the open to fire at Dick. Dick saw him moving and swung his arm in his direction. Vic didn't wait and fired at the gunman hitting him in the center of his chest. The impact forced a muscle flinch that fired his weapon, striking Vic in the left shoulder and he fell to the ground.

Clyde never took his eyes off Bob. "That was unnecessary, Bob. Your partner is hurt and it looks like mine is dead. Now tell me what I need to know and we can end this without you being hurt."

The two men were less than two feet apart. Bob took the pause as his chance and slammed headlong into Clyde's chest knocking him over backward. Bob used the moment to pull his Glock from its holster and fire at the man while he was struggling to regain his footing. Bob's bullet hit Clyde in the neck killing him instantly.

It was then he raced to where Vic lay on the ground, bleeding from a wound in his upper chest on the left side. Vic was conscious, but in a great deal of pain. Bob managed to put a makeshift compression bandage on the wound to slow the bleeding.

"I'll drag these two inside the tent to keep the bears and wolves off of them and load you up to get you to the hospital in Naknek. Relax a few minutes, Vic."

He finally returned to carry bleeding Vic to the Cessna. Bob strapped Vic into the right front seat so he could see how his friend and protector was doing during the flight. They took off in the direction of Naknek to get medical help. He would call Tony Harrison when Vic was in a doctor's care.

Chapter 19

As they approached the Naknek Airport, Bob radioed for someone to call an ambulance and meet them at the airport. A voice came on the frequency and said she would call it in. He circled once and landed on the north/south cross strip and taxied to the front of a large maintenance hangar where he shut down the engine.

Bob was pulling Vic from the seat when the ambulance arrived. Two medics helped him lift the injured man from the plane to the vehicle's stretcher.

"What happened to him?" asked one of the medics.

"One of my hunters shot him. He's pretty bad and lost a lot of blood. You need to get him to the hospital as soon as you can. If it's OK, I'd like to ride with you."

"Sure thing, Bob," said one of the medics who recognized the guide was eager to help.

It was a short ride to the hospital where a doctor was waiting at the ambulance entrance to treat the wounded Vic. "How did it happen?" asked the doctor as he examined the wound.

"I'd rather not say just yet, Doc. The guy shot him intentionally. I need a phone to call the troopers."

"The troopers have been notified already as we do with all gunshot wounds. Trooper Martin will be here soon." The doctor spoke without looking up from his task of cleaning the wound. He immediately ordered IV fluids and a shot to quell the pain Vic was suffering.

Bob stood back to allow the medical personnel space to do their job and work on Vic. They moved him into a small examination room to finish cleaning up the wound to determine the exact amount of damage done to his chest and shoulder. "Why don't you have a chair in the hallway until we can see what we need to do," said the nurse working with the doctor.

A few minutes later Trooper Martin arrived and saw Bob sitting in the hallway. "How is your friend?" he asked.

"I don't know yet. The doctor is still examining him. He was shot in the chest and it looks bad. He lost a lot of blood. I tried to stop the bleeding, but I couldn't."

"OK, let's get some paperwork done. Show me your driver's license or guide certificate and give me your name," the trooper ordered.

Bob dug into his wallet to produce both pieces of ID for the officer who took them and began to write on his notebook. "Do you want to call anyone?" he asked the guide.

"As a matter of fact there is someone. I need to call Lieutenant Anthony Harrison at State Troopers headquarters in Anchorage. I have his personal cell phone number if you need it. He is familiar with the issue that involves the shooting although he doesn't know about this specific incident yet.

"Before I call Tony, I need to have you tell me what happened. Exactly where did the shooting take place?" asked Martin.

"I have several camps out here on the Peninsula. We had just moved these two hunters from our Wildman Lake camp to a tent camp in the Jack Rabbit Hills. They had each killed a bear and we were moving to where they had a chance at some caribou. They overnighted in King Salmon and I flew them out to camp earlier today. I suspected they were hired thugs possibly connected with a recent crime and kept an eye on them. They began to threaten me and pulled out guns. Vic was in the tent and heard the commotion and when one of the men, Dick, was about to shoot me Vic called to Dick who turned to fire at him. Vic shot first and hit Dick, but Dick got off one shot and hit Vic. The other guy, Clyde Lyle, pulled his gun on me and I shot him. They're both dead. I dragged them inside a tent before bringing Vic to Naknek."

Trooper Martin was aghast at the story. "You say the Lieutenant knows about these two men?"

"We didn't actually know it was these two guys until they pulled guns and began to threaten us."

"I want you to wait here while I call Lt. Harrison. I'll be back in a minute." The trooper walked toward the back door where his patrol car was parked, carrying his notebook and Bob's licenses.

Bob waited in the hallway. Soon, the doctor came out of the examination room to speak with him.

"Mr. Halstead, your friend is badly wounded and needs surgery right away. Luckily, we have a surgeon on staff with experience in treating gunshot wounds. He's retired military. I had the nurse call him and he is on his way here now. We have stopped the bleeding and sedated your friend. There is a great deal of tissue damage, but I think the surgeon can repair most of it with very little loss of use in his left arm and shoulder."

"Thanks for being with him, Doc. He's a good friend and he actually saved my life today. He shot the man who was about to shoot me. We believe these two men were professional killers. We're both lucky to be alive."

It was then that Officer Martin came from his patrol car. "OK Bob, I just spoke with Tony and he said he would be here tonight sometime if he can get a flight from Anchorage. He vouched for you and said the same as you that these men were suspects from the start. He told me you have a truck to use in King Salmon and I'll give you a ride over there if you would like. We still have some things to talk about. We can do that on the way to your truck. Tony said he wants you to fly him out to your camp to recover the bodies first thing in the morning."

Turning back to the doctor Bob asked, "When do you expect the surgeon to operate on Vic?"

"He didn't say, but my guess is it will be first thing in the morning. Give me your contact number and I'll call you when I learn the time."

Everyone exchanged phone numbers and Bob accepted the ride to his truck parked in front of Lindsy Gibson's home in King Salmon. Bob stayed in the house for the night, sleeping fitfully, worrying about Vic. He slept late the following morning and was awakened by his cell phone chiming.

"Hello," he answered, half asleep.

"Bob, it's Tony. I'm in King Salmon. Can you meet me for breakfast at the hotel?"

"Yeah, Tony, I'll be there in fifteen minutes."

At breakfast Bob gave Tony the entire story from start to finish, leaving out nothing. Tony made notes as he listened and ate his ham and eggs. At the end he closed his notebook and shook his head.

"I wish there were something we could have done to keep Vic from being injured, but there was nothing concrete with which to measure the danger. It appears you boys did everything possible to avoid a confrontation and they chose to have one anyway—too bad, they lost. What time do you want to go out to view the scene and recover the bodies?" asked Tony.

"I need to drive to Naknek and speak with the doctors first, then fuel the plane. I left it parked in Naknek by the big hangar. Do you want to ride over there with me?"

"Sure. It will save a lot of time that way. Let's go." Tony picked up the check for breakfast and paid it with a state credit card.

At the Naknek Hospital the men spoke with both doctors. They were told the surgery would take half a day and there was nothing the guide could do to assist and advised him to take the day to help the troopers. Bob and Tony drove to the airport and fueled the Cessna for the trip. Clouds were building over the coastline indicating the weather was about to make a change. The flight was bumpy, but not terribly so as they flew to the camp in Jack Rabbit Hills.

After they arrived, Tony photographed everything he could see to indicate what had happened. He measured the distance from where Bob said the shooter, Dick, was standing to where he said Vic was when he shot. An hour and a half later they placed the bodies in plastic body bags they had brought with them and loaded them into the back seat of the Cessna. It was a tight fit, but they managed to get it done.

Bob secured all their gear, guns, sleeping bags and food as well as possible. He would return later to retrieve all the remaining camp items, leaving the camp clean. Trooper Martin met the men at the Naknek Airport and took possession of the bodies.

Bob and Tony went to the hospital to check on Vic. The doctors met the men in a small conference room to give them a report. "I believe things went well for Mr. Lamar. He's in recovery now and still feeling the effects of the anesthesia. We'll keep him there a couple of more hours and move him to a private room. There was a lot of damage to his muscles and bones in his upper chest, but his lung was not penetrated. His shoulder is broken and we fixed that. We rerouted some muscles and tendons to secure the area damaged by the bullet. We believe he'll have a full recovery but will have to do some therapy when he is well enough. There is no point in visiting him at this time because he will not be awake. Please come back later this evening." It was a short, but thorough briefing by the surgeon.

Bob drove Tony back to the King Salmon Airport where he planned to catch the evening flight out to Anchorage. "I don't mean to be all doom and gloom, but the people who ordered this are not the kind to stop. We need to find a way to get to the men at the top of the company, at least the branch in Anchorage. I'll meet with the major in the morning and see if we can come up with a plan. Call me when you pick up your gear and head to Kenai. Do you have any idea when that will be?" asked the trooper.

"I may go out and get the stuff from camp just to keep it safe, and I'll have to go down to Wildman Lake to get Ernie and bring him out so he can get a flight home. He's worked his buns off this year. I need to give him a little bonus for what he's done for me. I think it will be at least two weeks before I'll be able to take Vic out of here and back to Kenai. If I'm in King Salmon I'll have cell coverage and you can call me. Let me know if you come up with a plan to get that labor union bunch."

After dropping Tony at the terminal he drove to Lindsy's house to relax for the first time in several days. What troubled him now was the fact the threat still existed. The people who sent the killers were still in place. All this thinking made it difficult to sleep peacefully.

In the offices of AmerAsian Labor Union the following morning Li Tan waited for a call from his two men in the hunting camp. It could possibly be another day before the call came, but Li Tan knew his job and possibly his life were hanging in the balance. He was becoming uncomfortable in this situation and unable to control any part of it. The two men Ang Wei had ordered sent to the office were professionals and fully capable of handling any situation that could arise. In the end they would dispose of the guide and his helpers. Just the same he was made uneasy by the lack of information coming from the two hunters. He was pondering this problem when his desk phone rang. It was the receptionist in Mr. Wei's office.

"Li Tan, Mr. Wei would like you to come to his office immediately."

Li Tan knew this could not be good news and also knew he could not refuse to go. He walked slowly down the hall toward the main office wondering what had happened to prompt this summons.

As he entered the front office the receptionist lifted her phone to notify Mr. Wei. "You may go right in, Mr. Tan," she said without being asked.

Li Tan entered the office to find Ang Wei on the telephone. He pointed to the chair in front of the desk but never quit listening to the telephone in his ear. Finally, he said something in Chinese and hung up the telephone. Wei made a note on the legal pad in front of him before looking up at Li Tan. "Your replacement will arrive in the office in two days. You have been promoted to the home office in Jakarta. Congratulations, Li Tan," announced Ang Wei.

"To what do I owe this honor, Mr. Wei?" asked Tan.

"It is the good work you have done for this office. I expect you to brief the new man in every aspect of your office when he arrives. You will leave for your new assignment in three or four days, depending on transportation schedules. That will be all, Li Tan."

"Thank you, Mr. Wei. Since I am here I would like to tell you I have not heard from the two men I sent to the Alaska Peninsula to take care of that problem."

"I just received word two men were killed in a gun battle east of King Salmon yesterday around noon. Alaska State Troopers are investigating. The camp where this incident took place is leased by a guide by the name of Bob Halstead. Is the name familiar to you, Mr. Tan?" Ang Wei did not look up from his legal pad. "That will be all, Mr. Tan."

Li Tan only bowed slightly but said nothing before exiting the office. He walked slowly to his own office and sat in his plush office chair thinking about what had happened. He thought, 'How did Ang Wei get this information and he did not?' He summoned his two men to the office.

When Chin and Hua arrived he met them at the conference table where Tan took the head of the table for perhaps the last time. "I have received word the two men we sent to deal with the hunting guide have been eliminated. I have no further information on the matter and I want to know exactly what took place. I don't care how you get the information, but I need it right away."

Li Tan sat at his desk the rest of the morning brooding over his sudden dismissal. The outcome would never be good for him. He thought of options the entire morning and found none that would be to his benefit. At noon he went to his car in the parking garage.

When Chin and Hua returned to the office complex they found Li Tan in his car with a small hole in his right temple. Without ceremony they loaded him into a body bag for disposal and called two men to go to Mr. Tan's car in the parking garage and eliminate it.

Chapter 20

Tony Harrison called the ICE agent, Greg Beason. "Hello Greg, Tony Harrison here. We need to talk right away. There has been an incident you will want to know about. How soon can you come over to my office?"

A half hour later Tony escorted Beason to his office, stopping for coffee in the break room. "What's the big news, Lieutenant?" asked Greg when they reached the office.

Tony took the time to explain all the facts he knew about the attack on Vic and Bob at the Jack Rabbit Hills camp. He also gave an update on the condition of Vic Lamar.

"Wow!" said the federal officer, "Your friend Bob is either very good or very lucky. The labor union, both local and international, almost never fail to complete a task like killing someone. The bodies are seldom found. You should advise your friend that it may not be over. These guys don't quit."

"I wish there were some hard evidence to connect the labor union to the attempt on Bob and Vic. We can't go into their offices and accuse them of the attack without some sort of evidence," Tony remarked while thinking out loud.

"I have a couple of pieces of information I just received that may be a possible link. First, the two goons that were killed at the hospital were identified and traced to the labor union's parent company in Indonesia. They worked for the local union as enforcers. Locally they call themselves security, but they do a lot more than security. There are three more licensed security men listed who work for this office. My source at Interpol said there were two new security men sent to this office from Jakarta and it sounds like they may be the men your friend Bob shot. They were described to me as world class big game hunters using the names of Clyde Lyle and Dick Morris. Both are former mercenaries who once worked for the CIA in Africa. It seems people die wherever they go hunting."

"Those are the two names Bob said they used to book the hunt on the Peninsula. Do we have any pictures of them?" asked Tony.

"I don't know, but I'll check." He made a note on his pocket pad. "You know, Tony, police all over the world have been trying to find something on these unions. Wouldn't it be ironic if that came from here in Alaska?"

"They've probably figured out by now who I am and what I was doing looking around their offices, but it may be time to go down there and have a talk with the big boss and his head security guy. They won't tell us anything, but it could make them nervous," mused Tony.

"I had better clear that with my bosses first. I wouldn't want to inadvertently step on an undercover operation if they have one going." Beason was making more notes in his notebook.

"I shipped the two hunters' bodies back here to the crime lab for the medical examiner. They should arrive this afternoon if you want to go see what they look like," commented Tony.

"I wouldn't recognize them, but I would appreciate it if the medical examiner could get me some pictures for our files." Greg Beason made another note in his book and stood to leave. "I have to get back to the office, but keep me posted on your progress, Tony."

In the hospital in Naknek Vic had come around and was sitting up in his hospital bed, groggy from pain meds, but awake when Bob came in to see him. "You look pretty good for a used target," said Bob.

"I don't want to work for you any longer. You don't treat your help very well." Both men laughed a little.

"I talked with the doctor a minute ago and he thinks you'll have a full recovery after you heal and go to therapy. He claims you'll be back to your old sweet self in no time."

"He should observe the case from my point of view," muttered Vic.

"I went out to the camp and loaded everything up and took it all to my place—all the guns and gear and everything. I'll keep your stuff locked up until you get home to do with it whatever you want. I also stopped by the Wildman Camp and picked up Ernie. He wanted to come to Naknek to see you, but the day was too short. I paid him a little bonus for his efforts this year and he deserved it. I'll do the same for you when you get out of here."

"No need," claimed Vic. "Except for that one little thing, it was fun."

"Lindsy called and I talked with Jenny for a few minutes. She was glad to hear her dad was doing so well. I asked her not to tell me where they were for her own safety, so I don't know where they are right now. The school has sent her some new schoolbooks to study to get her ready to go back to class. That little girl is really smart."

"I have never spent much time around kids, but I really enjoyed my time with Jenny." At that moment Vic had suffered a spasm of pain, flinched and reached for his wounded shoulder.

"I'll tell the nurse to come and give you some pain meds as I go past the desk in the hall. If you need anything, anything at all, you call me, Vic."

Bob stood and walked out of the room as Vic closed his eyes in pain. He drove to the airport to fly to Anchorage for a visit with his brother, Don. As he did his preflight check he thought about the number of people injured and killed in the past weeks. It had to end soon and without any more innocent folks being injured or killed.

Back near Anchorage and with cell phone coverage, he dialed Tony Harrison to ask if he would pick him up and drive him to the hospital to see Don. Tony agreed and asked how long it would be before he arrived.

A half hour later Bob taxied to the transient parking area where Tony was sitting in his patrol car, waiting for him. Once Bob climbed into the front and strapped the seatbelt into place, Tony put the car in gear and headed the short drive to the hospital.

"Have you heard anything new about the men in my camp?" asked Bob.

"Nothing much, but my friend from ICE learned they were probably men the international police had been looking for in several cases of murder and disappearances around the globe. The medical examiner is sending him some pictures of the bodies which he will forward to Interpol. You realize that you and Vic were very lucky to get out of that one alive. It scares me to think about it."

"I knew that whoever the shooter was going to be I needed to be prepared, and Vic and I did just that. He covered my back all the time. When we got to the Jack Rabbit Hills camp they began to make threats and ask questions about Don and Jenny. They physically positioned themselves in such a way I was going to be vulnerable while they asked questions. As soon as they started asking questions concerning Don we knew it was time to get ready. Vic did a great job. He stayed inside the tent and waited. When Dick Morris moved into position to threaten me Vic was able to get his gun out and make a move on him when Dick was about to pull the trigger. The confusion of Dick being shot gave me the chance to take out Clyde Lyle. I'm still shaking from that deal."

"Just be aware there may be further threats. I'm learning just how ruthless this group is all over the world. They keep their power by killing witnesses. Greg Beason, from ICE, and I are trying to come up with a legal way to interrogate the head of the security unit of the labor union. I met him once when I went to the office pretending to be a possible renter. The atmosphere there is really sterile. The head of the office is a man named Ang Wei. He is the coldest fish I have ever met; all business and no nonsense. Since I have met him once I must be careful about how I approach him. Beason and I are working on that one." Tony had reached the hospital parking garage.

The two men walked to the secure area of the hospital and were permitted to enter Don's room. A therapist was working on his legs when they entered and he told them he was just finishing and he would be leaving the room. When he was gone Bob walked to the wheelchair and took his brother's hand but was afraid to attempt to shake it.

"How are you doing, Bro?" asked Bob.

"Better; the pain is going away and the therapist has my arms and legs beginning to move a little. He thinks I'll be up and walking within a month at the rate I'm improving."

"That's great news, Don. I talked to Jenny. Of course, I don't know where she is right now, but I do know the school sent her some schoolbooks to study. She's having a good time traveling around with Lindsy Gibson."

"I just feel so helpless, Bob. I've never had to depend on anyone but myself. Look at me, I can't even wash myself or go to the bathroom without someone helping me." There was deep sadness in his voice. "I want you to be careful, Bob. I don't want you to wind up like this."

"Can I bring you anything, Don?" asked Bob.

"No, I'm fine. I have been reading Kindle electronic books. I don't have to turn the pages, only squeeze the button." Don seemed proud of being able to do this little thing.

"I've closed my camps and moved back home, so I'll be able to come see you more often. Have your nurse call me if you want anything." Bob and Tony both stood to leave, but Don only nodded with a tear in his eyes.

The following morning at the AmerAsian Labor Union offices the receptionist was preparing her office for the day when a tall, handsome man with reddish hair entered the office. "May I help you?" she asked.

"Yes, I'm Paul Milan here to see Mr. Ang Wei. I believe he is expecting me." Milan was a tall Irishman and a veteran of the Irish Rebellion where he was arrested and jailed for more than fifteen years by the British. Once released he used his prison contacts to become one of the most successful hit men in Europe. It was during this time he was hired by an international labor union to do the dirty work the union needed done. He was very good at his job and became a noted employee by the home office. When Ang Wei notified the Jakarta office that he needed a new security chief they sent Paul Milan.

"Have a seat, Mr. Milan, while I notify Mr. Wei." He sat in the waiting area while she called her boss on the office phone. When she hung up the telephone she called to Paul, "You may go in now, sir." She pointed at the doorway leading to Ang Wei's office.

Wei stood as the visitor entered. "How do you do, Mr. Milan? I am Ang Wei. I've been expecting you. Please have a seat. You will excuse me if I must ask you for some form of identification."

Milan smiled, "Of course, sir." He reached into an inside pocket of his sport coat for a wallet and an envelope. He opened the wallet to show a picture identification originating in Europe. Once Wei had inspected the card he nodded and seated himself behind the large office desk. Paul Milan handed him the business size envelope. "This is from our employers and explains everything."

Wei took the envelope and opened it to read the single page of text. "Ah, then you already understand our problem and why I asked for assistance?"

"Yes, Mr. Wei. I have been thoroughly briefed prior to making this trip. If you will show me my new office I will get started right away. I will need a temporary secretary to familiarize myself with the office protocol and phone system. My first task will be a meeting with the present members of the security staff. I have been to North America many times and understand their systems, but I will need assistance with the local topography and law enforcement systems. One of the present security men, if qualified, will be able to take that position. I had late word you need two more men and they are on the way from Jakarta as we speak. I plan to make a quick end to the present problem as it has cost us too many personnel, time, and money.

Ang Wei was not used to having anyone speak to him in this manner, but knew the man ranked as high in the union as he did. "My receptionist will show you to your new office and introduce you to the staff. I expect nothing but the best work from you, Mr. Milan. Welcome to Alaska." Without speaking Paul Milan stood and walked to the door as Wei picked up the phone to give orders to the receptionist.

In the outer office the secretary hung up her phone and stood. "If you would follow me, Mr. Milan, I will show you to the security offices." She led the way out of the main office and down the hall to the far end where the sign on the door stated Security Office. "I have notified the two men who work in this office and they will join you in a moment. Is there anything else I can do for you, sir?"

"No, that will be all for now, thank you."

While he waited he walked around the office, opening doors and familiarizing himself with the office layout. He found the security chief's office and went inside to inspect it. It was well appointed and well stocked. Prior to arriving he had been told there was an office staff to do clerical work for him and they would contact him when he was settled into the office. He was opening and inspecting desk drawers when his door opened and two men entered. It was Chin and Hua, his two security men.

"Have a seat at the conference table and we'll get started," he said as they entered. There was no question who was to be the new security chief. The meeting lasted most of the afternoon with Milan asking a hundred questions, not accepting partial or incomplete answers. This man wanted clear facts and nothing more and nothing less. He chose Chin to be his right-hand man for the time being and to help him become familiar with the local police workings as well as to help the new security boss find his way around the city of Anchorage.

During his briefing in the home office in Jakarta they had informed Milan that the office came with a nice apartment close to the office. "Chin, I want you to show me my living quarters. I understand they are close by."

"Yes, sir. There is also a company car for you, but I advise you get an Alaska driver's license before driving yourself. Either Mr. Hua or I will be available to drive you at any time until then."

"My bags are in the lobby downstairs. We can pick them up and you can drive me to my new home. I expect we will get along fine." Chin noted this deep Irish accent when he spoke.

Chapter 21

The next two weeks were productive for all the parties involved in the case begun when Don was beaten and left to die. Don was making significant progress during this time. He was now able to move his arms and legs without assistance, and while strength was returning quickly to his legs standing was not possible yet. Pain medications were no longer needed since the nagging pain in his limbs was beginning to dissipate a little more each day. He ached a little after therapy each day but only for a short while as he became stronger over time.

Bob Halstead had been in to visit once this week and to tell Don he had readied a room at his place for him to stay while he recuperated. There would also be room for Jenny. He had not heard from Tony or the ICE agent but said he was going to stop at Tony's office while he was in the city. Bob said he had finished cleaning and storing all his camp gear and equipment for the winter. The process would begin again early in the spring to ready the camps for spring bear hunting.

Vic Lamar was now out of the hospital and temporarily living in Bob Halstead's home. The investigation into the shooting at the Jack Rabbit Hills camp had been completed and it was determined both Vic and Bob had acted in self-defense, but the reason for the attack had not been confirmed. Tony and Greg, the ICE agent, were continuing to investigate that aspect of the case.

In the lower 48 states Jenny Halstead and her now very good friend Lindsy Gibson were visiting Yellowstone National Park. They planned to see all the sights in the park before leaving in the motorhome to drive south toward Zion National Park in Utah. Jenny was keeping a journal of her trip in addition to doing her daily school studies as they traveled the highways of America.

One person in the Halstead case was not relaxed but was very busy learning his way around Anchorage and the surrounding areas. Paul Milan proved to be a restless and intense individual. His guide during this time was Chin, the security man from the office. The two men spent the first two days driving all the streets and roads around Anchorage, Palmer, Wasilla, and the Sutton vicinity. Milan had obtained a driver's license, and after the second day he began to do the driving to get used to the traffic flow and habits of local drivers.

He also spent many hours in the office studying the files that had accumulated concerning the attack on Don Halstead. He learned that this case had snowballed from a simple suspicion into an avalanche of death and loss. This Halstead person was hired as a business agent to oversee all the other agents in this company. These included agents in Japan, Hawaii, all the Pacific Islands, and the west coast of the United States. The office in the Philippines was managed by this office because of the number of laborers coming here to work in the commercial fishing industry. Paul knew from his work in Jakarta that young Filipino girls were a major portion of the prostitution and slavery trade. These young girls were usually sold to the union by their own families. Though it was not documented in the files he knew this illegal human trade accounted for a high percentage of the annual revenue generated by the labor unions.

Paul had made a name in his short time here for being a hard-working person, keeping early to late hours every day, never taking a day off and never making a joke. The two security men in the office were unable to form any type of social relationship with the new boss. This morning he called for a meeting in the office to discuss the case and make a plan for ending the need for spending more time justifying what had already been done. It seemed beyond his comprehension that four men from his security team had died in pursuit of information that could not be verified.

To Milan, this had gotten out of hand because the local superintendent had hired Don Halstead, someone outside the company, to supervise local managers around the Pacific Rim. Since this new man knew nothing of the covert activities of the union he was prone to asking embarrassing questions about things he was not supposed to know about. In the mind of Paul Milan this was a gigantic error on the part of the local boss. An outsider should never have been allowed to come into contact with the information he would learn in the performance of his daily duties as a supervisor. The more he studied the problem the less he believed Don Halstead had learned anything about the human trafficking business, but the paranoia of the man who had hired him was at fault. All that aside, it was still his problem to correct; a job at which he was very good.

When the meeting convened there was a tall pile of file folders on the table in front of him. "Mr. Chin, as you know we are very short-handed in this office. Therefore, some of the tasks I will be assigning to a single security officer would ordinarily be handled by two men. That being the case the tasks become more dangerous. We have lost too many men already and I don't want to lose any more. If either of you senses a threat you are to cease for the moment and call me." Milan stared coldly at his men.

"Mr. Hua, I have not had time to work with you yet, but I must assume you are a competent officer, but I repeat, take no chances," Milan continued. "This situation was started to verify an error made by management. Each step taken has deepened this error. We will now make a policy change regarding individual decision making. All actions will be approved by me and not dictated by managers of other departments in this company. Is that understood?"

Both Chin and Hua had puzzled looks on their faces. "Are you saying that if Mr. Wei orders us to do something we are to refuse?" asked Hua.

"That is exactly what I'm saying. You only follow orders given by me and me alone. Our loss of personnel has come from not following that rule. I don't want to lose any more officers. I will let Mr. Wei know of my orders." Milan could see the men here were not used to disobeying Mr. Wei. "As we discuss the case at this point you will see the need for this change."

Chin was both curious and relieved by the order. "Two of the men from this office were killed at the hospital by orders given by Mr. Wei. Li Tan gave the orders, but they came from Mr. Wei. I think this is a very wise decision. Thank you, Mr. Milan."

"I have read the files and I believe the order to deal with the business agent, Halstead, came directly from Mr. Wei. You will find I learn about a potential victim before I attack him. This was not done by Mr. Li Tan. Many mistakes were made, and I don't intend to make any more of them. Now, let's get down to business."

Milan began taking the files from the stack and began questioning every aspect of them. If he asked a question and the answer was 'we don't know', the officers took notes and were ordered to find out. The meeting lasted into the evening hours until the last file was reviewed. At the end he looked at the two men across the table. "You can see I have many questions. Attention to these details is what has kept me alive all these years. I intend to stay alive for many more years and I intend to do it by keeping my men, you two, alive as well. Now let's call it a day and start to get the information we need first thing in the morning."

Chin and Hua left the office and Paul put the files back in the drawers they had come from before leaving the office for the night, all the while pondering whether to meet with Ang Wei about his conclusions in this matter. Milan was aware of the fact Mr. Wei didn't like to be confronted or challenged about anything, let alone be accused of causing the problem.

The following morning he considered the question again and again decided such a meeting with Wei would not end well. He sat at his desk making a plan for what to do next and waited for his two officers to come to the office. They entered on time and seated themselves at the conference table to wait for instructions by Paul Milan.

Milan came to the table with a legal pad in hand. "Good morning, men," he commented as he sat. "I have two areas I want you to look into today. The first is of the past. Mr. Hua, I want you to learn everything you can about Don Halstead, our injured business agent. Specifically, I want to know what was the justification for the attack on Halstead? What information prompted such an order? I want to know why this happened to begin with. I want you to examine every fact. Do you understand your assignment?"

Hua was making notes, but said, "Yes sir, I understand."

"The other side of this question has to do with the future and how to go about dealing with it. Mr. Chin, this will be your assignment. I want to know where the daughter is at this time. My information says she has disappeared, and I want to know where she is at every minute. This is in case we need to use her as leverage. We will need to know the family habits and friends. I understand the business agent has a brother who is a hunting and fishing guide. I want him checked out as well. I will check with personnel and see if there are any local security people we can use to fill the empty spots on our roster. I will get you help as quickly as possible. Any other questions or comments?" asked Milan. There were none and the meeting was over.

Greg Beason had called to tell Tony he was on the way over to give him some new information. A half hour later he came into Tony's small office.

"Good morning, Greg. What's the big news?" he asked.

"Do you remember the name Li Tan, the head of security for AmerAsian Labor Union?" he questioned.

"Sure, a pompous little guy, boss of the men who kidnapped and beat Don Halstead. Why?"

"I just had a notification from Interpol saying his body has been shipped to Jakarta. There was no paperwork with the body, only a delivery address. Interpol did an autopsy on the body and determined the cause of death was a small caliber bullet to the right side of his brain. They said it looked self-inflicted, but that was still being investigated. The point, there has been no notification of his death by either his family or the corporation. The shipping notice said it was shipped from Anchorage, Alaska but with no return address." Greg smiled. "Does that seem a little odd to you?"

Now Tony was smiling. "It sure does," he replied. "I think it may be time for me to pay a visit to the union offices and have a talk with Mr. Wei in an official capacity this time."

"Want some company?" asked Greg.

"Sure. You can ask all the embarrassing questions." Tony picked up his hat and put it on. "I have to tell the major where I'm going. Let's go."

The two officers stepped into the main office lobby without advance notice and asked to see Mr. Ang Wei. This demand flustered the receptionist very badly. After stuttering a few times at the uniformed Lieutenant Anthony Harrison, she picked up the office phone and called her boss. When she hung up the phone she stood and said, "Please follow me to Mr. Wei's office."

They followed her to Wei's office, and she opened the door for the two men. Wei was at his desk. "Call Paul Milan to my office, please," he ordered. She closed the door behind her and went to her desk.

Wei stared at Tony. "You were not a trooper the last time we met," commented the union boss.

"I was conducting an investigation on my last visit and could not disclose my identity," explained Tony.

"I see," said Wei. "You were investigating our company?"

"I'm sorry, but I can't tell you that at this time." Tony could play the coy game with Wei.

"I have sent for my security chief to join this meeting if you don't mind. We will save further discussion until he arrives. It will only be a moment." Wei looked back at the top of his desk and studied the papers there. He said nothing until the door opened again and a tall, red haired man entered. Wei looked up and smiled, "Gentlemen this is Mr. Paul Milan, my new head of security." Milan stepped forward and offered his hand. Both Tony and Greg shook it.

"May I ask what this is about?" asked Milan.

Tony skipped over the question saying, "You're new here, aren't you? It seems there was another gentleman in charge of security the last time I visited this office."

"Yes, I have only just arrived in the past few days. Mr. Li Tan, the previous security chief, left rather suddenly and I was chosen to replace him."

"That is a coincidence; we're here to talk about Mr. Li Tan. We have located him in Jakarta. It seems he must have died and someone shipped his body back to Indonesia without any paperwork. We're here to find out why." Tony studied the eyes of the new security chief for any indication he knew about this.

"I'm sorry, but I never met the other security chief, and I cannot give you any information about his leaving the labor union. I am told he was very good at his job and two of his men still work for me. Can you tell me who claimed the shipment in Jakarta?"

"That's a strange thing," commented Greg. "The shipment was unclaimed and there was an odor coming from the container. It was opened by the police and there was a body inside. The police have identified the body and learned the cause of death was a bullet to the head. We are trying to determine if it was murder or a self-inflicted wound. Can you shed any light on his death?"

"I'm sorry, but as I said, I never met Mr. Tan. He left before I came to Alaska." Milan was convincing in his statement. "Perhaps Mr. Wei can tell you what happened."

The three men all turned to the desk where Wei was seated.

"What about it, Mr. Wei? Can you add anything about his death?" asked Beason.

"I'm, sorry to say I cannot. He failed to come to work and I could not reach him; therefore, I called the home office for a replacement and they sent me Mr. Milan. Mr. Milan is doing an excellent job, by the way. If you have further need for information, I suggest you contact him in the security office. Good day, gentlemen." With that curt dismissal the three men were sent out of the office by the executive.

When they were back in the patrol car Tony asked, "Well, Greg, what did we learn?"

"This is a cover-up and we need to learn why."

"I thought you would say something like that," replied Tony. "Want some lunch?"

Chapter 22

It was two days later when another meeting took place in the security offices of the labor union. Paul Milan called the meeting to follow up on the tasks he had assigned his two security officers. Milan was seated at the head of the large conference table with the two officers seated side by side to his right.

"I will begin with you, Mr. Hua. I asked you to investigate the circumstances surrounding the attack on the business agent, Don Halstead. Were you able to complete the task successfully?" asked the security chief.

"I believe I have recovered all the facts available, sir, but I can give you a report on what I have learned to this point," stated Hua.

"Have you reached any personal conclusions?" asked Milan.

There was a short pause before he answered. "Yes, sir, I will give you the facts I have learned and if you wish I can give you my opinion of the result."

"That is exactly what I want, Mr. Hua. Please continue."

Hua issued a huge sigh before continuing, "I can provide dates and times for all these meetings if you wish to have them for the files." After another huge sigh, "Mr. Li Tan was summoned to a meeting with Mr. Wei in the CEO's office. He came from that meeting and scheduled a meeting with the security staff. I was present at this meeting, as was Mr. Chang. During this meeting we discussed ways to get information from the new business agent. Mr. Li Tan revealed he had information that Don Halstead was a spy for another labor union. Li Tan was adamant that we get the truth from Halstead any way we needed.

That is exactly what we did. The four of us took Halstead to a warehouse and used extreme measures to get him to confess his part in a scheme to spy on the AmerAsian Labor Union. He insisted he did no such thing. As it became late and he gave us no further information, he was seriously injured from the interrogation, so we took him to a remote spot and clubbed him to death, or at least we thought he was dead. We left him there and someone found him. He was examined by police and found not to be dead, but severely injured. We reported back to Mr. Tan that we obtained no information about his spying on our company.

Mr. Halstead was taken to the hospital and placed in ICU under a fictitious name. We have associates working in the hospital and it was reported to us he was alive. Li Tan ordered Mr. Chang and Mr. Aluan to silence him. They were discovered entering the hospital and stopped by hospital security. Our men engaged in a short fight and took one of the security policemen's gun and fired a shot, but the other security officers killed them both. Mr. Halstead has not been seen since, but we suspect he is alive and in another part of the hospital under 24-hour guard. Those are the facts as I am able to gather them."

"Very good report, Mr. Hua," said Milan. "Now I want to hear what you have deduced from these documented facts. I want your best opinion."

Again, another long sigh, "You may not like what I think, sir," said Hua.

"I will evaluate and make my own opinions. I asked for your best assessment of the facts. I want you to give me yours."

Hua looked at his partner, Mr. Chin, then back at their boss. "Very good, sir. It is my opinion that Mr. Wei called Li Tan to his office and asked him to interrogate the new business agent out of personal paranoia. For some reason he didn't trust Halstead and wanted Li Tan to get the truth from him. My personal feeling is that there was no truth in the suspicion. No man could have taken what we did to that man without talking. As I said, we thought we had killed him.

After the incident and our men were lost, Li Tan became sullen. I think he knew Mr. Wei was going to replace him. Li Tan was a proud man and after considering his options he killed himself. Mr. Wei had people come in and remove Li Tan's car and crate up his body to be shipped to headquarters in Indonesia. I do not know the reasoning behind the fear Mr. Wei had, but we found nothing to justify any part of this act." Hua stared at the new security chief. Again, sir, this is only my personal opinion."

"I appreciate your candor, Mr. Hua. For what it's worth I agree with almost all of what you have said here today. I will document your findings in the files, but your personal assessments will remain between us."

Milan made notes on a pad before turning to Mr. Chin. "Your turn, Mr. Chin. What did you learn about the brother and daughter of the business agent?"

Chin glanced at Hua before speaking. "I was unable to learn the whereabouts of the daughter. Her name is Jenny Halstead. I spoke with several of her neighbors and they all seem to think she is now in the lower 48 states somewhere, but no one knows just where. As near as I can learn the move was directed by Don Halstead's brother, Bob Halstead. He is a noted big game and fishing guide here in Alaska. He is also very successful in his business. Those I spoke with and know him say he is a very strong person. He is protective of his family and a dangerous man to make angry.

We have yet to hear from the two hunters sent from the home office in Jakarta, but the rumor is that they were killed in one of Bob Halstead's camps by Halstead and his friend who worked with him. I have heard of the men sent to hunt with Halstead and they have a reputation of being very successful in their line of work. He has closed his camps for the season and is now at his home near Soldotna, Alaska. He comes to Anchorage on a regular basis to visit his brother in the hospital. Halstead leads a quiet life and is not married nor does he date a steady girlfriend. He is also good friends with an Alaska State Trooper stationed here in Anchorage."

"I'll wager he is the trooper I met here in our office a few days ago. I think he, too, is a dangerous man to make angry." Paul Milan made more notes before asking Chin another question. "Tell me, Mr. Chin, what is your personal assessment from what you have learned about Bob Halstead?"

"Like Mr. Hua I can only give you my opinion on the matter, but that opinion says to be very careful of Bob Halstead. I think he is a very cautious man and will do whatever it takes to protect his family. That means his brother and his niece, Jenny Halstead. I find it easy to believe he and his friend were capable of getting the best of the professionals assigned to get Bob Halstead while on their hunting trip. I believe if we are to make a move on either of the Halstead brothers we need to get Bob first and quickly. Again, this is only my personal opinion, sir."

"We cannot let this situation linger much longer," commented Milan. "I will take all your comments into account when making my decision about how to go about resolving our dilemma. I thank the both of you for your comments and honesty with me. I will get back with you as soon as I can with an answer as to what to do. I want to think about a plan that will not jeopardize the company or any of our personnel. And speaking of personnel, we will be hiring two new men for this office, but their responsibilities will be limited to security in this building They will be in and out of this office, but they are not to learn what we do outside this office. Do you understand?"

"Of course," agreed both men.

"Take the rest of the day off and come to see me in the morning. I will try to have a plan by then. The two of you did a good job on this and I thank you." Now it was up to Milan to decide what course of action to take.

Milan remained in the office until after eight in the evening. His decision would require careful planning for which he referred again and again to the notes and files in his office. He considered both the facts and the opinions presented by his men. Finally, he closed the office and went to his apartment for the night.

Early the following morning he was back at his desk making notes for the 9:00 a.m. meeting with Chin and Hua. Once they were briefed, he would have a meeting with Mr. Wei. At precisely nine o'clock the two men entered the conference room.

"Do you men want coffee while we talk?" asked Milan. Both men refused. "I want you both to know I found great value in the reports you gave me yesterday. My course of action is based on those reports. For your own safety I want the two of you to work together on this. I think you are both correct in your assessments, both factually and personally. I want you to find where Bob Halstead lives and where his hunting camps are located. I agree he is a dangerous man. I do not agree he should be eliminated just yet. It could lead to unwanted attention for us. I want the two of you to find his home and give him a warning he will understand. Do either of you fly?"

Chin held up a hand. "Yes, sir, I'm a licensed pilot and I have a small plane to get us to his camps."

"Good, that simplifies things a little. I suggest you find a time when he is gone from his home and destroy his airplane. Not his home, just his airplane. He should take this warning seriously, but if not, we may need to eliminate him. I also want you to find one of his camps and burn it to the ground. I suggest you find the closest one to save time and effort."

"He may not take kindly to this much loss," advised Hua.

"In that case we will eliminate him, but we will warn him with these losses," said Milan. "I am meeting with Mr. Wei this morning to let him know what we are doing. The two of you can get on with the project when we end this meeting. Be very careful."

The drive to Halstead's home would take nearly three hours. Another hour was needed to gather the equipment they would need for the first part of the operation, burning Halstead's airplane. After changing into work clothes they left town in a rented pickup truck.

Milan called the receptionist in Mr. Wei's outer office to let her know he wanted a meeting with the boss. She said she would arrange a time for him to come to the office. Minutes later she called to say Mr. Wei would see him right away and to come to the office now.

Paul Milan gathered a thick file folder and a large yellow legal pad and walked to the other end of the long hallway where the executive offices were located. Inside he smiled at the receptionist.

"Good morning, sir," she said pleasantly. "Mr. Wei is expecting you."

Milan nodded and smiled at the girl, turned, and walked purposefully toward the door to the inner office of the boss. Inside he closed the door quietly and moved toward the large desk near the rear of the room. The view from the office windows was spectacular this morning. Wei did not look up from his work, giving Milan the feeling that this was his form of power play. He stood in front of the desk for several seconds until Wei glanced up and motioned for him to sit in the large leather chair in front of the desk, but he continued to work for several more seconds before saying anything to the security man.

"Sorry, Mr. Milan, but I am very busy these days. What is so important you must have a meeting first thing this morning?" asked the executive.

Milan held up the file in his hand. "I have completed my investigation of the Halstead mess and I'm here to give you a report."

"Security is your responsibility, Mr. Milan. I have no need to know what you do at the other end of the hallway. That is, unless it affects me, my office, and the operations at this end of the hall. Please don't waste my time."

Milan's irritation was written on his face. "It is obvious to me that you don't fully understand my position here, sir. First of all, I don't work for you. My position in this office is equal to yours. I report to the headquarters of the company and the board of directors, not to you. I am here this morning to update you on what we intend to do next and to summarize my suspicions regarding what has taken place up to this point. Some of these suspicions involve you and some of your decisions. Would you rather hear it from me, or do you want me to send it to the home office and let them discuss it with you?"

"Your attitude is very presumptuous, Mr. Milan. You must remember I do have the power to fire you and send you back to the home office." Now Wei was showing his anger.

"That, Mr. Wei, is an error in your thinking. I was sent here to fix a problem which I believe you created. I have the authority to send you to Jakarta today. It is not my intent to do that unless you fail to listen and correct some of your policies and practices. If you doubt my word you may call the board chairman and ask him who is the real authority here? Don't challenge me, Mr. Wei. You will lose."

Ang Wei was astounded by both the news and the attitude of the security chief. He spoke with anxiety in his voice. "What is it you have to say, Milan?"

Paul opened the file folder he had placed on the front edge of the huge desk and began to review the entire case of Don Halstead and the related facts up until today. This included his order for the burning of Bob Halstead's airplane and his remote camp. Wei sat silently listening to the entire presentation.

"All that is very interesting, sir, but why do you think I created this problem?" asked Wei.

"I have reviewed this situation and every fact I could gather. All indications are that you, in your authoritarian way, created the situation causing life to become more than Mr. Li Tan could endure and he shot himself to get away. I can find no indication your new business agent, Don Halstead, was spying on the company or passing information to anyone. This leads me to believe you have become so paranoid you trust no one. I will explain one more time, you are no longer an autonomous authority here. The home office and the governing board sent me here to correct some of your management practices. You can listen and make these changes, or I will recommend we change the CEO in charge of AmerAsian Labor Union."

Ang Wei was now slumped in his chair. "I will check with the board of directors and confirm what you have said, but I cannot tolerate your attitude. Leave me alone now. I shall make a call to the board chairman."

"I will be in my office, sir, responded the security chief. Come to my office when you confirm my authority. We will discuss this further as well as outline the future of this agency." Paul stood, gathered his file and legal pad from the desktop, and walked from the room leaving Wei to ponder his fate.

Chapter 23

After Paul Milan left his office Ang Wei sat in his chair staring out the windows at the Chugach Mountains towering over the city. He sat in that pose for nearly two hours attempting to reconcile his conversation with Milan. He was confused and angry. His anxiety level was beyond measure. Milan had guessed what no one else had suspected: Wei ordered Li Tan to attack Don Halstead. Milan had also guessed the reason for the attack. Ang Wei had suspected Halstead was spying, but not for another labor union but for the home office and the board of directors. Every CEO skimmed a little cash from the total profits for extra monies to help with the cost of running an office. Wei, however, had taken more than a little from his vast collections. Since his area was so vast he accepted cash payments from members. This cash was paid in China yuan, Japan yen, Philippine peso, Tia baht as well as the U.S. dollar. His large accounting department deducted a "service fee" from all foreign currencies which were deposited in a bank in Jakarta in an account registered to a fictitious company owned by Ang Wei.

As he sat at his desk he pondered the problem of being able to retire and spend the enormous amount of cash he had amassed. Wei didn't know what Milan had told the governing board or exactly how much he really knew or if he only suspected. How to go about getting to the bottom of this dilemma was a problem he must solve immediately. He picked up the office telephone and ordered the receptionist to get the chairman of the board of directors on the phone. He knew it would not be office hours in Jakarta, but this had turned into an emergency for him.

Wei picked up the telephone and was met by the sleepy voice of his immediate supervisor and chairman of the board of directors. Both men spoke in the local Jakarta dialect of Betawi language, the dialect was Cocos Malay. "Sorry to have awakened you, Mr. Wang, but a situation has arisen with which I must deal immediately. It concerns Mr. Paul Milan and his mission here in Anchorage, Alaska. He has informed me he does not take his orders from me. Can that be true?" asked Wei.

There was a moment of silence before the chairman answered. "Yes and no, Ang. He was sent there to clean up a tragic situation that had gotten out of hand. It is true he has authority over you, but he was instructed not to interfere with your operating the union unless you were a part of the problem he was sent to resolve. Tell me, has he interfered with your position as head of the labor union?"

"Not exactly, but he has threatened me and told me he didn't work for me and would not take my orders. Surely this is insubordination in the highest order."

"Don't worry about him, Ang. Just stay out of his way and let him finish his work and I will replace him when he has finished. You know we demand excellence from our district managers and, up until now, you have performed admirably. I hope you are not losing control of your office." Wang was making a carefully veiled threat.

"My office is functioning perfectly, Mr. Wang. I am calling because I do not take kindly to being told I am not in charge of my own office. If this practice is going to continue, I will demand either he or I be replaced. Right now I am considering retirement."

Wang could hear the anger in Ang Wei's voice. "Calm yourself, Ang. I will look into it in the morning. I am going back to bed now. Good night."

The line went dead and Wei sat holding the hand set for a long moment before hanging it up again.

Once more he sat staring at the mountains, thinking about what to do. He finally turned around and picked up the office phone again. He ordered the girl at the front desk to tell the security chief to return to this office.

Less than two minutes later she opened the door and stepped into the office. "What is it?" demanded Wei.

"I don't really know how to tell you this sir, but Mr. Milan said he didn't have time to come to your office, but he would make time for you if you came to his. I'm sorry sir, but that was his reply to my call."

Wei realized, like the Dall sheep on the mountain, Milan was lowering his head for another challenge in this head-butting contest for control.

"I understand. I will see him later," replied Wei, seething with anger. When he calmed down a little he decided not to press the issue until later when he was more prepared to deal with the dangerous Irishman.

On the other side of Anchorage Bob Halstead and Vic Lamar were leaving the hospital after visiting Don who was improving quickly now. Vic, too, was mending as his shoulder wound began to heal. He could move his arm, though not in a full range of motion yet. The two men were walking from the main entrance of the hospital to the parking lot across the street when Bob's cell phone rang.

"Halstead Guide Service," he answered.

"Bob this is Tony Harrison. I just had a call from the Soldotna office and they told me there had been a fire at your place. It looks like someone torched your airplane. The investigators are there now."

"How did it start, Tony?"

"The investigator said it looked deliberate, but that's as much as I know right now."

"OK, Tony. Vic and I are just leaving the hospital and I'm headed home now. It will take me about two and a half hours if the traffic isn't too bad. Tell your investigator I'll be out of cell phone range most of the trip, but he can call me if he can reach me. By the way, how is the rest of my property?"

"I was told the only damage was to the Cessna, but it was totally destroyed. I'll talk with you later. I want you to take care driving home." Tony was worried the guide would put his foot to the floor all the way down the 150 mile trip.

Tony had been partially justified in his worry as Bob broke every speed law from Anchorage to his home. When he drove into the driveway in front of his home black smoke was still drifting off the charred remains of his aircraft. He leapt from the cab of his truck and ran to where the investigator was making notes and taking pictures.

The trooper looked up at the sound of a vehicle on the property and saw Bob approaching. "Are you Bob Halstead?" he asked.

"Yes, and the other man behind me is Vic Lamar. He worked for me this fall. Is it OK if I take some pictures right now?"

"Sure, but please don't move or touch anything just yet. I haven't finished taking pictures and documenting all the damage. Do you have any idea who may have done this to your plane?" The trooper continued to make notes while talking.

"I have a suspicion, but there is no way to prove it. I assume Tony Harrison told you about my brother being beaten and left for dead?" asked Bob.

"Yes, he told me. Do you think this was done by the same people?"

"I'd bet money on it, but we still don't know who it was. They even attacked my brother in the hospital. Hospital security was on guard and killed both the men. They never got to my brother, but he is still in the hospital under 24-hour guard. I don't know why they want me out of the way, but this is the second time they have attacked me. Last time was in one of my hunting camps and they shot my friend Vic in the left shoulder. He and I were able to take them out before they could get us." Bob was becoming angry while talking and the trooper saw it coming.

"Easy, Bob, I know this is a difficult time and you have suffered some great losses, but you have to leave the investigating and retribution to the law. Getting angry can only get you into trouble. Why don't you and your friend go into the house and wait until I finish my work. I'll come inside to talk with you when I finish."

Bob threw up his hands and turned to walk toward the house with Vic following. An hour later the trooper knocked on the back door. Bob invited him inside. The three men sat at the kitchen table.

"Is your airplane insured?" asked the trooper.

"Yes, but I don't know if this will be covered. I'll call them in a while to ask that question," answered Bob.

"Would you mind calling to get an answer?" asked the trooper. "I would like to have the information for my report."

Bob stood and walked to his desk in the dining area. He searched a drawer for a business card with the phone number of the insurance agent. Bob spoke with the agent a few moments and then stood to wait while the agent looked up the policy. He finally came back on the line and gave him the information. Bob wrote it all down on a note pad on his desk. He thanked the agent and returned to the kitchen table with his notepad.

"Here. This card has the name and number of my insurance agent. He said I was covered, but if it was arson they would investigate and attempt to find the arsonist and recover the amount from him. The agent, Jim Westmore, wants you to call him."

"Thank you, Mr. Halstead. I'll get out of your hair now. I advise you again that this is a trooper matter and you should leave the investigating up to us." He reached into a pocket in the back of his notebook and came out with a card with his name and office number. "I promise to call you if I find anything on the man or men who did this. I'm sorry for your loss, sir." He shook hands with Bob and walked to his trooper car.

Bob sat at the table rubbing his temples and sipping his cup of half-warm coffee.

"Well, Bob, what are we going to do?" asked Vic.

"I don't know, Vic, I really don't know. I ..." at that moment the telephone rang. He picked it up and answered. It was Tony.

"Bob, Tony. I just had a call from a federal wildlife officer and he reported your camp on the west side is on fire. They called a crew to put it out, but he said they were only to stop the fire from spreading to the woods and brush surrounding the site. Do you want me to come down and pick you up and take you to the camp?"

Bob was dumbstruck. "That does it, Tony. You had better stay out of my way now. I'm going after these people and when I find them it won't be pretty. From now on there are no rules."

"You can't go off angry like this, Bob. Let the troopers take care of it. I realize this has become personal for both sides, but you have to leave it to us."

"I'll tell you what you can do for me, Tony. Go down to that office building and warn those criminals there will be no appeals from my legal decisions." With that curt reply he slammed down the telephone and turned to Vic.

"How do you feel about going to war, Vic?" he asked.

"What's happened now?" asked the wounded Vic.

Bob explained the last phone conversation with Tony. "I'm going to rent a plane from my neighbor and go over to help fight the fire and salvage as much as possible. If you want to help you can go to the shed and gather some sleeping bags and a food box. I'll gather some firepower in case we need to defend ourselves. Is a .45 auto Colt OK for you?"

"You bet, Bob. I'll meet you at the truck."

Bob called his neighbor who also owned a Cessna 185 and often rented it to Bob when his needed repairs or an annual inspection on his own plane. He explained what had happened at his camp and at his home strip. The neighbor agreed to rent the plane to Bob. Once the deal was set he picked up two .45 Colts and two .338 Winchester Magnum rifles to take along on the trip. With his and Vic's guns the same it would cut down on the variety of ammunition they would need to carry. Vic had chosen well for a food box on an emergency trip. Everything was loaded into the back of the truck and they climbed in to drive the mile to the other airstrip.

"Are you sure you want to be involved in this adventure, Vic?" asked Bob Halstead.

"I feel they owe me a little revenge, too," he replied.

The owner of the rented Cessna met them at the grass airstrip to give them some help loading. "She's gassed up and ready to fly. There are a couple of cans of oil in the baggage compartment, but you shouldn't need them. Just bring her back in one piece along with yourselves."

Bob made his preflight inspection and checked the fuel and oil even though he had been told they were full. Vic climbed into the cabin and slid to the passenger side to lock his safety harness. Bob shook hands with his neighbor and climbed in, fastened his seat belt, and started the engine. With a wave of his hand he said goodbye to the airplane owner and pressed the throttle forward, taking off directly down the short grass airstrip. Once in the air he turned west toward the inlet and climbed to 5,500 feet.

Approaching the west shoreline they could see smoke rising from the vicinity of his fish camp a few miles ahead. Two twin Otter aircraft were parked on his airstrip and men were attacking the fire lines behind the cabin which had been partially burned. Bob circled once and landed to park near the larger twin engine airplanes.

As they climbed out of the Cessna a man in firefighter garb approached. "Are you Halstead?" he shouted.

"Yes, that's me," Bob called back.

"I'm Dave and I'm the crew chief here. There are shovels and polaskis (firefighting axes) over by the Otter. We are almost contained on the fire line, but if I were you, I would check to be sure there are no smoldering embers in the cabin. We used a pump and hose to fight the fire in the structure, but when it looked to be safe we moved it to the grass and brush. The wind helped us a little and kept the fire pushed toward the river instead of it travelling into the wooded area out back. We should finish up here in about an hour. I'll come talk with you before we load up and leave."

"Thanks, Dave. If you don't need us on the line we'll stay here and see what we can salvage at the camp." The fire captain waved and marched back to where his men were mopping up the smoking grass and brush.

An hour later the fire crews picked up their gear and loaded up for the trip back to Anchorage. The fire captain gave Bob a business card and asked him to call him the next time he was in town. Bob and Vic stood and watched the two larger planes take off to the north.

"Well, pardner, let's try to get this place closed up so we can sleep tonight. By the way, Vic, are you still of a mind to go all the way with me on this?"

"I'm with you up to the point you want to drop bombs on the office building in Anchorage. I have a hole in my shoulder given by them and I'm kinda mad about it. Yeah, I'm in.

Chapter 24

The following morning the two men did their best to patch the back wall of the cabin and make it sound enough to keep the bears out of the structure. They found some old chain link fencing and nailed it over the temporary rear wall of the cabin. Bob surveyed his work and decided it was as good as they could make it for now, but he would have to bring new materials to repair the rear of the cabin before next season.

"OK, Vic, let's load up and get out of here. I'll call Tony and have him meet us at Merrill Field. That is if he is still talking to me. I treated him pretty badly the last time I talked to him." Bob Halstead was not the kind of man who abused friendship but had been angry at the losses he had suffered in a few short hours. He dialed Tony Harrison's cell phone.

"Harrison," was the short answer.

"Are you still speaking to me, Tony?" asked Bob.

"Oh, hi Bob, sure. You know I never stay mad at you for long. Where are you?"

"Vic and I are at the west side camp. The fire did a lot of damage to the cabin, but we were able to patch it up for now. We're getting ready to take off and I thought I would like to meet with you at Merrill Field if you have time. I need more information before I decide what I'm going to do next. Can you meet us there?"

"I have a meeting in ten minutes that will last almost an hour, but I can be there after I finish. Is that soon enough?" asked the trooper.

"That will be great, Tony. How about Vic and I buy you lunch at the Olive Garden on that side of town?"

"It will take you almost that long to get here anyway. See you for lunch."

Bob turned to his new partner, "Tell me Vic, do you have any ideas about how to get these crooks? They already disabled my brother and shot you. I don't want any more damage on our side of the ledger."

Vic smiled, "I'm relieved you aren't going to go into the office building with guns blazing. I prefer to be a little more subtle than that. We will be meeting with Tony and he has a lot more information than we do. We might have a better plan if we wait until we have more facts."

"Good idea, pardner, let's load up and get to town."

An hour later they touched down on the north/south runway, landing to the south into the slight breeze. Bob taxied to the transient parking area and saw the state patrol car coming their way.

Tony got out of his patrol car to greet the men. "How are you doing, Vic? Is the shoulder getting healed up?" he asked as he reached out to shake hands with Vic.

"Sorry I blew up on you yesterday, Tony. You didn't deserve to be treated that way." Now he reached out to shake hands with the trooper.

"Forget it, Bob, but you have to buy lunch. Climb in and we'll go." Tony was chuckling as he climbed into the driver seat.

At the restaurant they were shown to a booth away from most of the crowd as they requested for privacy sake. They were given menus and asked what they wanted to drink. They waited for the server to step away before speaking again.

Tony spoke first. "We confirmed the identity and the employer of the bodies we shipped back from the Peninsula. They used their real names when they booked with you. They listed the parent company of all those labor union companies as the employer. The company has yet to get back to me with any conversation about the men. I'm having Interpol police pay them a visit and ask questions directly, but again that hasn't happened yet. Another development is that the head of the local union security, Mr. Li Tan turned up in Jakarta in a box with a hole in his head. It looked like suicide, but with all the other deaths in this case he could have had some help. I hear there is a new head of security here now, an Irishman with a reputation and a police record in Europe."

"It sounds as though you've been busy on this investigation, Tony," commented Halstead. Just then the server arrived at their booth with a tray of soft drinks, took their orders and headed to the food prep kitchen.

"I stopped by the hospital to see Don and the doctor told me he would release the patient if he had a place to go where he could have some minimal care. I said I would ask you about taking him to your place. He's getting out of his wheelchair and walking some. While not running a marathon yet, he is up and walking around. He can only lift a few pounds, but he can dress and eat on his own now."

"That's good news, Tony; How soon will it be until he's released?"

"You will have to ask the doctor about that." Tony chewed on his food a moment just after it had arrived, before speaking again. "Bob, I don't mean to preach to you, but I'm worried about you trying to get even on your own. I'd like to know what you plan to do?"

"The first thing is to meet with my insurance agent and find out what I have to do to get paid for my airplane. I have a lot of flying to do and I need another plane as soon as possible. That's the first thing on my list. The second is to get prepared. The only reason Vic and I survived the attack at Jack Rabbit Hills was that we had an idea it was coming and were prepared. This new attack, I think, is a warning. These folks don't intend to quit. I plan to be ready when they come again. I don't plan to attack them, but I fully intend to defend myself, Vic and my property. Those are my rights and I fully intend to exercise them." There was deep anger in Bob's voice.

Tony set his fork aside and wiped his face with a cloth napkin. "I can't blame you for being angry, Bob, but I do have to warn you once again. Leave the police work up to us. I am asking this as a friend. I don't want to have to arrest you."

"Do you have time to drop Vic and me off at the hospital? I can get a cab back to the airport." Bob didn't want to comment on the warning he had just been handed. "I have to get to the insurance company before they close today."

"Thanks for lunch. I'll drop the two of you at the hospital," said Tony in an unfriendly tone.

After a short visit with Don and a conversation with Don's doctor, Bob and Vic returned to Merrill Field and flew back to Bob's private airstrip. He had not lied to Tony, he really did need to meet with his insurance agent. Once the airplane was parked Bob asked Vic to keep an eye on the place while he went to town.

"Keep that .45 handy, Vic. Call me if you need me." Bob was in the office of the insurance agent for almost two hours. The final value of the burned Cessna was still to be determined, but the pictures showed the extent of the damages and his logbooks spoke to the condition of the airplane. Insurance adjusters have a phobia about paying full amount out on any casualty claim and this case would result in court time before the claim was paid. Bob wasn't happy about the delay and needed to find another Cessna 185 in order to complete closing all his camps. He also submitted a claim for the cost of the rental plane he was using.

As for the fire at the west side camp he was out of luck and the cost out of pocket. He had been unable to insure the property or cabin because of the remote location. Bob realized he was going to have to dig deep into his savings to repair all the damages even if the insurance company paid him the full value of the Cessna. The agent finally finished asking questions and making phone calls. He told Halstead he should have an answer and a check for him by the end of next week.

Frustrated and angry he drove back to his home. A trooper patrol car was parked in the drive when he arrived. When he entered the house he saw Vic and the trooper who had investigated the burned airplane sitting at the kitchen table drinking coffee.

"Have you caught the arsonist yet?" asked Bob.

The trooper looked up at Bob and smiled, "Not yet, but we have some leads and identified the manufacturer of the road flares used to set fire to the plane. We also found remnants of a five gallon gas can which we sent to the lab. They have identified the contents as car gas, not avgas. The can is common at all the big box stores and we can't trace it, but the flares were bought at a safety equipment outlet in Anchorage. The clerk said she didn't sell many of them and remembered the sale. The men paid with a credit card and she was able to look up the name and address of the buyer. He works for AmerAsian Labor Union in Anchorage. I have passed this info on to State Trooper Lieutenant Harrison and he told me he was going down there right away." The trooper chuckled. "He also told me not to give you this information because you have a bad temper. He also told me to tell you he would contact you as soon as he had finished talking with the suspect."

Bob went to the cupboard for a clean cup and poured some of the fresh coffee. "Just so you don't think I'm a total nut case, both Vic and I have had contact with men from the labor union. The outcome was good for us, bad for them, even though Vic was shot in the shoulder in that encounter. I think we've earned and deserve a bad attitude."

"The LT told me the story and you're right; you do have a right to be angry, but our job is to arrest bad guys. We don't want you going out for revenge."

"I understand your position, but I also know these men and they won't quit. I fully intend to defend myself and Vic as well as my property and equipment. We won't be out looking for trouble, but I'm betting it will come here again and very soon. We'll be ready and we probably won't have time to call you. We survived last time because we were ready for them and we're still ready."

The trooper stood to leave. "I'm just passing on the warning from Lieutenant Harrison, but between you and me I think you're wise to take precautions."

Bob and Vic sat at the table, not speaking for a very long time. Bob looked at his partner. "Well, Vic, I think we need to get ready for a war. Let's stash the .338 rifles, one in the hangar and the other in the meat shed. We'll keep a box of ammo with each rifle. I want to put a Mossberg 12 Gauge Shotgun in each of our bedrooms and one down here in the kitchen. Carry the .45

with you all the time and keep two extra magazines in your pocket. When we finish here let's go to town and find a motion-operated camera system for the yard and driveway."

"I wish I had some C4 and some splitter cord," said Vic.

"I don't know where to get any, but we can make up a few Molotov cocktails, put them in plastic bags and stash them around," suggested Bob. "I guess it's time to get to work, then. I'll get the .338s from the plane. If you get the shotguns ready I'll take care of planting them here in the house and in the parking area.

"One in the garden shed where you keep the lawn mower might be a good idea." Vic was thinking of a defensive plan.

In Anchorage Tony had met with Paul Milan and asked for one of his men by the name of Chin. Milan admitted Mr. Chin worked for him but denied any knowledge of the man buying road flares. "I'll ask him about it when he comes back to the office in the morning," said Milan. "He and Mr. Hua are working on some business in the Wasilla area today."

"I would like to talk with the two men when they come in. Have them give me a call as soon as they're in the office. Right now I should go to the other end of the building and speak with Mr. Ang Wei." Tony spoke as he rose from his chair to leave the office.

Once the trooper was out of the door Milan called the receptionist in Wei's outer office and told her to warn the boss of the approaching trooper. She was still talking with Wei when Tony walked in and asked to see the union CEO.

"He cannot see you right now, Trooper Harrison. Perhaps you can come back tomorrow," she advised.

"Tell him this is an urgent matter and I must see him immediately." Tony spoke to her in an official and stern tone.

Again, she called her boss to inform him the trooper was not going away without seeing him. He paused a long moment before allowing her to admit him to his office.

Inside Tony greeted Mr. Wei, "We meet again, sir. I don't mean to cause a disruption in your office, but I'm investigating an arson crime and the evidence has led me to this office once again."

"What kind of evidence do you have that came from this office?" asked Wei.

"Items found at the arson scene were apparently purchased by one of your security men. He's out of the office, but I want to speak to him when he returns." Tony watched for a reaction from the big boss.

"If the items were purchased by one of the security men then you must speak with Paul Milan. He is head of our security department."

"That is another question I wanted to ask you, Mr. Wei. I've learned your previous security chief has disappeared. Is that true?" asked the trooper.

"Yes, it is true. That is why we have hired a new security chief. That is nothing unusual."

"It wouldn't be except the body of Mr. Li Tan has turned up in Jakarta, Indonesia. It would seem that if he had disappeared someone from your office would have been curious enough to file a police report, but that wasn't done. I only learned of the fate of Mr. Li Tan through a report and request for information by the international police. It seems he was not sent as a registered human body, but only a large wooden crate. It was opened by the police because of the odor emitting from the box. The examination of the body determined he had been shot in the head with a small caliber weapon. Did you know about this?" Again, Tony watched for a reaction, but this inscrutable easterner was not fazed. Tony bid Mr. Wei goodbye and left the office.

Wei had the receptionist contact Milan and ask for him to come to the office once again. A moment later the receptionist opened the office door and quietly commented that Mr. Milan again said he was too busy to come to this office. She then returned to her desk.

Wei decided to call Milan on the phone himself. When Milan answered the CEO repeated what the trooper had said and wanted to know what was going on in the security department. Milan refused to reveal any information and told Wei it was nothing he needed to worry about.

Ang Wei was now very worried about his position in the company and the lack of respect he was given by the new security chief. After much consideration he thought it was time for him to arrange his own retirement. He did not want to go back to Jakarta in a wooden crate like Mr. Li Tan.

Chapter 25

Bob Halstead and Vic Lamar were busy placing the firearms in strategic locations around the property and nearly finished when Bob's cell phone rang. It was the hospital wishing to talk with him about coming to the hospital to transport Don to where he would be staying. He was being released tomorrow afternoon around one o'clock. Bob agreed to be there to pick him up and take him to his home where he could look after his injured brother.

After the phone call Bob and Vic went to the tool shed and began to fill bottles and jars with gasoline. Into the wide mouth jars they dropped pieces of paraffin wax which would dissolve in the gasoline and make it more volatile. Each of the jars and bottles were affixed with a gauze rag which could be wetted with the petroleum mixture if the jar or bottle were shaken. Each container was placed in a gallon plastic bag for storage. Once done, the men walked around the property to find handy places to store the bombs until they were needed.

It was late when Bob and Vic came back to the house for dinner. Bob took two steaks from the refrigerator, stepped outside and lighted the barbeque.

"How about a beer, Vic?" asked Bob.

"A beer?" asked a startled Vic. "I've never seen you drink a beer."

"On rare occasions. Usually I have to stay ready to fly, but not tonight. This is the first time since fishing season opened that I can say for sure I won't have to fly tonight. Let's both have a cold one while I burn the steaks."

After finishing dinner the sun was down and it was a bit chilly outside so the men retreated to the living room of the house and turned on the television set. Bob opened two more beers and sat in his recliner to drink it and watch the late news. He was grateful for the friendship and protective comradeship offered by his old friend Vic Lamar. "Do you want to ride into Anchorage with me tomorrow when I go to pick up Don?" asked Bob, slouching in his recliner.

"If you think it will be OK to leave the place unguarded," replied Vic.

"I thought I would fly up to get him, but I'm not sure he would be comfortable on the flight home. This way we can stop if he needs to get out and stretch. Do we need anything from Anchorage?"

"I don't know of anything, Bob. We have all the supplies from the camps to use up and we can buy milk here in town," Vic replied.

"You know, Vic, I have a .38 Chief Special in a drawer upstairs. I think I'll take it with us and let Don carry it. If we get into a shootout while he's living here he needs to have protection. That little .38 doesn't have much recoil and shouldn't do him any damage if he has to fire it. What do you think of that idea?"

"I think it's a really good one. Should we stop at Great Northern Guns in Anchorage and buy some speed loaders for it? We don't know how well his hands are working just yet. We can load up the speed loaders and all he would need to do is press the button and drop five cartridges in the cylinder."

"The holster just clips onto his belt and he can carry it without much bother. We'll stop and get some speed loaders for it when we are there tomorrow." Bob stood, yawned, and stretched. "Right now, though, I think it's time for me to go to bed."

The following morning the two men prepared for the three-hour trip to the hospital in Anchorage. On the way about an hour into the trip Bob remarked, "There is a wonderful little restaurant on Kenai Lake owned by a friendly lady who, on her summer open days, rides a motorcycle. It's a good place to stop." Bob liked her and always looked forward to visiting with her when he passed through the little town of Cooper Landing.

She was sitting at a table composing a special insert for the menu when they walked inside. Bob walked directly to her table and gave her a great bear hug. "How the heck are you, Arden?" he asked.

"Huntin' season must be over if you have time to come see me," she said with a broad smile on her pleasant face.

"It sure is and I'm ready to relax. I suppose you heard about my brother Don being hurt. He's getting out of the hospital today and Vic and I are going up to Anchorage and bring him home to stay with me for a while."

"Stop by on your way back and have dinner. I'll buy the three of you the best dinner in the house. Dang, it's good to see you, Bob." She wrapped her arms around his neck and gave him a big hug as he had done to her.

"We just stopped to say hello and have some breakfast. How was your summer?"

"It was good. It's getting better each year. Go sit down and order. I have to finish fixing the lunch menus and then I'll come and talk with you."

Nearly an hour later Bob and Vic continued their journey to the big city. There was no need to refuel before the return trip and they drove directly to the gun store in Anchorage. Inside Joe came out of the back office to greet them. They found the speed loaders to fit the five shot cylinder on the handgun and bought five of them along with two boxes of .38 caliber ammunition to add to the inventory at the house.

It was just before one o'clock when Bob parked his truck in the loading zone in front of the main entrance to the large hospital. The two men rode the elevator up to the secure wing of the hospital and found Don sitting in a wheelchair waiting for his final paperwork. Hospital security men were still stationed at the door. Bob spoke to them as he entered to thank them for all the effort they had made to keep his brother safe.

Don was getting his final instructions from the nurse when a tall trooper lieutenant entered the room. Bob and Vic both turned to greet Tony.

"I didn't think you were going to make it," said Bob.

"I'm mad at you, not Don," joked the trooper.

With that remark Tony stepped over to where Don was seated. "Hi, Tony. I want to thank you for everything you've done for me the past several weeks. There is no way to repay you for the things you and your men have done for me. I wouldn't be here at all if it weren't for them." Don reached out a fragile hand to shake hands with the man in the blue shirt.

"I'm not allowed to give you any details, but with your help this investigation has turned into a giant international case. You gave us information we used to get information from Interpol and UNAFEI in Tokyo. We are working with the feds on this one. U.S. Immigration Custom Enforcement has been consulting with us too."

"I'm sorry it happened at all, but I'm glad I was able to help out. Come see me when you have a little time, Tony. Thanks again"

Tony turned to Bob and said, "I know he's anxious to get out of here, Bob. Take him home and take good care of him." They shook hands and Tony left the room.

"Where is your car parked?" asked the nurse.

"In the loading zone out front," replied Bob.

"You can go down now and I'll take Don in the patient elevator and meet you at the front door."

Bob and Vic walked to the public elevators and rode down to the lobby. Vic waited inside while Bob went out to bring the truck closer to the front door A minute later the nurse arrived pushing Don in his wheelchair. Vic led the way outside and pointed out the big pickup truck. With Don strapped into the front seat and Vic in the rear they headed out of town in the afternoon sun for a pleasant ride home. The conversation worked around to the fortification plan in place at Bob's home.

"It sounds as though you two have been busy. Is there anything I can do to help you out? I can't run or fight, but there must be something I can do to ease the space you have to cover." Don was feeling helpless and unable to add to the plan.

"I've been thinking, Don, since you can't run and can't fight, as you said, I plan to put you in the bedroom downstairs. If there is an attack you can get in there with your .38 and we'll make some kind of barricade at the door. You can stay in the main part of the house until they try to break inside. At that point you should go to your room and get behind the barricade to wait. Vic and I have the weapons and ammo placed all around the property and we can shoot and move. We don't know if, when, or how they will attack. Nor do we know how many men will be in the party. The one thing we are sure of is that they're going to come at us. We took them by surprise at the Jack Rabbit Camp and when they made their move we were ready. They won't be that easy this time. I think they'll try to ambush us and hit us before we can see them. Vic and I have put motion detectors and cameras around the property. That should give us a warning when an attack comes." Bob Halstead laid out the plan as best he could for his brother so he would know what to expect.

"All we can do now is wait and wonder," added Vic.

"Are you getting hungry, Don? We can stop at Sunrise Inn to eat if you are." Bob had remembered the invitation given by Arden.

"It might be a good idea to stop so I can use the bathroom and stretch my legs a little, replied Don.

After they stopped at the eatery they helped Don negotiate the stairs to the dining room. They enjoyed a tasty dinner and good conversation with Arden then boarded the pickup for the remaining fifty miles of the journey home. Once there they helped Don into the house and showed him his room. The trip had been hard on the injured man and he wanted to lie down for a while to rest up. The evening went quietly for all three men as they relaxed and waited for whatever was to come next.

The following morning in the security offices of the labor union Milan had called his two security men to the conference table for a meeting. "That trooper lieutenant was here. He came to the office yesterday and wanted to talk with you, Mr. Chin. He said the fire in the airplane had been started with car gas and not avgas and ignition was with a road flare they traced back to the ones you purchased in Anchorage. Missing details like this can get you arrested in this country. The trooper said he was coming back to talk with you today. You had better be ready to produce the flares you purchased to account for them and prove you did not set the plane on fire."

"Yes, that was careless of me, but I didn't think they could identify the specific brand of road flare after it had burned. Their crime lab here must be exceptional," Chin explained.

"I read in the newspaper there was a wildland fire on the west side of Cook Inlet. The article said the cabin on the property was damaged, but repairable." Milan needed answers from Chin in order to prepare the next chapter of their plan. "I think these damages will do what we intended which was to send a message to Bob Halstead. We need to be careful with this guide. He is clever and resourceful. He and his camp cook shot two of the best men in the world at this job. We cannot afford to take these men for granted. If they continue to bring attention to this office I'm afraid we will have to deal harshly with them."

The next comment came from Mr. Hua. "I had a note in my basket this morning to see Mr. Wei. You said we were not to take orders from anyone but you. Should I disregard the note from him?"

"He and I are having a policy disagreement at this time. I would prefer you only report to me and let me deal with Mr. Wei. I also wish to advise you that the trooper will probably come here today to speak with you and Mr. Chin. The two of you know how to deal with the law. Don't answer any questions you are not comfortable with. This trooper is clever. Have your meeting with him here in this conference room. I will be in my office if you need me. I'll call Mr. Wei and tell him you aren't coming to his office.

I shall be working on the next segment of our plan for Mr. Halstead. I would like to clear up this matter as soon as possible. Stay around the office until after the trooper leaves. Any further questions?" asked the security chief.

There were none and Milan returned to his office to call Ang Wei on the office phone. When he answered Milan barked his orders. "From now on you will not speak to my men. You can ask any question you wish answered, but it will be through me. You do not command my security team."

Wei was furious, "Perhaps you should come to my office and we will make a conference call to headquarters to see who is in charge of this office."

"You can call them if you wish, but I am not going to bother the men in Jakarta when it's this time of day for them. You seem to think I want to take over your position here. That is simply not true. I don't want your job. I only want to do my own. I have specific authority from the home office to do what I think is needed to clean up the mess you have created." Paul Milan would not back down from this pompous ass. He hung up the office phone without a reply from Wei.

An hour later the receptionist in the front office called to say Lieutenant Anthony Harrison of the Alaska State Troopers wished to see Mr. Chin and Mr. Hua.

"Send him to my office," said Milan who immediately called Chin and Hua to the conference room.

Moments later Harrison entered. "You said these two men would be in the office this morning. May I see them?"

"Of course, they are waiting for you in the conference room. It is through that door there." Milan pointed to another door in the office.

"You don't want to attend the meeting?" asked Harrison.

"It has nothing to do with me. You can interview them in there and come back to this office if you have further questions for me."

Thank you, sir," commented Tony as he stood to walk to the other door.

The interview lasted more than an hour with Tony taking notes the entire time. The one unanswered question was about the number of flares Chin had purchased and where they were at this time. Chin claimed he didn't remember how many flares he bought, but they were in the company garage for use in company vehicles. He said he would have one of the mechanics count the flares and give the figure to the trooper. Tony doubted he would ever get the information but had no reason to question Chin's story.

As he drove back to the trooper headquarters he called Greg Beason and asked him to come to the office for a short meeting. He then called Bob Halstead to give him a short report on the meeting he had just finished. It seemed this was about to become one of those days when nothing went the way it should.

Chapter 26

In Bob Halstead's kitchen the three men were drinking coffee and talking about the situation they were involved in when Don asked a couple of questions. "I wonder if the danger to my daughter has ended. When can she come home to me?"

Bob rubbed his chin and said, "I don't know, Don. I think they wanted her to pressure you to give them some answers to questions they thought you knew. If we knew what information they wanted perhaps we could strike a deal and get her off the wanted list, but we still have no idea what it is they want to know. Personally, I think she is safer on the road with Lindsy than she would be here. On the other hand, we might be able to find a way to send you to the lower 48 (contiguous U.S. states) to be with her. The problem is they seem to know where we are most of the time. It's possible they could find her if they followed you."

"Yeah, you're right, of course. I just miss her and want to be with her. This sitting around and waiting is driving me nuts."

Bob suddenly had another idea. "Hey, Vic, do you feel well enough to stay here and guard the place while Don and I go to the Peninsula and close the camps for the winter? It would take several days, but I think it would do Don a lot of good to get out for a while."

Vic was surprised at the question and said "That's a great idea, Bob. I was wondering how we were going to accomplish the job before winter sets in. I can handle the guard duty and call the troopers if I need backup. How soon do you want to leave?"

Bob turned to his brother. "What do you think, Don? Are you up to traveling for a while? We would be staying in camps and sleeping on camp beds and eating in real kitchens. I can do all the work and you can soak up some sunshine, even go fishing if you feel up to it. Being out in the field may be good for you and let you get some exercise to help your rehabilitation."

Don thought for a couple of minutes before answering. "It sounds like a great idea with one caveat. The flight down there is over three hours and I don't know if I can sit that long without getting out of the seat to stretch my legs. Can we make a stop somewhere for me to move around a few minutes?"

"Sure we can. I can stop in Iliamna and in King Salmon where I should fuel up anyway."

The plan was made with the departure set for tomorrow morning. The rest of the day was spent loading the needed tools and gear for the trip. Bob called Kenai flight service to file a flight plan which included stops in Iliamna and King Salmon.

He also spent a long while talking about the plan with Vic. He was to be their eyes and ears while they were away. The plane was loaded and fueled for the flight and final plans made with Vic being given a written schedule of where and when he and Don would be during the trip. That evening the trio went into Soldotna for dinner at Froso's restaurant and visited with the owner.

It was early in the cool morning when the two men took off in the rented Cessna 185 for the trip scheduled to for six days and two stops while going each way.

AmerAsian Labor Union has thousands of members in every walk of life doing the menial tasks and maintenance in offices around all the Pacific coastal areas. One such team worked at night in the offices of the Federal Aviation Administration as contract labor for janitorial service. Early the following morning Milan received a call from one of the workers to report the aircraft leased and piloted by Bob Halstead was leaving to fly to the Alaska Peninsula this morning. It was followed by a computer copy of the flight plan.

With this information in hand Paul Milan, AALU Security Chief, called his team of enforcers to the conference room. "Using this flight plan do you think you can use your airplane to follow and find him?"

Chin read the copy of the flight plan. "Yes, it will be easy, but he flies much faster than I can in my airplane. If he is in the air he will cruise much faster than me, but he will be stopping several times and we know where he is going. I can be in King Salmon shortly after he arrives and follow him to his camp. There are many places to land an aircraft in the tundra. I am confident I can find them and land out of their sight but close enough to walk to within rifle shooting distance. I have heard this Halstead is a dangerous man and the use of the rifle may be warranted."

"You had better get moving then," said Milan. "Do you have enough gear for the trip—food, gas, warm clothing and other things you may need?"

"I'll be loading all the items first thing along with several cans of gasoline for the airplane. We will be close to maximum allowable weight on the trip down there, but we will use a lot of fuel for the return trip. I have flown in that area many times in the past. The only unforeseen obstacle I see is the weather. It can change quickly in that part of Alaska."

"Stay in contact with me as much as possible, Mr. Chin, and good luck to you and Mr. Hua."

Chin owned a Piper PA-18 Super Cub capable of flying at about 90 miles per hour as opposed to the Cessna 185 Halstead was flying. The Cessna could cruise at 140 miles per hour. Chin checked the weather and decided the winds were not in his favor at altitude and chose to take the low route through Lake Clark Pass and fly direct to the Wildman Camp from Iliamna. The flight for Halstead would be longer and he was not only stopping in Iliamna, but planned to stop in King Salmon, too, presumably for fuel. Chin had brought enough fuel to take him back to Anchorage without stopping. He knew flying today would be governed by the size of his bladder and not the size of his fuel tanks. With Hua in the back seat they took off on the long trip to the Alaska Peninsula.

Bob Halstead had landed in Iliamna to allow Don a chance to get out and stretch his legs a while before continuing on to King Salmon where he intended to buy fuel. There were no fuel stops south of King Salmon and the country is wild. There are hundreds of miles of beaches and hundreds of lava cinder airstrips all the way down the Peninsula enabling a pilot to land safely at almost any given point. The problem was that if you needed fuel or parts they were a long way off and there would be no telephone for him to call for help.

In King Salmon the two men took a cab to the hotel where they each ate a huge steak. Don said he was holding up well and was ready to continue. Another cab ride back to the transient parking area, a preflight check and clearance from the tower was all they needed to continue on south. It was still more than a hundred miles to the camp and the winds were beginning to pick up. This would slow their arrival at Wildman Camp a little and make the trip a little bumpy from time to time.

Don had to grit his teeth a couple of times to keep from crying out from pain when the turbulence made the Cessna bounce around in the sky. It took a full two hours to make the trip, but at the camp the winds on the ground were just a breeze. Don stepped out of the airplane and walked or rather limped around the area.

"Are you going to be OK, Don?" asked Bob.

"Yeah, Bob, I'm just a little stiff and sore right now."

"You go ahead and walk around while I open the lodge and get us set up for the night. There are fishing rods in the lodge building and we can catch some fish for breakfast in the morning." He hoped Don was not suffering from the flight.

Bob started a fire in the oil stove for heat during the night. It was going to be frosty here later when the sun went down. The sleeping bags were placed on the beds and the lodge was warming when Don came inside.

"I don't see any bear sign around the camp," reported Don.

"Good, but just the same be careful if you have to go outside during the night. Have a seat, Don, I'm going out to tie the airplane down for the night and then I'll be back."

Outside the wind had picked up a little and the sun was down. The sky was clear with stars shining brightly in the heavens. Bob loved it out here, in his heart it was his home. As he walked back to the lodge he heard the sound of a Super Cub somewhere in the distance. It was a common sound and he paid no attention. "Perhaps a trapper is readying his area for winter," he thought.

"It's a beautiful evening out there," commented Bob as he entered the lodge building. "It would be easy for me to stay here all winter. I love the solitude and peacefulness I get when I'm out here." Bob chuckled and grinned at his brother, "I must be turning into a recluse in my old age."

"It is nice here I have to admit. But you know me, I'm a city guy. I like the social side of life."

Now it was Don's turn to grin. "I like it when the guy in the car behind me toots his horn and calls me names."

Both men laughed. Bob filled his coffee cup one more time and sat at the table to relax awhile before retiring. He would sleep well tonight.

The sun was up when they arose in the morning. Don had made the coffee and poured two cups which were sitting on the large table when Bob awoke and came into the dining area.

"How did you sleep?" asked the guide. "I don't think I even rolled over all night."

"I slept like a log, too, and this was the first night I didn't have to take pills to kill the pain to be able to sleep. I feel like we could walk to the little lake and catch a fish for breakfast." Don rotated his shoulders and bent his back as a stretching motion. "I must be getting better."

"The rods are in the closet by the door. I'll wash my face and we'll walk down to the lake. We can catch and release some fish, but we'll only keep a couple to eat."

With that short statement Bob drank his remaining coffee and stepped away from the table to reach the kettle of warm water on the stove and pour some into a metal basin in the sink. Don dug two rods from the closet and found a small plastic box of lures. He affixed a lure to each rod and put the box of lures inside his shirt. Bob stepped into his small bedroom, put on his gun belt and holster then added the .45 Colt that was lying on the table next to his bed.

As he stepped out of the room he exclaimed, "I guess I'm ready."

Each man picked up a rod to carry and stepped outside. They walked around the lodge building toward the lake which was only two hundred yards away. They were almost to the water's edge when Bob made his first cast. "Don't look up, Don, but there is someone on the hill over there watching us. Where's your .38?"

"In my pocket," said Don, not looking in the direction Bob had mentioned. "Can you make out how many there are?"

"No. but I think there are two. There could be more, but I only see two. They're lying on the ground and watching with binoculars.

"Let's get a couple of fish and go back to the lodge. There is a window on that side with a shutter to keep the bears out, but there's a peep hole in the shutter. I can see them from inside with my binoculars. If they approach we have to be ready."

Back inside the lodge Don began to prepare the fish for breakfast while Bob found his binoculars and went to the window he had described to look through the hole where he could see who was on the hill above the camp. "I only see two men. Just watching us. I don't like it. If they get out of sight I want you to go to the plane and get in. I'll lock the lodge and come out, untie the plane and start the engine. I'm hoping they are the ones flying the Super Cub last night. If they're in the Cub we can outrun them without any problem. I don't want to go outside until they're out of sight and can't shoot at us or see me untie the plane. I'll only run the engine to warm it up as long as they stay out of sight."

"Shall I go ahead and cook the fish?"

"We might as well eat. It looks like they are just watching us for now."

A half hour later Bob was finishing his fish, eating with his fingers while still watching the men on the little hill above the lodge. Don was gathering the utensils to wash them in the sink when Bob spoke.

"They're moving, Don. Leave the dishes in the sink and go to the plane. We'll come back when we can to finish cleaning up. I have a friend in Pilot Point we can visit for a while. I don't think they want to take us on in public. When you get inside the plane put you holster on your belt to make it more accessible. Go, go now," he ordered.

Don moved as fast as he could to the plane while Bob locked the lodge building and followed. At the airplane he untied the ropes and slid into the pilot seat. He primed the engine and hit the starter button. The Continental engine caught and started on the second revolution of the turning propeller.

"Do you see them, Don?" asked Bob as he warmed the oil in the engine.

"Not yet, Bro."

Bob idled the engine for about two minutes when Don spotted the men walking stealthily down the stream bed on the upper end of the small lake.

"Here they come, Bob. They're carrying rifles."

"Hang on; I'm not taxiing to the end of the airstrip. It's going to get bumpy about the time we lift off. I want to get out of here before they can get a good shot at us. I'll be jinking around when we get off the ground to keep them from getting a good target. Here we go," he said as he applied the throttle.

The Cessna bounced on the tundra and began moving faster down the runway. Bob lifted the tail to reduce ground friction and seconds later jerked the nose into the air and the plane was airborne. Bob had enough airspeed now to maneuver and banked the plane hard to the left, then immediately hard right.

Don could see the men shouldering their rifles and saw them firing at them, but they could not predict which direction the plane would move next. Seconds later Bob nosed the plane out of sight behind the hill they had used to spy on them.

"We should be safe for now. Look. It's the Cub parked over there. I wish we had time to stop and disable it. Oh well, let's just go to Pilot Point and visit my old pardner."

Chapter 27

After landing at Pilot Point, Bob taxied to a large commercial hangar. The business was operated by his old hunting partner, Ed Cusak, for the commercial airlines operating in the area. He shut down the engine and climbed from the cockpit and was immediately met by Ed. Bob explained his need to hide from the Piper that was following them, and Ed responded by telling him to push the plane into the hangar when he opened the huge overhead door. Ed helped with the labor of moving the Cessna inside and closed the hangar door once again.

"Come on into the office and we'll have coffee. By the way, who is this other guy with you?" asked Cusak.

"Sorry, Ed, this is my brother Don. We were down at my Wildman Camp when these guys showed up in a Cub. I'll tell you the whole story later."

Cusak held out his hand to greet Don, "Pleased to meet you, Don. Your brother and I have indulged in a lot of mischief in our day."

Don took the hand and shook it weakly. "I've heard some of the stories," commented the other Halstead brother as they walked to the front offices of the hangar business.

There were three people in the waiting room scheduled to leave on the next flight to King Salmon which was due to arrive at the airport in twenty minutes.

"Grab a cup of coffee and we'll go to my office to visit," said Ed. With cup in hand they walked to an office behind the ticket counter in the front office. Ed closed the door behind them and sat at his desk.

"Now, Bob, what kind of trouble are you in this time?" he asked.

Bob proceeded to relate the entire story finishing with the fact the men in the Cub had shot at them as they took off from the camp.

"Wow! That's crazy, Bobby. What can I do to help you out?" Ed was amazed at the story and had genuine friendship for Bob Halstead. "I can put you up here for a few days if you want, or I can loan you my Cherokee Six to go wherever you need to go. What do you need most, Bob?"

"To tell you the truth I really don't know. We came out here to get away from those people and somehow they knew where we were anyway. I'm going to have to think about our next move. What I do know is that these men are dangerous and intend to kill us if they catch us. I don't want to put you in danger, Ed. I think we should hole up a couple of days until they get tired of looking for us. It would give me time to think of a plan. If you let me use your telephone I'll call my trooper friend in Anchorage and let him know what's going on."

"Go ahead, Bob, use whatever you need. I have a flight coming in right now and I have to go to work. Use the phone on my desk," said Ed as he stood to leave the office.

Bob dialed the cell phone number for Tony Harrison.

"Where are you," asked Tony.

"Right now Don and I are in Pilot Point. I have my plane hidden in a hangar here." Bob then went on to inform Tony of the incident at his Wildman Camp.

"You saw a red and white Super Cub parked on the tundra a mile or more from your camp? Did you get the registration numbers on the plane?"

"Sorry, Tony, I was too busy dodging rifle bullets to see them. I was able to watch them for a while with my binoculars while they were checking out the camp. I think both men are Asians. They were too far away to get a good look, but they were definitely Asian looking. I don't know how many shots they fired, but it was a lot."

"You say they looked like Asians?" inquired Harrison.

"They looked like it to me and I watched them for quite a while."

"I wonder if these men are the same two I interviewed in the labor union office a couple of day ago.

I'll call over there and see if they're in the office. What is your plan now, Bobby?"

"I'm still working on that. I need to go back to the Wildman Camp and finish closing it up for the winter, but I don't dare go there until these guys are gone. Don is feeling better and getting stronger, but he still isn't moving very fast. Ed says we can stay here a few days and I think that's our best option right now. Store this phone number in your cell phone for now. It's the airline hangar in Pilot Point."

"I'll do that, Bob. Keep your head down and be safe." Tony was worried for the safety of both Halstead brothers.

Four days later Mr. Chin and Mr. Hua entered the security offices of AmerAsian Labor Union in Anchorage. Paul Milan met with them in the conference room to hear the report of yet another failed plan.

"Did you search thoroughly?" asked Milan.

"We checked all his camps and checked every landing strip on the map. He was nowhere to be found. Of course he knows the countryside better than Hua and I, but we searched every inch of the Alaska Peninsula as far down as Port Moller. With hunting season now closed there was very little aircraft traffic down that way. The country is flat with little cover making it very difficult to hide a big Cessna 185 like his. I have no idea where he went. We overnighted in King Salmon and looked around there as well as Naknek. We even checked the hangars there. Nothing; and no one we spoke with has seen them either."

Milan sat, thinking, "You say there were two men in camp. There were three when they left the hospital. The third man must have stayed behind to watch the home place. Check it out and if he's there you might convince him to tell you where they are as well as where to find the girl. If we had her we could control the men. Drive to Soldotna instead of flying. It will take longer, but he may not see you coming this way." Without further comment Hua and Chin stood to leave the office.

Three hours later Vic was doing domestic chores around the place. He had finished making beds and washing breakfast dishes. Next, he moved outside to gas up a mower to cut the large front lawn. He returned to the house to change his shoes when the motion detectors began to ding and notify of movement in the front drive. He walked to the living room where the camera monitors were displayed on a television screen. A vehicle was parked far out on the driveway and was visible on one of the cameras. Another camera showed two men walking behind the trees along the drive. Both men had weapons visible.

"Oh, crap," Vic muttered to himself as he picked up his cell phone and dialed 911.

"What is your problem?" ask the dispatcher.

"This is Vic Lamar at Bob Halstead's place." He gave the address. "There are two men coming toward the house with handguns and sneaking through the trees. I need troopers right now!"

"Please hold while I send a trooper your way." He could hear her dispatch several patrol cars to his location.

"They are approaching the house I'm going to have to move, said Vic."

"Please keep your phone with you if possible. Help is on the way." The dispatcher stayed on the line without talking.

Vic watched the cameras track the two men to the rear of the house, checking the outbuildings as they moved. When he saw them approach the back door of the house he moved to the bedroom where a barricade of mattresses and boards had been devised. He stepped behind the fortification and kneeled down, his .45 Colt in his hand and ready to fire.

As he watched the door slowly open, no one was visible at first. Suddenly he saw the side of a head peek into the room. The head became more exposed while he watched.

"OK, come out from behind the fort," called the voice outside the door. He spoke with a slight accent.

Vic didn't move, but he heard the dispatcher on the telephone say help had arrived at the property.

"I said come on out," demanded the voice again.

"Go to hell," shouted Vic.

The voice outside poked an arm around the corner with a semi-automatic weapon in its hand. "Last chance, buddy," he said.

At that moment Vic heard another voice in the kitchen area, "This is the Alaska State Troopers; come out with your hand in the air. Drop your weapons and come out now."

The arm with the gun pulled back from the door to where Vic could no longer see it.

"The troopers are out there and I'm in here; you're surrounded," shouted Vic. "It would be in your best interest to give up and drop your weapons."

Vic heard the voice outside the door of his room talking to someone else in a foreign language. They spoke back and forth a couple of times when the trooper, once again, ordered them to drop their weapons.

"You had better do as they say," said Vic to the voice outside his bedroom door.

Now Vic heard the back door open and a voice order: "Drop the gun, pal." It was the trooper at the back door with a gun aimed at Hua who was standing in the doorway between the kitchen and the living room.

Vic heard Hua say, "Don't shoot, I'm putting it on the floor."

At that moment Vic heard another voice at the front door, "You in the back, drop your weapon and come out where I can see you."

There was no reply from the man outside Vic's door. The trooper in the kitchen now shouted at Hua to get on the floor and put his hands behind his back. There was a pause in the sounds until the trooper in the kitchen shouted to the one at the front door, "OK, Mel, I have this one cuffed."

At that moment the voice outside Vic's door gave an audible sigh, "OK, troopers, I'm putting my gun down. Don't shoot."

Vic heard the gun being placed on the floor and stood up from behind his fortified position and called to the trooper. "I'm in here trooper and I'm armed. I'll put my gun on the bed, but I want to see both these guys in cuffs before I step out."

He now heard the trooper outside his door and the handcuffs being applied to the man there.

"Who are you?" asked the trooper from around the corner.

"Vic Lamar, I've been staying here with Bob Halstead."

"Step out toward the door where I can see you," commanded the trooper.

Vic stepped to the doorway where the policeman could see him.

"Leave the gun on the bed and step out here."

Vic complied with the order. Now the dispatcher was shouting at him.

"Mr. Lamar, Mr. Lamar, do as the trooper says. Give him the phone and let me talk with the dispatcher."

Vic handed the telephone to the trooper who took it and confirmed the situation was in control.

The prisoner in the kitchen was still on the floor and the trooper was in possession of the apprehended person's handgun. The second trooper speaking with Vic had now picked up the weapon on the floor in front of him belonging to the second apprehended person. Both troopers got the prisoners on their feet and into chairs in the kitchen.

Vic walked to the doorway leading to the kitchen but didn't go inside.

"Tell me, fellas, exactly what are you doing here?" asked Mel, the trooper.

Neither of the prisoners spoke.

Finally, Mel read both men their rights from a card and both men nodded that they understood. "You really don't have to say anything to us, but you are about to go to jail for some serious felony crimes. This is your last chance to explain what you were doing."

The two men looked at each other but said nothing.

"Mr. Lamar we will need a statement from you," informed trooper Mel. "I'm going to have my partner take these men to the booking facility. As soon as we have loaded them in the patrol car I'll come back to get your statement."

Vic nodded and entered the kitchen to sit to wait.

Minutes later Mel came back to the kitchen to interview Vic. The interview took more than an hour as Vic told him the history behind the attack today. When the trooper left to go back to his office Vic picked up the phone to call Bob Halstead in Pilot Point.

Bob answered his cell phone while sitting in the small living quarters at the back of the hangar.

"What's going on at home?" asked Bob.

"That's what I called to report, Bob. I was just attacked here at the house. I'm OK and the troopers showed up to help me out and arrest the two guys. The motion detectors and cameras saved me this time. I heard the signal from the motion detectors and saw them coming on the cameras. Two men had parked at the end of the drive and sneaked up through the trees to the back of the house." Vic related the rest of the encounter and the arrest by the two troopers.

"What did these men look like, Vic?" asked Bob.

"They were probably of Asian descent, both short and muscular, not fat, but muscular built. They looked like martial arts experts or weight lifters. They wouldn't talk to the troopers while they were here, so I don't know any more about them."

"It's OK, Vic. I'll call Tony and ask him to check them out. If it looks like these are the men who came after us I'll head home right after I close the rest of the camps. It's getting frosty at night and I need to get this done before the winter storms hit."

When Vic hung up Bob made a call to Lieutenant Anthony Harrison. "Hey, Tony, I just got a call about an attack at my home in Soldotna. I'm trying to learn if these are the same men who tried to get Don and me at Wildman Camp. Have you heard anything?"

"Yes, I have. I just got off the phone with one of the arresting officers and when they finally got ID on the two, the officers learned they work for the labor union security office. I was about to call my new friend at ICE and confer with him, but it looks like this whole thing is related to your brother's incident. This could be the link that proves AmerAsian Labor Union was responsible for your brother's beating and evidence we need to take the union down. Interpol has been investigating the parent corporation for a very long time but could never come up with anything concrete or any witnesses. This may be what they need to break the case. It involves human trafficking, prostitution and slavery. It's a very big deal, Bobby."

"Then do you think it will be OK for me to come home when I get the camps closed up?" asked the guide.

"I'll have to get back with you on that, but it looks like it to me. Can I call you back in an hour?"

"I'll be waiting, Tony."

After hanging up the phone Bob walked to the front of the hangar where the commercial office was located to find Don and Ed. They were alone giving Bob an opportunity to relate the story to his brother and friend. "Tony said he would call me back within an hour, and if the men that the troopers arrested at my place in Soldotna are security men from the labor union we may be able to go back and finish shuttering the camps and then go home."

"That's good news, Bob," commented Don.

"I'll say, Don. This means we can tell Jenny she can come home and go to school." Bob chuckled, "Oh yeah, and see her father."

Chapter 28

An hour later Tony Harrison called Bob Halstead on his cell phone. "Your suspicions were right, Bob. The men arrested at your place in Soldotna do work for the labor union. I've called Greg Beason from ICE and he's coming to the office to help with a plan to confront Ang Wei, the CEO, and Paul Milan, the security chief. I don't expect them to admit to anything, but we might make them nervous enough to make a slip. I suspect they are running out of big guns in this company's security department, so you should be OK to go out and close your camps. I still think you need to be very vigilant, though."

"We still have about four days' work to do at the camps and they are all away from cell phone coverage. I'll try to check in each time I move from camp to camp. I'd appreciate it if you would keep an eye on Vic and my house while I'm out of contact."

"Sure thing, Bob. I'll have the local trooper check in with him periodically. Good luck with your job." Harrison was not at all sure this was over.

After Bob hung up he said to Don, "It looks as if they have the men who shot at us in custody. I think we can go back to the camp and finish closing up for the winter. We still have to do the same at all the camps, although we just need to be sure they're locked up and clean. Let's get the plane out of the hangar and fly down to Wildman Camp and spend the night there. We can do a little fishing as long as no one is shooting at us."

"Sorta takes the challenge out of it, doesn't it?" laughed Don.

The two brothers found Ed and filled him in on what had taken place. He helped them get the big Cessna 185 out of the hangar and fuel it up for the short flight to the camp.

"I'll fly out there in the morning in the Cherokee. I can land on that strip with it. I just want to check on you and be sure you're safe." Ed, too, was concerned for the safety of the guide and his brother. "Martha, my neighbor, brought me some homemade bread and I have a couple of nice steaks in the freezer to send with you for dinner tonight."

"Thanks, Ed, you're a good friend and I appreciate what you did for us. I'll never be able to repay you for your help or for hiding us out." Bob reached out to shake hands with his old friend.

Don climbed into the cabin of the plane and Ed handed him a large grocery bag of food. Bob was doing his preflight check and checking the fuel tanks for moisture. When he finished he climbed into the left seat while Ed stood at the open door.

"Thanks again, Ed, for everything."

"No problem, Bob. Have a safe trip. I'll come by in the morning to check on you. Have the coffee on the stove." With that comment he stepped back, and Bob called "Clear," closed the door and started the engine.

The flight to the camp was short, only about 30 minutes by direct route. The air was smooth and the trip pleasant. As they neared the camp Bob circled the camp to check the place out prior to landing. On the ground Bob took the grocery bag and some of the gear to the lodge building. "There isn't much left to do here, Don. We can relax and do some fishing this evening if you feel like it."

"As tense as I've been over the last few days it might do me good." Don had been so worried about his situation he hadn't noticed the aches and pains in his body. "I think the first thing I am going to do is go lie down and take a nap."

Bob laughed, "Go ahead, you earned it. I'll go out and close up the out-buildings and bring in some firewood for the stove in case someone needs to come in during the winter."

Don went to the crew bedroom and laid down to rest. Bob went outside and tended the chores around the camp. There were three caribou on the other side of the lake and Bob took the time to watch them feeding along the ridge. Few caribou were left in this part of the countryside these days. They had migrated to the north and joined the big Mulchatna herd. It always amazed him at the way they could move such long distances while feeding. The animals were aware of his presence but didn't seem to mind him watching. In a few minutes they had moved out of sight behind the little rise, and Bob went back to work.

The temperature was dropping as the sun dipped low in the western sky. The peace and quietness were relaxing as he finished his work around the camp. Don came out of the lodge building to see what the guide was doing carrying two fishing rods. "How do you feel about fishing for a while until dinner time?" asked Don.

"Good idea. I'm finished with everything but closing up the main building and we will do that in the morning after Ed leaves. Have you ever been down inside the volcano, Mount Veniaminof?"

"Gosh no. Where is it?" asked Don.

"It's due east of here. The crater is fantastic to see. It's about six miles across the opening and there is a cinder cone and a lake in the bottom. A lot of wildlife lives there, including bears and small animals. It's unusual in that there is a huge crack in the north end of the crater and a stream runs out of the lake and flows out through the crack in the crater wall. In the little canyon outside the crater the creek splits and flows in both directions, east to the Pacific side and west to Bristol Bay. Red salmon migrate to the lake to spawn from both sides of the Alaska Peninsula. It's really something to see. If you want to take a look we can check it out when we leave."

"Wow, Bobby, I'd love to see it."

The two men walked to the small lake and fished until the sun went down in the west and it was getting dark. As they walked back to camp Don spoke to his brother. "These last few weeks have been terrible for both of us and for my daughter. I can never repay you, Bob, for what you've done for us, but my experiences with you out here have been priceless. They are some of the best days of my life. I've always worked in an office and been happy doing it. This time out here with you has made me see what I never knew I was missing. Do you think it would be possible to get you to bring Jenny and me out to Wildman Camp sometime? Just to fish and relax and enjoy the peace and tranquility of it? I didn't know there were places like this. Even though I've heard your stories I couldn't imagine how wonderful it is. I can see why you chose this way of life, Bobby. I envy you."

"I would love to bring you and Jenny out here, perhaps in the spring after bear season closes. We can open the camp and spend a couple of days fishing and sightseeing. Did you know the walrus herd hauls out on the beach near here each spring?"

"You're kidding me, really?" asked Don in wonder. "Have you seen them?"

"Oh yes, many times. It's quite a sight."

"Wow! That would be something to see." Don was limping slightly.

"Are you OK, Don?" asked his brother.

"Yes, just a little sore from the exercise I've been getting. The walking I've been doing is good for me and is making me stronger, but by nightfall I get a little stiff and sore."

"Let's make some dinner and call it a day," suggested Bob. "We can close up this camp and move on in the morning after breakfast. Ed will be here first thing to check on us and we can catch an extra char to feed him. How are we fixed for eggs?"

"We have plenty for breakfast," replied Don. "What is the food supply in the other camps going to be like?"

"There won't be much left at any of them, but we will only be at each camp for a few hours. We'll clean the camps and pack out all the perishables. The main thing to do is make each camp bear proof. Local hunters sometimes break into the camps for shelter during the winter, but they seldom do any real damage."

With dinner finished and the dishes cleaned and back in the cupboard it was time to go to bed and rest up. Don's aching body told him he was ready for the rest.

The following morning Bob loaded most of the things he was taking from the camp into his plane. He was making coffee when Ed flew by in his Cherokee Six. The plane circled once and landed on the tundra airstrip and parked next to Bob's Cessna.

Ed climbed from the low wing aircraft and greeted Bob.

"About time you got out of bed, Ed. Breakfast is ready." Bob greeted his old partner with witty sarcasm.

"How is the camp work coming along?" asked Ed.

"We will be locking up as soon as we finish breakfast and start moving up the string of camps toward King Salmon. I'm going to fly into Veniaminof crater on the way just to show Don how beautiful it is."

"I guess we had better go eat so you can get on with it."

The two men walked to the main lodge building where Don was busy cooking Arctic char with eggs and fried potatoes for breakfast. The coffee was hot and the conversation lively as they ate. Once again Bob thanked Ed for taking them in to protect them from the attackers. The brothers each admitted they would be glad to get back home and contact Jenny.

After breakfast Ed climbed back into the Cherokee and took off to his business in Pilot Point. An hour later the brothers locked the lodge and took off toward the east and the active volcano Bob had described to his brother Don.

Two days later they closed the final camp in Jack Rabbit Hills. The bloody sleeping bags and tarps as well as the blankets and coats used to cover the bodies of the two assassins would need to be cleaned or replaced. Those decisions would be made at home with the help of Don and Vic.

It was early afternoon when Bob helped his brother into the Cessna to take off in the direction of Lake Clark Pass and home. Once over the inlet there was cell phone coverage and he was able to contact Vic to let him know they were on the way home and would be landing in less than an hour. He planned to call Tony when he arrived at the house.

Days before, when Ed was at Wildman Camp having breakfast, Tony Harrison had been in his office with Greg Beason developing a plan to interview the two bosses at AmerAsian Labor Union headquarters. One of the big concerns was whether to go in with a force of troopers or interview the CEO, Ang Wei, and Security Chief Paul Milan, one on one. Since they had no real evidence of wrongdoing by either of these men, but only on men who worked for them, they decided to make an official call and ask for certain files from the company. They could get a warrant and return at a later time if the request was refused. They took the plan to the major who agreed with the strategy.

"What does your supervisor say about this plan?" asked Major Gatsby.

Beason chuckled, "He is anxious to see evidence that ties this labor union with the illegal activity around the world by their affiliates. ICE and Interpol have never been able to come up with any evidence in all the years they have investigated them. He wishes us luck."

"I'll have a couple of troopers hang out in the area until you men come out of the headquarters building. I want frequent check-in calls. I'll be waiting to hear how it goes."

Beason and Harrison drove two separate cars to the labor union offices in mid-town. They met in the lobby and rode the elevator together to the fifth floor. The office door across from the elevators was the lobby to the main office of Ang Wei. The two officers entered and marched to the receptionist desk. She was startled when the two men with badges demanded to see her boss, Ang Wei.

"I'll ask if he can see you now," she said, reaching for the office phone.

"You don't understand, ma'am, we're here to see your boss," said Beason, placing his hand over hers, stopping her from lifting the handset. "We're here under federal authority while investigating your company employees." She pushed back from the desk, frightened. Beason and Harrison turned and walked to the office door at the back of the little lobby.

Harrison opened the door and looked inside. Ang Wei was instantly angry at the intrusion.

"How dare you barge into my office. Get out!" shouted Wei.

"Sorry sir, we can't do that. We are here to gather information concerning wrongdoing by your company employees, namely Mr. Chang, Mr. Aluan, Mr. Chin and Mr. Hua. Under your corporate charters you are required to furnish these files. If you will give us the files we will be happy to leave your office. By the way, Mr. Wei, did you give the orders to enter the hospital here in Anchorage and attempt to kill another man who worked for you, a Mr. Halstead?"

"Of course not, how dare you come in here and accuse me of such things. I only heard about it after it had happened. We at this office do not indulge in such behavior." Wei was now becoming frightened of Beason. "If you need information about our security personnel you must go to the security office at the other end of the hallway."

"I'm told nothing happens in that office without your permission. I want to see the files in this office regarding all contacts made with the business agent, Don Halstead."

"There are no such files in this office," said Wei.

"You are part of an international corporation and we came here without a warrant to request the files we need in an investigation. If you don't want to cooperate with us we will seal the office until we can have a judge sign a search warrant." Harrison was the one delivering the sermon now.

"If I had a file I would give it to you," said a frightened Wei. "The only files in this office are my private files in that cabinet over there," he said pointing to a large file cabinet against the left, windowless wall. You may look if you wish. They are only personnel files."

"Then, you are giving me permission to look for specific files in those cabinets?" asked Harrison.

"Yes, you may look for the files you listed as the ones you are wanting."

"Thank you, Mr. Wei. If you would be so kind as to unlock the file cabinet we will look to see if the files we want are there. If they are not we will leave the office and not bother you further." Again it was Tony Harrison speaking to the CEO.

Wei stepped behind his huge desk and opened a drawer to retrieve a set of keys. He then walked slowly to the file cabinet and unlocked the drawers. When he stepped back behind his desk again both Tony and Greg approached the cabinet to open the drawers and look inside for the files they had requested. Wei had returned to his desk and seated himself there to wait.

Tony did the actual searching of the well-kept alphabetical filing system. One by one the files were plucked from the drawers and handed to Beason. Once all the files had been removed the two men closed the drawers and walked to Wei's desk to write a receipt for the documents.

"Thank you, Mr. Wei for being so helpful. We will return them to you when the case is closed."

Wei said nothing, but sat behind his desk, seething.

"We are now going to the security offices, and we would appreciate it if you didn't call and warn them. Remember we can close this office and get a search warrant. We will want to talk with your security chief and would like to surprise him. Do you understand?"

"Yes, I will not call them." Wei was somewhat gratified by them moving to the other office to confront the arrogant Mr. Paul Milan.

Chapter 29

Carrying the seized files, the two officers walked from Wei's office past the receptionist at the front desk, thanking her as they passed. "I hate to take these files with me to the security office, Greg. Would you take them to the car and come back up and meet me in the office at the other end of the hall?"

"I think it's a good idea, Tony. I'll do that while you go down the hall and introduce yourself to Mr. Paul Milan. Be careful, he's a dangerous man."

Tony handed the stack of files to Greg who pushed the button on the elevator. Tony walked the long hallway to the last door on the left which had a small brass sign on the door, Security.

When Tony entered the outer office there was no one in it. The door to the inner office was open and a voice called out, "Come in."

Milan was seated at his desk at the back of the office and looked up when the uniformed officer appeared in the doorway. "Ah, Officer Harrison, isn't it?"

"Yes sir, and you are Paul Milan, the new security chief."

"That's correct; what can I do for you?" he asked.

"We, my partner and I, have just come from the office of Mr. Ang Wei and he said the information we need would have to come from you and your office. I would like to wait a moment until my partner comes back from downstairs. I understand you were sent here by the parent corporation to take over after the disappearance of Mr. Li Tan."

"Yes, his death was a tragedy. The stress was just too much for him and, unfortunately, he shot himself. Like I said it was tragic. Did you know Mr. Tan?"

"I met him once here in the labor union office. He was a very intense man," said Tony.

"I never met the man, but I understand he was very good at his job."

"It's my understanding he is the one who had the business agent kidnapped and beaten and ordered the attack on the injured agent in the hospital." Tony was just making conversation and attempting to make the security chief uncomfortable. It didn't seem to be working.

"I don't know anything about all that. It took place before I arrived."

"You have a distinctive accent, Mr. Milan. Are you from the United States?"

"No, I'm Irish by birth. I have an Irish passport. Would you like to see it?" asked Milan.

"No, that won't be necessary. I'm just waiting for my partner to return from our car."

At that moment Greg Beason entered the outer office. Tony stepped into the open doorway and motioned for the ICE officer to come in.

"Mr. Milan, this is federal officer, Greg Beason. He and I are working together on this case. As you undoubtedly know the two men killed at the hospital some time ago were traced back to being employed by your labor union. They were licensed and employed by your department. In addition, there were two men arrested in Soldotna, also licensed and working for your security unit. Officer Beason and I are here to learn what capacity they operated under in the union. It is highly unusual to have four men from the same department involved in such a manner. We have come to inspect the personnel files of these four employees. Are you willing to give me those files?" asked Tony.

"As you already know I have only recently come to work in this corporation. My employer is the home office of all the labor unions in Jakarta, Indonesia. I have no personal knowledge of what took place prior to my coming here. I will give you those files, but as I said, I have no personal knowledge of that incident." Milan was building his own defense in the matter.

"Yes, Mr. Milan, I understand that. Mr. Li Tan was in charge of this unit when that took place. I'm told he may have committed suicide in remorse for the incident and you were brought in to take over as head of security for the labor union. I once met Mr. Li Tan. He was very committed to his position."

"I can't speak as to Mr. Li Tan. I never met the man. I was sent here after his demise. The files are in the outer office and conference room. If you will follow me I'll get them for you."

"Thank you, Mr. Milan. Those would be the files for Mr. Chang and Mr. Aluan, but I will also need the personnel files for two current employees, Mr. Chin and Mr. Hua. These are the two men arrested for felony assault yesterday in Soldotna. They are being held in the pre-trial facility at Wildwood Correctional Center in Kenai." Tony was attempting to chip away at Milan's defenses.

"I will have to check with Mr. Wei before I can give you those files," said the security chief.

"He has already given us his copies of the employment files. You should call him." Tony could see Milan was becoming uncomfortable.

Milan picked up the telephone to call his "boss". The conversation was short. "Mr. Wei said it was permissible for me to give you the files."

The three men walked to the conference room where there was a bank of filing cabinets. Milan led the way to the cabinet containing employee files and searched inside for the files Harrison had requested.

"Would you like me to copy those files for you?" he asked.

"That won't be necessary, Mr. Milan. We will need the original files for court purposes. I will give you a receipt and you will be able to get the files returned to you after the case is heard in court. Do you have any questions for Mr. Beason or me?" Tony sat at the conference table writing the receipt for the files.

"No, but since you have arrested my men I should call our attorneys to represent them."

"I suppose you should since they were arrested while doing AmerAsian Labor Union business as instructed." Tony hoped this was a frightening assumption aimed at the security chief.

With that statement Tony stood to gather the large stack of files, which he shared with Beason, and the two men made their way out the door and to the elevators on the other end of the long hallway.

The lawmen had not yet reached their car when Paul Milan stormed into the private office of Mr. Ang Wei, slamming the door shut behind him as he entered the inner office.

"What were you thinking when you gave those officers private employee files? Why didn't you demand a warrant?" asked the irate Irishman.

"You cannot come into my office and speak to me like that. I am the head of this office and you will treat me with respect. You seem to think you have omnipotent powers in this company, but you work for me. I am planning to retire, but until I do you will show me the courtesy this office deserves. There is nothing in the files I gave them to incriminate anyone in the union. The acts they committed will speak for themselves and will not reflect on this office." This was one of the longest speeches Wei had ever made.

"Get off your high horse, Wei. I was sent here by the office in Jakarta because things have gotten out of hand. I didn't come here to interfere with your administrative duties, only to correct mistakes made by the security office. As I see it the entire episode was brought on because you didn't trust one of your new employees. I have not been able to find one reason why any of these actions were taken. It is now up to me to control the damage done by you. I think retirement would be a good option for you at this point. This situation is like a giant snowball and grows with each revolution. This cannot and will not continue. There are going to be losses within the company and you could be one of them." Milan seldom gave in to anger, but he had suffered enough of Wei's arrogance.

"What do you plan to do?" demanded Wei.

"I am not going to discuss this with you. I will be calling Jakarta when the office opens. Until then you will oversee the administrative duties of the office and not interfere with the security division in any way. Do you understand what I said?"

Wei nodded weakly which was Milan's signal to turn and leave the office, passing a shocked and dismayed receptionist as he strode from the lobby. On his way to his own offices he stopped by the legal department to speak with the head lawyer about the men who were being held in Kenai Pretrial Facility.

Tony and Greg had each come in their own vehicles. The files were loaded into the trooper's car for the trip to the office. Greg followed closely behind in his. Both cars were parked in a secure area at trooper headquarters, and they unloaded the files they had seized from the union offices.

"It's going to take a lot of time to search all these files, Tony," said Beason. "How about some lunch first?"

"Good idea, but we need to secure these files and report to the major before we leave." Both men were feeling good about the morning's work.

Bob and Don Halstead had arrived at home in Soldotna late the previous evening, exhausted and out of ambition. The pair had coffee with Vic and went to bed early. The following morning they awoke to the smell of bacon, eggs and hash browns cooking in the kitchen. Bob shaved and showered before leaving his bedroom. He was dressed in a clean shirt and jeans when he came down the stairs for breakfast.

Don was sitting at the kitchen table drinking coffee when he arrived. Bob poured a cup of coffee and sat down beside his brother. Vic was busy dishing up breakfast to put on the table. No one had said a word yet this morning.

It was Vic who broke the silence, "You fellas must have been tired last night. I've never seen you sleep this late."

"It's the first good night's sleep we've had in two weeks, Vic," commented Bob.

"I don't think there is a reason to get in a hurry this morning. I'm guessing we will need to unload the plane and put all the gear where it belongs." Vic was speaking between bites of bacon.

"We have all day to get it done. I want to thank both of you for sticking by me during all this turmoil. I'll call Tony and ask if the danger is over and if we can bring Jenny home now." Bob spoke while spooning jam on a piece of toast.

"I'm not able to earn my keep just yet, but I'll do what I can to help out," said Don.

"I've been grateful for the company this time. You've been a big help, Don," said Bob as he bit into the toast and jam.

"Where do we start today?" asked Don.

"Unload the plane and store all the gear where it belongs. I'm hoping we can do the job without getting shot at." Bob sipped his hot coffee. "I'll call Tony later and see how he's making out with his investigation. With any luck this thing is over."

After finishing breakfast Don said he would take care of the dishes and clean the kitchen while Bob and Vic unloaded the airplane. Bob was pleased to have the help during this chore. He usually had sent his help home by now and was doing all this alone. It was past noon when they finished and Bob turned to the task of changing oil in the engine of the Cessna before pushing it back into the hangar. He would soon have to begin shopping for another Cessna to replace his and return the rented one to his friend. It was becoming expensive to keep this plane around.

In Anchorage Tony and Greg had just returned to the office when Bob called him on the cell phone.

"Got time to talk, Tony?" asked Bob.

"Yes, for a minute. Are you home?"

"We just finished unloading the airplane and changing the oil. I have a few things to catch up on, but the hectic pace should slow down now. How is the investigation coming along?" asked Bob.

"Greg Beason and I are in the office going over all the personnel files we took from the labor union offices. It's a tall stack."

"What about the men who attacked Vic? Are they still in jail?" inquired Bob.

"Yes, but I'm guessing the company lawyers are going to attempt to bail them out today. Beason and I caused a big to-do at the offices this morning. I got the impression there is a shake-up in the works at union headquarters in Anchorage. Milan was the only one in the security office when we were there this morning. The CEO threw a fit when we demanded the personnel files he had. I think they have enough internal problems to keep them busy for a few days." Tony couldn't reveal specifics to Bob, but he deserved some explanation.

"I have to ask, Tony, do you think we're safe here now, or not?"

"I wish I could give you a good answer, Bob, but I just don't know. I believe they're too busy with internal problems to worry about you, but I can't guarantee it."

"We were wondering if it was safe to bring Jenny home to be with her father, but it doesn't sound as if we can do that yet." Bob was disappointed in the answers.

"This case can drag on for a very long time. I wish we could speed it up, but most of what happens from now on is up to the court. I suspect their lawyers will arrange for bail on the two we arrested at your place and it's anyone's guess what the union will do then. I have to suggest you stay alert and be careful, at least for now."

"OK, Tony, keep me posted on what is going on. I'll call again in a few days. You call me if there are any changes on your end." Bobby hung up the phone and turned to Vic and Don.

"Well, is there any good news?" asked Vic.

"I'm afraid not. He thinks the two guys who came here after you will get bailed out today. I think we need to stick together for a while longer."

Both Don and Vic were disappointed by the news but understood. They realized how dangerous these people were and had no wish to let their guard down any time soon.

Chapter 30

After Tony and Greg left the union offices with the personnel files in hand Ang Wei sat in his office for a long time thinking of what to do next. For over two hours he sat and planned. His first order of business was to walk to the legal department to discuss defense and release of the two security men in jail in Kenai. Wei told the lawyer he would furnish a specific time to meet as soon as he could arrange it.

The second thing on his list was a call to San Francisco where a company airplane was housed. He had company authorization to use the Gulfstream G600 to travel on company business. He chose the G600 for its long range and speed. It had a range of 7,500 nautical miles at a cruise speed of 550 mile per hour. For a private business jet it is large, with a 95 foot wingspan and a 96 foot fuselage length.

When speaking with the aircraft director he specified the G600 fly directly to Kenai, Alaska where it could refuel and load three passengers for the long flight to Jakarta. The aircraft director said it could be done, but there would be a need to make a stop in Seoul, Korea to refuel for the final leg of the journey. He also informed Wei there would be a need for three pilots and three flight attendants and that he would stock the airplane with provisions for the long flight. He made a note to get back with Ang Wei with arrival and departure times.

The next item on Wei's list was to prepare a box for mailing to Jakarta. He used an international mail priority shipping box. In the bottom of the box he put rows of $100 dollar bill packs, positioning them tightly in the box. He found he could put two rows and two layers of bills, $250,000 in all, in the bottom of the box, covering the cache with several file folders filled with blank paper. He addressed the box to his personal address in Jakarta and sealed the top with shipping tape. Wei called the receptionist to his office. When she arrived he ordered her to mail the box Priority Mail and insure it for one thousand dollars. She said she would take care of it right away and carried the shipping box to her desk.

By late afternoon he had a call from the head of the legal department. "We have a bail hearing in the Kenai court tomorrow morning at nine a.m. How do you want me to handle the hearing?"

"I want you to stay with the two company security men as much as possible. Get the bail set as low as possible and pay it. They will want to take the prisoners back to the jail to be formally released and allow them to change out of jail clothing. You will wait there and pick them up to take them to Kenai. Later today I will set a time for them to meet me at the Kenai Municipal Airport. I will take them with me and your job will be done." Wei's plan was now coming together.

It was five p.m. in San Francisco when the aircraft chief called back. "We have filed a flight plan leaving here and landing in Kenai, Alaska at ten o'clock tomorrow morning. The crew will refuel in Kenai and be ready for your departure at your pleasure. Do you have a specific time of departure in mind?" he asked.

"There are some legal matters to be attended in the morning, but I suspect we will be able to depart before noon. Will that satisfy your schedule?" asked Wei.

"Of course, sir. Is there a number where you can be reached if there is a problem?" Wei gave the aircraft chief his cell phone number.

He did not intend to notify Jakarta of his arrival until they were nearing the islands. He and the two security men would be met by someone from the board of directors of which he was one. The lawyer would see to it he had possession of their passports when he took them from the jail to the airport. It was Wei's plan to fly on a commercial airliner from Anchorage to Kenai to avoid being noticed by anyone from his office. He would need no luggage or personal items for travel on this trip, since he was going home.

Wei drove to his small apartment where he settled in for the night. Sitting in his favorite chair he watched the evening news eating a microwave frozen dinner and drinking the last of a bottle of Johnny Walker Blue Label Scotch. His mind kept going over his plan but could find no flaws to discourage him from following through. The two security men were an unnecessary burden, but he could not leave them for the police to question. They were not privy to the inner workings of the labor union but knew enough to cause a disruption while the police investigated.

Relaxed by the liquor he went to bed early and planned to take a cab to the airport early in the morning. He had only just climbed into bed when the telephone rang. It was the board member in Jakarta he had called earlier in the week. Both men spoke in the same dialect used the last time they talked.

"It is now business hours here in Jakarta, Ang. I called your office and did not get an answer and called your private number. Do you have time to talk a minute?"

"Of course," replied Ang Wei. "I was going to call you tomorrow to let you know I was coming to Jakarta for a meeting. There has been a small setback here and I am bringing two security men in order for them to avoid being interrogated by the police about some things they have been arrested for. I suspect Paul Milan will be calling you about all that very soon. I don't have an arrival time yet, but I will call you when we are close to the Indonesian Islands. Was there something you wished to speak with me about?"

"If you are coming to the office it can wait until you arrive. I am pleased you decided to come in person to discuss any problems." The director was too friendly, thought Wei.

"One of the things I wish to speak with you about is my retirement. I feel the Anchorage office needs a younger man in charge. I don't have the energy I once had, but we can speak of that when I arrive in Jakarta. I will be arriving in the company jet." Wei had not asked the home office for the use of the jet, but knew they would approve.

"Very good, Ang, I will see you soon. I am looking forward to our meeting." With that the director hung up the phone.

Wei now had some trouble getting back to sleep and worried about the sudden end to the phone call. His position on the board of directors gave him certain privileges and entitlements not available to most regional CEOs.

It was early next morning when Wei drove his private vehicle to a local restaurant for breakfast. After eating he went back to his apartment to review his plan and prepare for the long trip ahead. He called the local airline to book a seat on the flight to Kenai before showering and putting on a clean suit and tie. Satisfied he had tied up all his loose ends he called a cab for a ride to Ted Stevens International Airport in Anchorage.

It is only a short half hour flight to Kenai from Anchorage. When he was inside the terminal he called the attorney for the two security men.

"Is the hearing on schedule?" asked Wei.

"Yes, nine o'clock at the Kenai Court House. The local Judicial Services officers will bring them to court and return them to the pre-trial facility after court. The court clerk said the judge would review the case prior to the hearing making it a much shorter time in court. I expect the DA to object, but state law says they are entitled to bail. The amount is the only question. I have their passports in my possession, and I'll swear I won't release them to the prisoners." The lawyer was optimistic. "As I said before, even if we get bail they will have to go back to jail to be released. I'll pick them up and bring them to you."

"I will wait in the terminal for you as well as the arrival of our transport. Bring them to me when you finish."

Wei sat in the lobby of the air terminal reading a newspaper when he heard the big private jet arrive and taxi to the fueling station several hundred yards north of the terminal. It wasn't long until one of the pilots came into the lobby looking for him.

"Mr. Wei?" asked the pilot.

"Yes, I'm Ang Wei. I assume you are one of my pilots."

"Yes sir, I am the chief pilot on this flight. I believe we are ready for the long trip. We have plenty of food and other provisions for you and your guests. Do you have any special requests to make your trip more comfortable?" asked the uniformed pilot.

"No, I'm sure you will have everything I need. I am waiting for the other two passengers to arrive. It will be a few minutes, so if you and your crew want to come into the terminal and have breakfast in the café you are free to do so."

"Thank you, Mr. Wei, but we have had breakfast and are anxious to get on with the flight as soon as possible. Our route will be similar to the route used by commercial airlines. We will follow the Aleutian Chain to the end leaving only a short distance to Japan, then down the west coast of Japan until we cross the Sea of Japan to our refueling stop in Seoul, Korea. When we leave there we will fly directly south to Jakarta. This will be a long flight, but we have three pilots for safety. Do you have any questions about the flight?" asked the pilot. His nametag said his name was Warren.

"No, thank you; it sounds as if you have it all worked out. I expect my passengers to be here in about a half hour, but it could be a little longer. A lawyer is bringing them here. Do you have a cell number I can use to notify you when they arrive?" asked Ang. Warren gave Wei a business card with the number listed and walked back to the flight line.

An hour later the lawyer came into the terminal with the two men. They were dressed in jeans and heavy shirts, the same ones they were wearing when they were arrested. The lawyer gave Wei the passports he had been holding for the two men. "The judge said they were not to leave Alaska or a warrant would be issued for their arrest. I will also lose my bail deposit. I will send the bill to your office. Is there anything else, Mr. Wei?"

"No, that will be all. I thank you for being prompt. I would appreciate it if you would find an airline clerk to escort us to our plane."

A moment later the lawyer returned with a pretty, blond ticket agent to lead the way through the security doors and across the short distance on the tarmac to the boarding stairs for the large private jet. Wei thanked the girl and walked up the airstair and into the cabin of the plane. He introduced the two passengers to Warren, the pilot and followed them into the luxurious cabin. A flight attendant came to be sure their seatbelts were fastened properly and welcomed them aboard. Once strapped in she began her safety speech while the pilot began to spool up the engines. Once done she took a seat near the galley and secured her seatbelt for takeoff.

The pilot taxied to the far north end of the runway, was granted clearance and pressed the throttles ahead. The powerful Pratt and Whitney G600 engines roared to life and the airplane suddenly became a living entity, leaving the ground and soaring into the heavens like a giant magnificent eagle. The landing gear was retracted and the plane climbed at an amazing rate. Several minutes later there was a small ping in the cabin and the flight attendant unsnapped her seatbelt.

"We will be climbing to 33,000 feet, and the air should be smooth the rest of the way to our first stop. Can I get you gentlemen anything to drink or to eat?" asked the flight attendant. Wei declined the offer, but he two security men asked for beer, even though it was not yet noon. Wei dozed off and on for most of the flight to Korea. The two security men whispered to each other most of the time. Wei guessed they were discussing their fate once they arrived in Jakarta.

They were five hours into the flight when the flight attendant came to them to offer a full dinner of baked salmon, au gratin potatoes, salad and white wine. There were now two flight attendants on duty preparing their dinner.

The two security men had yet to approach Wei or ask him what was about to happen to them. By the same token, Wei had not taken it upon himself to explain it to them. The truth was that he had no idea what would happen to them. He suspected they would be put to use in another place on the globe.

The pilots landed in Seoul, Korea to refuel and immediately took off again. Wei was satisfied to get more rest, a luxury he had been missing for several months. The two security men drank a great deal of beer each time they awoke.

The sun was coming up from behind them when Wei awakened. The pilots were flying westward toward Jakarta and descending from their cruising altitude. Another, different flight attendant was working in the cabin now. She approached Wei and asked, "Would you like something to eat or drink, sir?"

"I would like a coffee and a sweet roll or toast," answered Wei. The two security men were still asleep.

The flight attendant brought Ang Wei a huge sweet roll with thick frosting and a cup of black coffee. She asked if there was anything else she could do for him and he said "No, thank you."

Wei finished his breakfast and stood to go to the lavatory to relieve himself and find a razor if one was available. There was an electric razor on the bathroom counter which he used to clean up after the long night of flying. Then he washed and combed his black hair, which now had much gray appearing in it. He went back to his seat somewhat refreshed and picked up his cell phone to call the director for a ride to the office. He had been told they would land in less than an hour. It was time for Wei to prepare his case for the board of directors. It would be difficult to justify all the mistakes that had been made, but he thought he could place a majority of the blame on the security unit. He only hoped it would work for him.

Chapter 31

As Ang Wei's flight was en route, Greg Beason and Anthony Harrison worked to sort out all the files they had collected. There was little in these files about the crimes these men had committed or who had ordered them. On the third morning Tony looked across his desk at Greg, "I think we need some help with this research, Greg. Why don't I get someone from the District Attorney's office to give us a hand and a fresh mind in looking at the files? There must be evidence in them somewhere that would incriminate the head guys at the AmerAsia offices."

Greg rubbed his chin, "That might be a good idea. I agree with you that there has to be hard evidence somewhere and we're just missing it. Those two thugs arrested at Bob Halstead's place will be convicted, I'm certain, but getting the bosses who sent them is unlikely at this point. Call down there and see if one of those lawyers can come over here and lend a hand."

Tony thought it would be better if the major made the call to the DA's office and probably render better results. Greg agreed with the plan and walked with him to Major Gatsby's office. After several minutes of filling the major in on their progress he succumbed to their pleas and called the courthouse to ask for legal assistance. The clerk said one of the assistant DAs would be right over.

One cup of coffee and half a cinnamon roll later the lawyer arrived. She was a tall, thin, and intelligent woman. Her name was Nola Wilson. Tony had worked with her in the past and had confidence that if there were links to crimes to be found she could find them.

"Hi Tony," she said as she was escorted to his office. "Gosh it's been a long time since we worked together."

Tony shook her hand, "Yes it has, Nola. I'd like you to meet Greg Beason; he's with ICE and has been working this case for a long time. He can fill you in on the worldwide implications of this case. Have you been briefed on the background in the case?"

"Somewhat, but no specifics. I would appreciate it if you would bring me up to speed." She turned to Greg, "Pleased to meet you Greg. Tony and I are old friends." She put out her hand for him to shake.

"Tony was happy when he heard you were the one the DA's office was sending over. He said you were very smart and easy to work with. While we're getting acquainted let me fill you in on the world view of the labor union."

For the next several minutes Greg outlined the sex trade, human trafficking, and slavery conducted by the labor unions all over the world with the majority of the victims being very young girls, many of whom were sold into the trade by their families. Legitimate union activities being conducted were quickly described but added that these same union employees were being used to spy on governments and companies worldwide. He also outlined the disappearances of witnesses in many of the cases being mounted against the labor unions. Finally, he described the relationship between the several labor unions around the world that were being directed by a board of directors in Jakarta, Indonesia. He mentioned that the investigation by Interpol and UNAFEI had always failed due to the lack of witnesses. "I'm involved because of the Immigration and Customs violations being committed."

"Gee Whiz! I didn't understand the complexity of this case. I thought it was a simple assault, but I can see conspiracy, murder, money laundering and many other crimes to look at. Where do we start?" she asked, taking a seat at the small table.

"I have a friend whose brother was a victim of the assault, which was an attempted murder. My friend is a big Alaska game and fishing guide. The local labor union of the international labor union hired my friend's brother as a business agent. One afternoon they kidnapped him, took him to a gravel pit near Palmer and tried to beat him to death. They nearly succeeded, but he survived. Since then they tried again while he was in the hospital here in Anchorage. Hospital security shot the two attackers, killing them both. Since then my friend has been in one shoot-out, killed two more union security men and had his airplane torched along with one of his fish and hunting camps. And, in the last few days his home was attacked, but troopers had been alerted and arrested the two armed men. They were arraigned a couple of days ago."

"I can see these are all personnel files and all marked Security Department. What are we looking for?" she asked.

Tony answered her question, "Any link between these security people and the crimes they are involved in. Greg is interested in the international links and we both want to know if the AmerAsian Labor Union is conducting criminal activity or is it just a coincidence these men are all tied to the security department of the labor union company?"

For two days the team made graphs and charts, read files, invented scenarios and drew conclusions they could not prove for lack of witnesses. It was decided they would need to go to Kenai and interview the two prisoners in the Kenai Pretrial Facility.

When Tony called to set up an interview, he learned the two men had made bail and had been released; another disappointment for the team.

Tony turned to Nola and asked, "Do you think we have enough probable cause to bring Wei and the Irishman, Milan, in for interviews in our office?"

"Hmmm," muttered Ms. Wilson, "Not for an arrest, but for interview or interrogation I think we have enough, especially if you are polite."

Tony smiled and turned to his telephone to call the offices of AmerAsian Labor Union. Is it possible to get appointments with Mr. Wei and Mr. Milan, separately, but in the same visit?" he asked the receptionist.

"Oh, Trooper Harrison, there is something strange happening here. Mr. Wei hasn't come to the office for the past two days nor today. When he left the day before yesterday, he gave me a large box he wanted mailed to Indonesia. I forgot and it is still setting in my office. Mr. Milan is in his office, but he has only the building security men working now. All the other offices are working as usual, but Mr. Wei never takes a day off and I'm worried."

"Perhaps we should come down there and make some inquiries to be on the safe side," said Tony.

"Oh, would you please?" she pleaded. "I don't know Mr. Milan very well, but he isn't at all friendly and I don't know if he is in charge when Mr. Wei is out of the office."

"Yes, I think we'll check it out for you. We'll be there in a few minutes."

Tony turned to Greg Beason, "We have to go. Wei has disappeared and neither of the two security men has shown up for work this morning. The receptionist has asked us to check it out, for safety reasons, you understand."

Greg stood to leave, but turned to Nola, "Will you be OK here until we get back?"

"Go ahead I have a lot of files to read."

After a short stop to inform the major they both climbed into Tony's patrol car for the short drive to the office building and rode the elevator to the fifth floor main office of the labor union. The receptionist was waiting.

She ushered them to look into Wei's private office and showed them the box she was to mail. It was addressed to Ang Wei at a Jakarta address. They left the office, but in the hallway Tony turned to Greg. "I think Ang Wei has skipped. Can you call your office and have them talk with someone in Interpol in Jakarta to see if they can locate him?"

"Good idea, I'll catch up with you in Milan's office."

Tony walked the length of the hallway and entered the security office, which, as before, had no one in the outer office.

"Is anyone here?" called Tony.

"Yes, come in," returned a voice from the back office. It was Milan.

Stepping into the inner office Tony greeted Milan, "Can I have a minute of your time, Mr. Milan?"

Milan closed the file he had been working on and looked up at the trooper. "I'm pretty busy, Trooper Harrison. What is it you want?"

"A couple of things: First of all, do you have a home address for the two security men arrested the other day in Soldotna? It seems they have bailed out and we are having trouble locating them."

"Each of their home addresses are listed in their personnel files which you now have. It would be the only address I would have for the men. What is the second thing on your list?"

"Thank you. The second thing is we have had a request for a security check on the CEO, Mr. Ang Wei. He, too, has gone missing. Would you know his whereabouts at this time?"

"No, I was made aware he had not come into the office in two days. I was asked by Jakarta to take over as operations officer until he returns. I do not know the reason for his absence. Is there anything else?"

"One more thing; the two men who bailed out of jail had a lawyer. Do you have his phone number?"

"I believe I do," he admitted, opening the file on his desk. He wrote the number and name of the law office on a yellow sticky note and gave it to Tony.

"Thank you again," said Tony, taking the slip of paper. "Are you planning any departures from the office in the near future?"

"No, I have too many responsibilities and have no time to waste. Now if you will excuse me I have a lot of work to do."

Tony put the small slip of paper in his notebook and left the office. In the hall he found Greg still on the telephone. As he approached Greg held up his hand indicating he wanted Tony to wait until he had finished before saying anything. Greg stayed on the phone, making notes in a notebook with one hand. After several more minutes he closed his cell phone and said, "Let's go to the car."

They rode the elevator to the ground floor without speaking. Outside Greg spoke excitedly, "Get in the car I have a lot of news."

Inside the patrol car they sat without starting the engine. "OK, Greg, what is this news?"

"First of all Ang Wei is in Jakarta. He flew out of here on a private jet owned by the parent office of his labor union. Second, the two security men are with him. He picked them up in Kenai. The lawyer drove them to the airport after the bail hearing. This is a long-range private jet worth about 40 million dollars. Interpol was notified when they landed in Jakarta and checked in with Customs at the gate

Interpol had an alert out for him after the body of Li Tan was discovered. They didn't know who the other two men were until I informed them. Ang Wei is on the union's international board of trustees and they figured he would need to come there for a meeting sooner or later," Greg chuckled. "How's that for a shocker?"

"Hold on, Greg. You know that box we looked at in Wei's office? It was addressed to Wei in Jakarta. I think we should go back up and seize it as evidence. It might be interesting to see what he's mailing to his home address."

"What about a search warrant?" asked Greg.

"I'm betting the receptionist will give it to us, but we won't be able to open it without a warrant."

"Well, let's go back up and ask her." Greg was agreeing with the decision and excited to know there was progress being made in both the local and the international cases.

In the offices of AmerAsian Labor Union Tony saw the receptionist was nervous about their return. What can I do for you, Trooper?"

"Ma'am, I'm sorry, but as many times as we have spoken, I don't know your name."

"It's Costa, Rosita Costa. Everyone calls me Rosie."

"Thank you, Rosie. You can call me Tony," he replied in an attempt to put her at ease. "My partner just learned your boss, Mr. Ang Wei, has left the state with two security men. These security men are out of jail on bail and not allowed to leave the state. I don't want you to get into any trouble, but we wondered if you would release that box you were supposed to mail to Mr. Wei, into our custody. I will be happy to give you a receipt for the package. It may be evidence in a crime."

"Oh my," uttered Rosie. "There are so many bad things happening around this office I don't think I want to work here anymore."

"Now, now, Rosie, none of the illegal business we are investigating will affect you or your position here. As far as I know the labor union is a legitimate enterprise and you have nothing to worry about. We believe some of the officers in the company may have committed crimes, but the company itself is perfectly legal as far as we know. If you like your job here you should stay."

"Oh, Trooper Tony, that is so good to hear. I have a baby girl and I must work to support her. They pay me well and until recently it has been a good job." Rosie was now wiping her eyes of tears.

"Just out of curiosity, Rosie, are you a U.S. citizen?"

"Yes, I came here from the Philippines with my family when I was a girl. I have been a citizen for many years now. I am proud to be a citizen and proud to be an American."

"That's wonderful, Rosie. I'm proud for you." Tony took her hand and squeezed it gently. "Now, will you give us the box?"

"Yes, Trooper Tony. I will give it to you, but you must give me a receipt for it in case someone asks. If they do I will refer them to you. Is that what you want me to do?"

"That will do just fine. Thank you, Rosie." Tony wrote a receipt and handed it to her as she lifted the box onto her desk. Greg picked up the box and thanked her as well.

Back at the patrol car Greg put the box in the rear seat, "You really are a sweet-talking devil," he said as he strapped his seat belt tight.

Chapter 32

The two officers were back in the office working with Nola most of the afternoon. The postal box they had received from the receptionist was tagged and placed in the evidence storage room.

"Have you found anything in the files to indicate the men were ordered by the company or its officers to commit felony crimes?" asked Greg Beason.

"It's difficult to say; however, I ran background checks on all four of the bad guys as well as Milan and Wei. Wei came up clean, but Milan did fifteen years for murder in Ireland during the insurrection against Britain. It seems to be more a war crime than a felony. He has no current warrants anywhere. The two men killed at the hospital had long criminal records and it beats me how they were able to get licensed as security men. The two booked into jail in Kenai aren't much better. They have no warrants in the U.S. but are wanted in several other countries including France and Germany. Again I can't see how they were able to get licensed for security positions here in Alaska."

"We need those two security men back here. Without them we have no witnesses as to who ordered the guide's airplane burned and his fish camp torched as well." Tony was speculating out loud. "We have a lot of crimes and a lot of suspects, but we have no witnesses or solid proof they were ordered by either Wei or Milan. Taking it further, could they have been ordered by the home office in Jakarta?"

Beason was the next to speak. "I think we are becoming too frustrated and need some time to think. Let's take the rest of the day off and begin again in the morning."

"You're probably right Greg. Besides, I have a lot of paperwork to catch up on. Go home and I'll see the both of you first thing in the morning."

Tony knew Greg was right. Sometimes the most productive thing you can do is nothing.

Nola and Greg returned to their offices while Tony began to sort through the daily mess on his desk. It was late in the afternoon when the receptionist at the front desk of the trooper offices called him on the in-house phone.

"Lieutenant Harrison, there is a young lady out here and I think she wants to talk to you. She asked for Trooper Tony. Her name is Rosita Costas. Do you know her?"

"Yes, I know her, and I'll be right out to see what she wants."

Tony met Rosie at the front desk and escorted her to his office and offered her a chair.

"Hi, Rosie, I didn't expect to see you so soon."

"I know you can't tell me what you are investigating, but maybe I can guess. You see my parents have worked for the union for many years, mostly here in Anchorage after they came here from the Philippines when I was a baby. It isn't pleasant for me to talk about." She hung her head and was silent for several moments. "When I was young my father worked at many jobs for the union, mostly janitorial and groundskeeping jobs here in the city. My mother worked cleaning public buildings and offices. The union would come to get her when out of town officers from the union were in town and there was a party for them. They would pay my mother a lot of money to go to these parties and be nice to the visitors. She was encouraged to drink a lot and I think she did a lot of things she did not want to talk about." Rosie went silent again for several seconds.

"When I was fifteen years old there was to be one of those parties and Mr. Li Tan asked my mother to attend and said he would pay her well. He also asked her to bring me along to join in the party. She said she didn't want to do that, but Li Tan insisted. My mother finally gave in and had me dress in a fancy dress and high heel shoes. I thought it was going to be fun and I would have a good time. My mother never told me what to do, only that I could make a lot of money by going to the party."

She continued, "We arrived at the party and were met by Li Tan. He introduced my mother to a man I had never see before and she went to a table with him. Li Tan took me to meet another man, an older man, and told me to be pleasant to him. I sat at the table next to him when the food and drink was served. I had never had alcohol before. The man poured me and himself a cup of, what I know now is, sake. I sipped on the cup and it was pleasant to drink. We had another cup when the first of the food was served. I didn't know the effects of sake and drank all the cups he poured. By the time dinner was over I lost track of everything. I was told he took me to a private booth in the back of the dining room and began to feel of me. Each time I began to object he gave me more sake. When I awoke later in the booth I was hurt and bleeding. I had no underthings on and there were two one-hundred dollar bills in my shoe." She was now crying.

"My mother returned to the dining room and found me. She took me home and cleaned me. I was very sick for a couple of days after the party. A few months later she took me to another party and once again I drank too much sake. The man I was to entertain that night took me to a private room and fed me more sake and once again I passed out. And once again I awoke alone in a bed with no underthings on and three hundred dollars on the night table beside the bed. I dressed and cleaned myself in the room and returned to the dining room to find my mother. She came a little while later when no one else was there and took me home. I refused to go to any more of her parties after that, but it was too late; I was pregnant with my daughter."

"How old is your daughter now?" asked Tony.

"Three and a half," replied Rosie.

"I wish I had recorded this conversation, Rosie. This treatment is one of the reasons we are investigating the labor union. Would you be willing to repeat what you told me to a lady officer so we could record your statement?"

Rosie thought a few seconds, "Yes, Trooper Tony, I will tell her. I must say that until Mr. Li Tan died I was afraid to tell anyone. Mr. Wei was at both of those parties, but I never spoke to him while I was there. After I finished school I went to a business college and was able to apply for the job at Mr. Wei's office. He recognized me and gave me the job of receptionist. He always treated me well."

"You may not know this, Rosie, but your story could be the thing we need to put an end to this sort of behavior by the labor union. You're a brave young lady." Tony moved a box of tissue to the front of her so she could blow her nose and dry her eyes. "By the way, if I may ask, does your mother still work for AmerAsian Labor Union?"

"Yes, but she doesn't go to the parties anymore. She is too old and fat now. She is ashamed to talk about those days. My father still works as a groundskeeper for several local businesses, but he is getting older and can't do that work like he used to do."

"OK, Rosie, I'm going to call a lady officer down here and we can get this done." Tony offered her coffee or a soft drink, but she refused. He then called one of the female officers that was near the office and explained what she was to do. A recorder was set up and Rosie began to relate her story one more time. When she finished Trooper Tony asked if she needed a ride home and she accepted the ride from the female officer.

It was late in the evening now, but Tony dialed the private cell phone number of Greg Beason. It took several minutes to recite the events of the afternoon to his partner in the case. Beason was astonished.

"Can you make me a copy of the recording?" asked Greg.

"I will if you can guarantee Rosie's anonymity," he replied.

"The International Police have never had a living witness. I know if word got out she would be killed by the union. I don't want anything to happen to this witness. Once things are set I think we can get depositions from her and hide her identity. I'll talk with my bosses and they can contact Interpol to confirm we can do that. Damn, Tony, this is big!"

"That's what I thought, Greg. But just the same we must be careful. Once this has been sorted out by the big guns we can get warrants issued for Wei and, I think, some members of the board of directors of the parent labor union." Tony was still concerned for the safety of Rosita Costas.

"I think we may be lucky that AmerAsian is short on security men right now. We have got to get this done before they can send any more killers from the home office. Milan, I hope, doesn't want to do the job personally. I'll get with my supervisors first thing in the morning. Thanks for the call, Tony."

The following morning Tony took the information to the major. "We still don't have those two that attacked Bob Halstead's home. Do you think we will be able to extradite them from Indonesia?" asked Tony.

"I don't know, but we can ask your DA friend, Nola," the major remarked.

These events and the statement by Rosie set off a firestorm around the world. It was the first time in over a decade there had been a living witness. Interpol thought the two men with Ang Wei would trade information about who ordered the destruction of Bob's airplane and his camp for many years in prison. He wanted to call Bob and let him in on the good news but couldn't for the safety of his witness. If Chin and Hua did talk they would surely incriminate Paul Milan, and Tony and Greg would have the pleasure of arresting and booking him into jail.

At the Anchorage courthouse Nola Wilson was successful in obtaining a search warrant for the box Ang Wei had intended to be mailed to himself in Jakarta. Once she had the warrant in hand she personally delivered it to Lieutenant Anthony Harrison in his office. Tony called Greg and the trio gathered around the box in a small conference room where a large table was available.

"I've set up a video camera to record the opening of the package," Tony informed the assistant DA. "Do we need any other witnesses to this unveiling?"

"The videotaping is a good idea, Tony. With it we will have enough eyes and verification. Let's open the package." Nola was excited to be in on the opening and expected there to be some sort of real evidence in the box.

With everything set and the camera running, Tony took a sharp knife from his pocket and cut the tape sealing the box. Wearing latex gloves to preserve any fingerprints or other evidence, Tony pulled the flaps of the box aside. Inside there were many file folders which Tony lifted out of the box one by one, noting the names on the file as he placed them, one at a time, on the long table. Most of the names on the files were unfamiliar to Tony or Greg, but Nola recognized a few. Near the middle of the box was a file marked DON HALSTEAD.

"Bingo!" shouted Tony as he thumbed the pages but put it beside the other files on the table to dig deeper into the shipping box. Below the file folders was a layer of empty folders and once removed there were stacks and stacks of $100.00 bills bound with bank bands. Each banded packet proclaimed it contained $10,000.00. Once counted the witnesses noted there was a quarter of a million dollars in United States cash in the box.

"He sent all these dangerous files and a quarter of a million dollars to himself," commented Tony. "I don't believe he was planning on returning to Alaska. I'm betting this was his retirement fund."

"I think we need to dust these files and bundles of cash to see whose prints are on them," cautioned Greg Beason.

"Good idea," seconded Nola Wilson.

"How do you want to do this, Greg? Do you want me to have someone from the crime lab to come and do this? And do you want someone from your office to assist in the fingerprinting? We're only going to get one shot at this and we want to do it right the first time, right?" remarked the trooper lieutenant.

Greg scratched his head, "Nola, do you think the crime lab doing the work is enough verification?"

"In my experience in court the crime lab has always been the authority. I'm thinking they can do it while the scene is being videotaped, just like we're doing now." It was true that she had never had evidence obtained and examined by the crime lab disputed by either side or the judge while in court.

"OK, then, I'll call them over here right away. I want to get into the files and see if they document any of the crimes we are investigating." Tony stepped away from the table to call the crime lab techs.

It would take a long time while the three witnesses to the opening of the box watched the process. By mid-afternoon the printing was finished and cleaned up. The lab techs went back to their offices to finish the process while Tony, Greg and Nola began to read the files on the table.

Chapter 33

Nola, Greg and Tony drank sodas while the lab techs gathered their tools and left the small room. When the last of them had departed they began to assess the labels on the files. The one that caught Tony's eye was the file marked Don Halstead. He picked it up to read. Greg took the one marked Bob Halstead. Nola was left with the others labeled with names unfamiliar to her. An hour into this session of study Tony stood to stretch his back.

Greg looked up and asked, "Did you find anything interesting?"

Tony grinned, "Enough to extradite Mr. Ang Wei from Indonesia. He documented his order to Li Tan sending the four security men to kidnap Don Halstead. He also ordered Li Tan to send the team to the Anchorage hospital to 'eliminate' Don. I have never seen felony crimes documented like this. I suppose this is why he was mailing this box to himself in Jakarta."

"That would account for Li Tan taking his own life. He was going to take the fall for the two missed chances to get Don Halstead." Greg was making a note on a legal pad as he spoke.

"Well, listen to this," commented Nola. "I found a ledger in one of the file folders I first thought was empty. It is a listing of the amount of cash in this box as well as a list of bank accounts in Jakarta, Switzerland, Hong Kong, New York and four more cities I have never heard of before. I don't have an exact total for you, but the rough figure is something over six million dollars. Those four banks I mentioned have totals in foreign currencies and I don't know the exchange rates for those accounts. Either Wei had a very large salary or he skimmed a great deal of money from the company. Either way he has a lot of cash and the ability to disappear if he suspects we're on to him."

"Greg," asked Tony, "Have you found anything in that file about the attack on Bob Halstead and his partner, Vic Lamar?"

"Not a detailed entry, but there is a note from Wei about having a confrontation with Paul Milan in which Milan chastised Wei for ordering the two hunters to come here from Jakarta. I would like to copy these files and get permission to send copies to Interpol. I don't know how your file reads, but there is no reference to any felony crimes, only directing the movements of the men who committed the crimes. Ang Wei is a clever old goat. He kept track of every movement his men made but was careful to not mention that he was the one ordering the criminal activity."

"Did he make note of ordering Milan to torch Bob Halstead's airplane or his camp?"

"As near as I can piece it together, that was the reason for the confrontation between the two bosses. It read like Milan was not taking orders from Wei and Wei was mad about that. He called someone in Jakarta about it."

"Nola," asked Tony, "Do you think there is any further danger for Don Halstead or his daughter?"

"Hmmm," she muttered, "We have a pretty good case against Li Tan and Wei as well as the two men we arrested at Bob Halstead's home in Soldotna. The trouble being they've left the country with Wei. We don't know who is going to take over as the new boss in Anchorage, but it reads like Wei didn't trust Don Halstead from the beginning and that started this whole thing. I can't see any reason for them to continue to harass Bob or the daughter. Everything they have done so far has been totally bizarre and all leads back to Wei. With him gone I would like to think the threat is gone."

"What about you, Greg? Do you think it would be premature to call Don Halstead and tell him his daughter can come home and that he was no longer a target?"

"I don't really know, Tony. The one wild card we have is Paul Milan. I think he's capable of extreme acts, but he doesn't seem to be as intent on getting at Don. Of course, there is no guarantee he couldn't."

"The one piece we have on our side is that statement by Rosita Costas. It directly links Ang Wei to prostitution and human slavery. You say Interpol is investigating the parent corporation on that one. Rosita's statement gives us enough evidence to issue a warrant for his arrest here in Alaska, but the international police may take first claim on him, linking him to the international side of the trade. Those two henchmen Wei bailed out of jail and took away to Indonesia will have warrants, but home invasion probably won't be a heavy enough charge to get them extradited." Tony chuckled, "Now that we have the evidence we don't have anyone to arrest."

Nola was the next to add her comments. "Back to Don Halstead and his daughter; I think you can advise him it will, most likely, be OK to bring his daughter back to the state. Paul Milan is the only one in the company who was involved at all, is still here, but wasn't here when the initial assault took place."

"I'm going to have to think about that, Nola, averred Tony. I know you have a lot of case reports to write when you get back to your office and I think we are at a standstill here. You can go back to your own work if you want. Greg, like you have a lot of information to give to other agencies and I'm totally out of touch with my other duties. I think we should take some time to catch up and get warrants issued for Wei, Chin and Hua. I'll put this stuff back in the evidence locker. Any copies you want of the files I will see that you get them. This case is winding down and the two of you have made it a successful ending. Thanks."

Tony wasn't sure about this being the end of the case, but it seemed like it should be. He knew Don Halstead was still staying with his brother Bob and waited until late in the afternoon to call him. "Hello Don, this is Tony Harrison. I think I have some good news for you."

"I'll take some good news," replied Don.

"We think the men responsible for the attack on you and the threats against your daughter are now out of the country. We are issuing warrants for their arrest and extradition back to Alaska to stand trial for their crimes. What that means is it may now be safe to bring your daughter home. I must advise you that these men are very dangerous and are not under arrest at this time which means if you bring your daughter home you should exercise great caution to keep her safe."

"Thank you, Tony, I understand. I am reminded every time I get out of a chair. I'm healing quickly but it still hurts." Don sagged into his recliner chair with relief. "I'll pass this along to Vic and Bobby. It will be good news for them as well."

After finishing the phone call Don stood and walked into the back yard of the property to find the other two men. They were cleaning the fleshing shed when he found them. "Hey guys," he called out, "I have some good news from Tony Harrison."

The three men returned to the house to hear the story while drinking some fresh coffee. "And that's what he told me," said Don as he finished relating the details of the phone call.

Bob Halstead grew a huge grin on his weathered face, saying, "I guess this means you can finally go home, Vic.

"I didn't especially like the circumstances, Bobby, but I've had a great time out here with you. If you ever need me again I'll be ready."

Don asked Vic, "I want to know, Vic. Do you know where Jenny and Lindsy are right now?"

"Nope, I surly don't, but I can find out in a few minutes. I'll bet Jenny will want to talk to her dad, too."

"While you two talk to the girls I'm going over to see the fella who owns this 185 I'm leasing. He sent me a message saying he would consider selling me the Cessna and putting my lease payments toward the purchase price. If I can afford the total I'm going to buy it. It's a good plane and handles really well. I'll be back in a couple of hours." Bob was excited by the prospect of buying this newer and slightly more powerful airplane.

By the time he returned Don and Vic had made arrangements for the ladies to drive the motorhome to Soldotna for the reunion. Vic could drive the big machine back to Oregon alone, but he considered asking Lindsy to make the trip with him. Both Don and Bobby had been noticing that Vic was getting more and more attached to Lindsy as the days wore on. Bob suggested the three men go to Froso's restaurant for a celebration dinner.

Over the next several days Tony Harrison had made several trips to the offices of AmerAsian Labor Union to visit Rosita Costas and to gather information from Paul Milan who now occupied the office of the CEO where Rosita was the receptionist. Tony never mentioned her statement when he came to the office, only passed the time of day and pleasant greetings. Rosita seemed less tense with the new boss.

"Good Morning, Rosita," said Tony as he entered the office. "Is your new boss in this morning?"

"Yes, Trooper Tony, he is in. I will let him know you are here." She dialed the interoffice phone to notify Milan who asked her to send the trooper right in.

Milan stood as Harrison approached his desk, "Good to see you Lieutenant, what can I do for you?"

"Just a few details are all I need today. I'm curious, Mr. Milan, the promotion to this office; is it permanent?"

"The home office has asked me to take the position as CEO for AmerAsian but I haven't given them an answer just yet. I have spent my entire career as head of security units wherever I was needed in the world and I liked my job. But, the truth, I am getting older and the risks are becoming greater. If I can find someone to take the security officer supervisor position, one that I can trust to use good judgement, I think I will take the CEO position." Milan smiled, "Do you want the security chief position?" he chuckled.

Tony heard the offer. "I'm too close to my pension to quit the troopers," he said, still smiling. He collected his needed facts and left the building to return to his office where Greg was waiting for him.

"Good to see you, Greg. What's up?"

"Nola called me to say they have heard from UNAFEI that Chin and Hua will be extradited back to Alaska for trial," he said.

"What about Wei?" Tony asked.

"It seems Mr. Wei has fallen ill and cannot leave the hospital in Jakarta. It is said this will be reevaluated if Mr. Wei recovers from his illness."

"What sort of illness does he have?" asked the trooper.

"They didn't say, only that it was serious and he was ill. Interpol has information that Paul Milan is in line to take the local CEO position and if he does, he'll be appointed as the replacement for Wei on the board of directors."

Greg smiled again, "Local boy makes good," he said.

"I talked with Milan this morning and he has a whole different attitude these days. I'm hoping this leopard has changed his spots."

"Me too," commented Greg.

"By the way, Bobby said he wanted to go up river to do some trout fishing and asked if you would like to go along with Vic, Don, Bobby and me. The mornings are getting pretty chilly, but he said the fishing is reported to be good."

"That's the best offer I've had in a long time. Give me a date and time and I'll be there."

"I'll call you and let you know as soon as I talk with Bob. Good to see you again, Greg."

A week later Bobby and Don Halstead were with Vic Lamar at Bob's home, working on his newly acquired Cessna 185 when a huge motorhome slowly made its way up the driveway to the house. The three men saw the Winnebago drive into the yard and the engine stop. When the door opened the first out was Jenny rushing to hug her father. It was a joyous meeting.

Next out was Lindsy Gibson who waved at the small crowd and walked directly toward Vic to plant a huge kiss on his lips. This act drew a round of applause and laughter from the rest.

The reunion stopped all other activities and for the first time in months everyone was laughing and happy. Jenny had grown at least two inches and was becoming a young lady. Her education in that field had been guided by Lindsy.

A barbeque was planned as the homecoming grew more somber and all the members of the party hugged and talked. It was the first sign of normalcy seen at the Bob Halstead home in many months. As he broiled the steaks, Bob thought how wonderful it was to be back in control of his own life. It seemed that the past several months had been much like flying blind through the unexpected perils of international intrigue. Winter was on the way; preparation for the coming fishing and hunting seasons would all begin again in the spring, hopefully without all the drama forced upon them this year. When he went to bed tonight he would be sure to thank the good Lord for this happy reunion.